House of Blossom

Copyright © 2024 by Karen Raymond
All rights reserved,
Including the right to reproduction
In whole or in part in any form.
ISBN: 9798325301971

Cover Art by Karen Raymond
Edited by Marguerite Smith

Imprint: Independently published
1st Edition

Trigger warnings: Murder, Sex, and Adult Language

Karen Raymond

A flower blooms beautifully even when immersed in darkness.

As Always, In Loving Memory of
My mom, dad, and brother

Blossom Family

Nobility

Magnolia
Mother

Devotion

Father
Heliotrope

Deceptive

Hatred

Aconite
Youngest
Daughter

Snapdragon
Oldest Child
& Only Son

Anger

Power

Cruel

Petunia
Middle
Daughter

Gladiolus Marigold
Twin Daughters

Prologue

A gunshot rang through the night air, drowning out the noise of the SUV that sped off. Car horns blared and tires screeched as drivers frantically swerved and slammed on the brakes to avoid the black Ford Expedition with tinted windows that was unfortunately gobbled up by the immense hoard of traffic that crowded the Atlanta Buckhead streets as it turned onto Peachtree Road.

All of the Blossom children stood, frozen, as their mother exited the restaurant. She was oblivious to what had happened. As the social butterfly of the family, she had told her grown children to summon the car while she stopped to speak to City Councilwoman, Ga'Nessa Newman.

She had no regard for the up and coming politician, but she knew that she'd rather have her as an ally than an enemy as she had bested the entrenched Councilman, Ted Graham, in the election just two years earlier. The Graham family and the Blossom family were two of the oldest and wealthiest bloodlines in the state and had been doing business together for over a hundred years.

With his defeat, the Blossom's knew they had to ingratiate themselves with the newest city representative and secure a relationship from which they could continue to benefit.

Magnolia Blossom sauntered over to the Councilwoman's table and displayed her best Southern charm. They had met a handful of times previously, but Mrs. Blossom knew that a slight when exiting would be rude. She placed her delicate hand on Mrs. Newman's shoulder as she flashed her perfect smile to the other patrons at the table.

"Good evening Councilwoman, it is so lovely to see you again."

After dabbing the sides of her mouth with her napkin and wiping her fingertips, Ga'Nessa turned to face Magnolia and greeted her with her own pleasant smile. "Good evening to you, Maggie, it is so nice to see you again. I hope you had a lovely dinner."

"Oh, Ga'Nessa," Magnolia said with a drip of annoyance and revenge. Only her family and close friends called her Maggie. Ga'Nessa was neither. "Yes, dinner was simply divine."

At that exact moment, while the two women were shaking hands, a pop sound came from outside. Both ladies slightly glanced toward the front, as did others, but no one gave it a thought.

"Sounds like someone needs to get their car in for a tune up," Magnolia fained a proper, small laugh. She released Ga'Nessa's hand. "I didn't want to interrupt, I just wanted to say hello." She made eye contact with each person at the table before her eyes landed back on Ga'Nessa. "Have a wonderful evening and please, stop by the store anytime. I know our designers would love to create something for you."

With a smile and a nod, Magnolia left the table and headed toward the exit. Pleased with her interaction, she signaled the doorman with a single finger in the air that she was ready to leave. When she neared the door she was insulted that the doorman began to talk to her.

"Mrs. Blossom, I don't think you should go outside. There's been an incident."

"Nonsense, my family is waiting for me; open the door," Magnolia demanded.

The doorman knew from experience not to aggravate Mrs. Blossom. She'd had three doormen fired in the last ten years. One had looked at her the wrong way, according to her, and she refused to return until he was gone.

He reluctantly opened the door knowing what she was about to see. He dared not tell her. He didn't want to be the one to tell her that life as she knew it was over.

With her head down, looking into her vintage Hermes handbag, Magnolia stepped out into the crisp evening air. "Snapper, is the car here yet?" She hadn't looked up yet. She hadn't realized that Snapper, her only son, was cemented in place with his crying sisters clinging to him.

A crowd of people with their cellphones recorded the unfolding events circling the horrendous scene. When she saw them she began to pose, since she was wearing one of her latest designer dresses. The fall line from the House of Blossom had been a resounding success and she wore one of the pieces each time she was in public, which was her habit within the weeks after a show.

The crowd was horrified. Finally, one lady pointed to indicate that Magnolia needed to turn around.

In a gracious twist of her head, she took in the scene. Police sirens were screaming and getting louder as they raced down the street. But the screams of her daughters were so guttural and high pitched, that they are what caught her attention.

She glided over, still aware of the cameras that were on her, and stood in front of her son, who had his sisters wrapped in his arms and holding them from going to their father. Silent tears escaped his eyes as he looked down at the sidewalk.

"Snapdragon," Magnolia demanded his attention, "What in the hell is wrong with all of you? What is going on? Where's the car? I'm ready to go home."

He didn't reply. His eyes pleaded with her to look at the sidewalk in front of her. The police and ambulance arrived on the scene as she saw the blood that formed a perfect circle around her husband's head as he laid there in an awkward position on the ground with a hole in his forehead.

Chapter 1

The Atlanta Journal-Constitution
November 1, 2021
Front Page

House of Blossom Patriarch, Heliotrope Blossom, Murdered

At 9:02pm, Halloween night was rocked by the tragic and senseless drive-by shooting of beloved fashion designer, Heliotrope Blossom. Known to most as Helio, he was a pillar of the Atlanta community who through his charitable foundation, Blossom's Blooms, in partnership with Savannah College of Art and Design (SCAD), sponsored scholarships for students who wanted to work in the field of fashion.

His company, House of Blossom, has been a fixture in the Atlanta fashion scene since his great-grandfather, Clematis "Clem" Blossom opened a husbandry clothing store in 1890. In 1920 his grandmother, Sassy Blossom, started a woman's tailoring section in what was once a supply closet in the back of the building. With it decorated like a Victorian home, she called her little corner shop, House of Blossom. A legend was born.

By 1925, they phased out the husbandry apparel and officially opened the entire building as House of Blossom. Under the supervision of Sassy, the business flourished and has been a family business ever since.

Born March 16, 1972, Heliotrope Blossom was 49 when he was tragically shot in what police are describing as a random Halloween act of violence.

"At this time, we do not have a suspect but we are working diligently to find the person who did this to Mr. Blossom. He was truly an honorable man and he will be sorely missed," stated Sherrif Boland. "If anyone has any information we encourage you to contact law enforcement. You can also contact Crime Stoppers anonymously. There is currently a $100,000 reward for information that leads to a conviction."

Mr. Blossom is survived by his wife, Magnolia "Maggie" Blossom; twin daughters, Gladiolus "Dio" Blossom and Marigold "Mari" Blossom (25); son, Snapdragon "Snapper" Blossom (22); daughter, Petunia "Nia" Blossom (20); and daughter, Aconite "Oni" Blossom (17) all of Atlanta.

The family has asked for privacy during their time of grief. They understand how beloved Mr. Blossom was and will announce later this week arrangements for a public memorial. The family spokesperson added their desire for people to come forward with any pertinent information and expressed sincere thanks for all of the prayers.

The Atlanta Journal-Constitution
November 1, 2021
Front Page – Business Section

Who Will Become CEO of House of Blossom After Death of Heliotrope Blossom?

Rumors and speculation abound less than twelve hours after the death of Chief Executive Officer Heliotrope Blossom as to who will take the reins of the colossal and world-renowned fashion house. All of the Blossom children work for the company in various managerial positions and Magnolia Blossom is currently Chief Financial Officer.

It has been thought for years that the only son, Snapdragon Blossom, would one day take the reigns as he was appointed Chief Marketing Officer after graduating from Parsons The New School of Design (Parsons) in New York City a mere two years ago.

Blossom's father, Catkin Blossom, retired in 2000 and naturally Heliotrope Blossom was voted in as CEO. However, he was the eldest of his three siblings so the transition was a natural fit. That is not the case this time. Eldest twin daughters, Gladiolus and Marigold Blossom are known for their rivalry within the company.

When Marigold graduated a semester earlier than her sister from Parsons she was appointed Director of Marketing (currently she is the Chief Design Officer) upon her arrival back in Atlanta. When Gladiolus graduated she was relegated to serve under her sister as Assistant Director of Marketing.

Within a year, Gladiolus outranked her sister to become Chief Operation Officer. What neither of them could have anticipated was their brother outranking them both when he graduated.

There are also two other siblings that will be vying for the title. Aconite Blossom, who is the Chief Information Officer, and Petunia Blossom, the Chief International Affairs Officer.

It is worth noting that all of the siblings are students at Georgia Tech in the Executive MBA program. Their father insisted when at 16, Aconite Blossom was accepted into the program after completing her education at Parsons.

With her genius level IQ, she has had her eye on CEO since she was 13, she stated in an interview when she graduated high school.

House of Blossom (HOBL) was trading at 57.03 as of the closing bell Friday. There will be a close watch as to how the company fares as the news of Heliotrope's death hits the world markets.

Chapter 2

Magnolia huffed and groaned as she read the newspaper at the breakfast table. Her hand was shaking as she reached for her coffee. She slammed the paper onto the table and took a deep breath.

"These fucking reporters!" Magnolia said angerly.

Walking into the dining room, Snapper solicited his unwanted comment. "Mother! Is that the first thing you want the girls to hear the morning after their father has been murdered? They are beside themselves." He kissed her on the cheek and sat in his assigned seat at his mother's side.

Lydia, one of three housekeepers, was on kitchen duty that morning. "Coffee for you sir?" she asked.

"Yes, thank you," he replied.

"Will you have breakfast this morning?" she inquired.

"Just a piece of buttered toast will be fine."

She shuffled back to the kitchen.

Snapper took a sip of his coffee. "Umm, Mother, did you know the girls all slept in the loft? They had Hank move the mattresses out of their bedrooms and put them in the middle of the floor up there. Mrs. Kelly was on her knees putting sheets and coverlets on them." He took another sip of coffee. "Do you remember when Father had that oversized bed built up there after Oni was born. What did he call it? Daddy/daughter sleepover?"

"No," Magnolia replied annoyed, "he called it The Blossom Sisters Super Sleepover." She rolled her eyes.

"You're just mad because they didn't invite you," Snapper teased.

"You are dreadful." She allowed a small smile to reach the corner of her lips.

He patted the back of her hand. "What were you upset about when I walked in?" he asked.

Lydia placed the lightly toasted bread, gently brushed with butter, in front of Snapper.

"These damn reporters. Look at this," Magnolia turned the front page of the paper toward him, "your father is barely cold and they have plastered his name across the front page."

"If that makes you angry, you really don't want to read the front page of the business section. I read it online before I came down." he warned.

She quickly picked up the paper and flipped it to the business section. Her eyes grew wide as she read the article that made it seem like her children were at each other's throats to take over the company. The more she read the more furious she became. When she finished, she threw the paper onto the floor.

"Conjecture and lies!" she screamed. "He doesn't even consider that I will assume the helm." She looked up at Snapper to see his reaction. He didn't flinch. "Get me Phil Griffin on the phone. I want this reporter fired now!"

"Mother, I don't think Phil is involved in the daily reports. He just owns the paper," Snapper reminded her.

She slapped Snapper with her open palm.

"How dare you speak to me that way. When I tell you to do something, you do it. Don't think that your father's death leaves you as man of the house. This is my house and you need to remember your place."

"Yes, Mother. My apologies. I meant no disrespect. I'll get him on the phone for you." Snapdragon cowered and lowered his head as he dismissed himself from the table and went up to get his phone.

She sat there, staring out the massive floor to ceiling windows of her circa 1870 mansion. The enormous grounds helped to make the property a fortress. If she hadn't needed it to be that before, she needed it now. The media was camped out on the road just waiting for the gates to open in hopes of capturing the mental anguish of the family as they headed to the funeral home.

She checked her watch and sighed. They had to be ready to go in less than an hour. Figuring the girls weren't coming down for breakfast and were most likely getting ready, she sighed again, pushed herself away from the table and headed to her room.

Stepping out of the back of the limousine, no one would have known that Magnolia Blossom was a recent widow. Her long, tanned legs that ended with a luxurious pair of deep blue, almost black Louboutin heels slipped out first as the funeral director offered his hand to help her out. She wore a knee-length navy blue skirt with a buttoned up, oxford style soft pink blouse which was tucked into the waist where the outfit was bound together with a black Chanel belt. Her makeup was perfectly applied and not a single fly away dared to appear from her raven-black hair.

In contrast, the girls were all in jeans and oversized hoodies. There wasn't a stitch of makeup on any of their faces and they all wore large, dark sunglasses. Their grief was on display and they didn't care.

Snapper came around and took his mother's arm as he escorted her into the funeral home. He too was impeccably dressed. Wearing a dark blue Armani suit and black Santoni Oxfords, he looked as if he had coordinated with his mother. They looked more like a power couple than mother and son.

"Good morning Mrs. Blossom, my condolences for your loss. Mr. Blossom was truly a generous person. Over the years I believe his donations provided proper burials for thousands of our community's less fortunate." The funeral director was a pleasant looking, middle-aged man. He too was a family businessman. The Broadwater Funeral Home had served the area for over a hundred years. "Helio and I were school mates until high school when he went to Citadel Prep and I stayed in public school," Morris Broadwater continued.

Magnolia held out her hand to him. "Nice to see you again Mr. Broadwater. Yes, yes, I believe my husband mentioned that a time or two." Her smile exuded charm as she tried to hide her disdain. Helio had mentioned it to Magnolia many times. It was a dreadfully boring tale that she did not wish to hear again.

Mr. Broadwater smiled and took her hand in a stronger than expected handshake. "If you are ready, we can step into my office and begin discussing details." He gestured toward a hallway that led to a bank of offices and proceeded to the third one on the right.

It was cluttered with brochures, samples of vaults, woods, and miniature headstone models. To Magnolia, the most impressive item in the room was his antique mahogany desk which was in desperate need of a cleaning and polish, she thought.

In silence, the entire family sat and listened to Mr. Broadwater go through the obligatory options that every grieving family had the onerous duty to endure. There was a clear distinction between how the girls were handling the situation versus Magnolia and Snapper.

The girls were huddled together on a small sofa that was obviously old and made from dark tan pleather. Tears streamed down all of their faces and they were absolutely no help, to their mother's dismay. Magnolia was regretting her demand that they attend. On the other hand, Mother and son sat straight as boards in the two pleather chairs that matched the sofa. They were situated in front of Mr. Broadwater's desk.

They listened intently to every word and took in all of the information in stride. There was no reflection of their emotions on either of their faces. The distinction did not escape Mr. Broadwater's notice. It even made him feel slightly uncomfortable.

Once he finished laying out all of the styles, equipment, and accessories, as if he were an interior designer, Magnolia asked if the family could have a few moments to confer. Her sweet, Southern drawl was hard for any man to resist, so, of course, he excused himself and closed the door behind him.

Magnolia's façade of charm and grace dropped immediately. She visibly shook before she stood up. Not from grief, but from anger.

"This is so insulting." She ran her finger with her perfectly manicured blood red fingernail across the mahogany desk. She held it up and made a distorted face. "Disgusting. You'd think a funeral home would be more...sterile. At the very least some semblance of cleanliness." She looked around trying to find somewhere to dispel the dust from her fingertip.

She opened Snapper's suit coat and grabbed the handkerchief with the family crest embroidered on it from his inside breast pocket.

"Thank goodness your father taught you to always place a handkerchief in your suit pocket. It might be old fashioned, but that is no excuse for not being prepared for a lady's possible need."

She quickly wiped her finger and returned the handkerchief, neatly folded, back into the breast pocket of Snapper's suit. Then, with an audible huff, she looked over at the girls who had finally stopped crying but were still rendered mute.

Exasperated, Magnolia made a decision. "Snapper, the girls and I are going to take the limousine back to the house. None of us want to deal with any of this right now. Just pick out the most expensive of everything. I'll send the car back for you."

With that, she ushered the girls out of the funeral director's office and left Snapper to complete the transactional affairs of death.

One Week Later

Public Memorial

Magnolia looked elegant in a bespoke, vintage black dress from the exclusive vault of House of Blossom. It was a one-of-a-kind couture garment from the vintage 1972 collection. She wore it in honor of the year of Helio's birth. She made sure that the press knew this tidbit of information, but she would later swear that the details must have been leaked.

She had also insisted that each of the children wear a specific piece that she had meticulously selected for them from the vault. Just because they were grieving didn't mean that they couldn't look their best and represent the company at the same time.

Public displays, no matter the circumstances, were only meant to show strength, power, or altruism as far as Magnolia was concerned. To her, the public memorial was an exercise of her patience. She and the children stood by the closed casket as dignitaries, business colleagues, employees, family, friends, acquaintances, and strangers filed through to express their condolences and to pay their respects.

The memorial was held at the Mt. Bethal United Methodist Church as it was anticipated that more than 25,000 people would stand in line for hours just to say they were there.

Magnolia was wearing lace trimmed black gloves as she had no desire to tempt fate. The COVID pandemic had held everyone hostage for months the year before and she insisted that there be ushers handing out masks to everyone. No one was allowed in the building without one. Black tape had been laid on the floor at a measurement of six feet in all directions from Magnolia and the children. Everyone was informed, as they entered the building, to follow the black carpet runner that had been placed to designate the flow of movement. Once they had passed the area near the family, Magnolia didn't care where they went or if they wore a mask. Even though the CDC restrictions had been lifted, she wasn't taking any chances.

With the conspiracy theories and the anti-mask movement still lingering, she didn't come down on the matter one way or another. Her refusal to wear a mask was simply because it diminished her power and ruined her makeup.

Compliance during the memorial was not pro-mask or pro-social distancing. To her, it was just common sense in such a large crowd. She had the company publicist, Dawn, construct a script for the ushers to memorize as their reply, if asked or if there was push back.

"Just put together talking points or some bullshit to make us look good, but not controversial." Magnolia barked a week before the memorial. "I don't need *that* dumbfuckery right now. Make them memorize it to sound more genuine." She turned to Dawn, "Fuck! I hate having to do this shit. Oh, and Dawn, make sure that inept funeral director only has the family crest cloth draped on the casket. He was saying something earlier about a casket spray that had been sent by the governor," she scoffed, "he's just looking for a campaign contribution."

"Yes ma'am, I'll take care of everything. Text if you need anything else," Dawn, the company and family publicist, replied as she backed out of the sunroom, where Magnolia lounged, that overlooked the infinity pool in the backyard of Flora Fields.

For a brief moment of solitude, Magnolia allowed herself to drift to fond memories of Helio playing with the children in the pool while she soak up the sun's rays. That turned her thoughts to how annoyed she was that Helio favored the girls so much.

After Snapdragon was born, she was willing to have another baby thinking that having two sons to go with her twin girls would be worth the pain. To her horror, instead of the boy she would name Aster, she produced another girl. She gave her one of the most ordinary of floral names, Petunia.

The family tradition of everything, including the children, being named for all things floral was deeply rooted in the Blossom family from the days before they immigrated to America from England. Few people knew that Magnolia had legally changed her first name a year before she and Heliotrope had married.

This too was a tradition for the women who married into the family, which Magnolia fully embraced. She was born Margaret Ann Talbot. With most people calling her Maggie in those days. She had always hated her name. She decided that the name Magnolia allowed her a seamless metamorphosis into the high-profile life she would live as a Blossom.

Unfortunately for her, part of that high-profile life included four hours of greeting the public and accepting the same quintessential and customary expressions of condolence. Magnolia was done.

She leaned over to Snapper and in a whisper she announced, "You need to figure out how to end this. I'm sick of standing here. I need a break. Fix this!"

Snapper nodded with complete understanding that he was to act immediately. With a subtle look, he caught the attention of one of the security guards who walked over behind the family.

"We need a break. Please discreetly redirect the mourners to the sanctuary. We will join them in thirty minutes if they would like to stay. Have the minister lead them in prayer and whatever else he feels is appropriate to give us some time."

"I'll cover it Mr. Blossom," confirmed the guard. He turned on his heel and began his task.

Snapper took his mother's hand and kissed her on the cheek. "Let's go," he stated as he looped her arm in his. The girls saw the movement and it was apparent that it was a welcome reprieve.

"How much longer must I endure this?" Magnolia complained as she flung herself onto the pleather sofa in the funeral director's office.

"Mother," Snapper replied, "what can I do to make this more bearable for you?"

The girls settled themselves into the four available chairs, and although they had been able to control their emotions thus far, the exhaustion set in for all of them.

"Dragon," Mari addressed Snapper by her pet name for him, "can we get some food?" She pulled out her phone. "Who wants sushi?"

Mari was Snapper's favorite of his sisters. She was the only one allowed to call him Dragon, which made her twin sister's blood boil.

"Mother? Would you like something to eat?" Mari asked as she tapped on her phone.

"Ugh, No, Marigold, I do not want food." Magnolia replied as she rubbed her temples. Snapper, we have got to end this public display. Go tell the minister that I will speak and then this will be over." She stood up and headed for the door. "Why must I have to do everything myself? All of you are useless. SNAPPER! GO!"

Defeated, Snapper silently, but quickly left the room. Mari slid her phone back into her purse. All of the Blossom women sat in silence.

Chapter 3

Looking bored and uninterested, Snapdragon Blossom looked around the lawyer's office as he and the family waited for the reading of the will. It had been a month since his father had been gunned down. The police had suggested waiting before any monetary distributions were made while they continued to investigate. A compromise was reached that all aspects of the business and all non-monetary items would be open to the beneficiaries.

It all seemed like a waste of time to Snapper. He pretty much knew how his father had prepared his will. Mother would take ownership of the company as well as ownership of the house, all real estate holdings, and half of his monetary estate, sans the considerable charitable contributions. There were other minor items, but these were the ones that were most important to Magnolia.

The other half of the monies would be placed into a trust for all of the children until they turned 35. Helio didn't believe in instant wealth. While the children were wealthy in their own right, the additional funds would have elevated them to a new level. Helio worried that it might cause them to become complacent if they were not older and most likely had families of their own.

A few nieces and nephews would receive sentimental family items, Helio's brother would get Catkin's 1966 Ford Fairlane, and Heliotrope's best friend, Harold Gill, would get his prized 1969 Ford Mustang.

Everyone had known for years who would get what, thus the reason for Snapper's boredom.

With a thrust, the heavy wooden door opened as Attorney Nick Harvey entered.

He was a pudgy man with thick, large-rimmed glasses. His suit was ill-fitting and he wore New Balance walking shoes. Magnolia had never liked him, but as were most of Helio's confidants, they were friends before they ever did any business together.

"My apologies for the delay. With the legal restrictions and Helio's changes last month— "

"His what?" Magnolia interrupted.

"Oh, you didn't know. Um, yes, he came in three days before his death and drafted a new will, but we'll get into all of that here shortly," he paused, waiting for another reaction from Magnolia.

She had collected herself, but she was boiling inside. This was exactly what she had feared was going to happen, but she didn't know that it had.

"We are just waiting on the copies to finish…ah, here they are. Thank you Denise."

He checked to make sure everything was in order before he handed a copy to everyone present. "I'm glad everyone could be here today. The copies you have contain redacted sections that will be released once the police have completed their investigation. Does anyone have any questions before we start?"

Snapper felt himself begin to say something, but he thought better of it. His boredom had been replaced by utter confusion. What possible changes could have been made, but more importantly, why?

"Okay, if there are no questions, we'll get right too it. I, Heliotrope Oak Blossom, being of sound mind and body —"

To the attorney's annoyance, Snapper interrupted. "My apologies, but can we dispense with the formalities and get to why we are all here?"

"Very well," Mr. Harvey replied. "We will start with the real estate holdings. Mrs. Magnolia Blossom will inherit the property known as Flora Fields and all properties surrounding it in the total of 247 acres. Additionally, she will inherit the beach house on Tybee Island, the ski chalet in Vale, and the estate known as Blossom Manor in England. Mr. Snapdragon Elm Blossom will inherit the Hilton Head, South Carolina beach condo, the undeveloped land in Buckhead, Georgia, and the vineyard in Tuscany, Italy."

He continued with the distributions for the girls. Gladiolus would get the Los Angles house and the apartment on TriBeCa in New York. Marigold would inherit the apartment in NoHo in New York and the condo in Malibu, California. Petunia would receive the animal shelters in Houston, Texas; Atlanta, Georgia; Charleston, South Carolina; and Phoenix, Arizona. Aconite would get the house in Greece, the house in Sidney, Australia, and the ski chalet in the Swiss Alps.

With that, the real estate was divided and although Magnolia had expected to get all of the properties, surprisingly she did not seem upset by the massive change. Looks, however, were deceiving.

Helio had correctly believed in the value of real estate and had begun his collection at the age of eighteen. By twenty-five he had bought and sold enough to purchase the beach house on Tybee Island for cash.

Snapper asked Mr. Harvey to move on to the extended family and to what Snapper referred to as the trinkets portion of the will. He didn't have much love for his family outside of his parents and sisters.

Once that was completed, Mr. Harvey continued through the rest of the provisions.

"Lastly, a personal note from Mr. Blossom to all of you. My beloved and precious family, I know that my vote for who will be elected CEO of House of Blossom looms heavy on all of you. I had hoped I would live long enough to retire and the choice would be obvious. Unfortunately, if this is the letter Mr. Harvey is reading, then that did not come to pass. The Board of Directors will vote for my replacement and I will stay my vote unless there is no majority decision. If that transpires, then Mr. Harvey holds a sealed envelope to only be opened if necessary. I feel that this is the only way to be fair to all of you. I love each of you so very much."

All of the Blossom family members sat in stunned taciturnity while the attorney nervously thumbed through the papers like he was looking for something…anything else to say. He knew that the letter would not go over well. Helio had warned Mr. Harvey that Magnolia would most likely blow up as she assumed that she would be appointed the next CEO, but it was Snapper who was the first to lose his composure.

He stood up and looked pointedly at each of his sisters, then his mother. "Fine, if none of you will say it, I will. This is complete bullshit. He knows…knew the Board would follow his vote which would obviously be Mother. Now he has made it look like he does not have confidence in her to run the company. This is disastrous. Out reputation will be ruined. Who could run the company better than Mother?" He turned to Mr. Harvey, "If you will excuse us, ladies let's go."

Without hesitation and in unison, all of the Blossom women stood up. Snapper opened the door and they all filed out leaving attorney Harvey dumbfounded.

"Ms. Dobson, the Dictaphone is ready for transcription," Snapper's voice squawked over his executive assistant's phone intercom.

The leggy twenty-six-year-old, Venus Dobson, walked into his office wearing her usual House of Blossom Wednesday dress code – a deep purple Oxford and a black pencil skirt that landed right above the knee with a three inch slit up the right thigh.

Magnolia had instituted a dress code for all employees, based on colors of flowers that would be blooming during the season, many years earlier. Monday was red for amaryllis, Tuesday was yellow for winter jasmine, Wednesday was purple for pansies, Thursday was pink for cyclamen, and Friday was green for evergreens. Oxford shirts were provided for all employees. Pants, skirts, and suits were all to be dark in color from blue to black. Men were given ties that featured the company logo in each of the prescribed colors for the season, set on matte black.

When Ms. Dobson leaned over to retrieve the device, Snapper couldn't help himself but to stare at her young, plump breasts that tested the strength of the thread that held the buttons in place. He'd always had a thing for older women. His sisters called it 'mommy issues" which caused even more strife between the siblings.

Without a word, Venus Dobson turned to exit.

"Ms. Dobson," Snapper called out.

She turned back to him. Her bouncy, brunette curls framed her face and held his attention.

With a slight shift in his voice, he continued. "I have a lunch meeting at noon, please make yourself available to attend."

"Yes, Mr. Blossom. Do I need to make reservations?"

"No, they have been arranged. That will be all."

Tony, the limousine driver, pulled up to the By George Hotel at 11:55am. Snapper and Venus casually walked in and headed to the bar. After ordering an afternoon cocktail, they chatted about business for a few minutes before Venus excused herself. Snapper ordered another drink. He walked toward the restaurant and over to the concierge for a brief conversation.

He lingered for a few moments in the lobby before heading to the elevators to attend his meeting. He wasn't in a rush since he and the person he was meeting had a standing engagement once a month in the company's penthouse suite that was mostly used for out of town guests, informal meetings, and business associates.

He unlocked the door with his phone and entered to find Venus sitting on the cherry red leather loveseat waiting for him. With long strides he made his way to her. She presented her luscious neck to him and he placed his lips in the soft curve.

"So, what are you in the mood for today," she asked with a coy smile.

"I need to blow off some steam. Take your clothes off," he replied in a gruff voice.

Theirs was not a romance. He had no desire or need for relationships. When he hired her, he had her sign a standard company million dollar non-disclosure agreement before he offered her what he called a bonus program.

If she voluntarily entered into a private arrangement with him for sex, she could set the terms and boundaries. If either of them wanted to terminate the contract, only 24 hours of notice needed to be given. There would be no backlash or interference with employment at any time as long as job performance was done properly, effectively, and efficiently. In exchange, a $25,000 bonus would be paid at the end of their contract or at the end of each year, whichever came first. An additional $10,000 would be added for each additional year the contract was in effect.

Venus agreed immediately that first day on the job. She had been with him for two years. He had rounded up and given her $70,000 as her Christmas bonus for a job well done. She was very thankful and showed her gratitude at the stroke of midnight New Year's Eve.

They undressed and as she stood there naked, he picked her up and wrapped her legs around his waist. He took her to the credenza and began to have his way with her. Biting her nipples and pounding into her at a frenzied pace.

Chapter 4

The Board of Directors meeting for the election of a new Chief Executive Officer was scheduled for four that afternoon. It was January 12, 2022, and the first Board meeting of the new year.

Tensions had been running high between all of the Blossoms and there had been backstabbing and arguments since the reading of the will. His father's letter had the opposite effect of his intensions.

His pure heart was not contagious in the Blossom household. Magnolia had groomed Snapper from day one to have her decisive and cold demeanor while her lack of emotion toward her daughters could not be quelled despite Helio's constant attempts at family bonding and unity.

Even the night he was killed was one of his famous family outings. He had bribed Magnolia with the promise of a trip to St. Barts if she would just be pleasant enough to join the family for dinner.

Snapper had suspected over the last year that their marriage might have been less than perfect, not that they would have let on to anyone, especially him or his sisters, but he'd heard spats and tense conversations.

While it was stressful waiting for the meeting, there was one thing that hung over the family even more – the police investigation. Detectives still had no answers despite reviewing CCTV from every camera up and down Peachtree Road and the interstate. The vehicle had been seen, but the license plate had a tinted cover, making it impossible to read, and the Ford Expedition was non-descript. It was quickly lost as it exited the interstate onto a road that did not have any CCTV coverage.

The only thing the police would divulge to the family was that the shooting was most likely a hit, not a Halloween prank gone wrong. Each one of the Blossoms had been brought in for questioning shortly after the murder, but one by one they all handed the detectives a business card with the names and numbers of their attorneys.

With all of the turmoil, Snapper had begun to grow suspicious of the people who slept under the same roof as him. He would ask subtle questions, in passing, to each of his sisters and even his mother, although with her they were phrased very carefully. He knew he was beyond reproach, but he couldn't say the same about the women in his life.

Magnolia sat at the head of the twenty-foot long Ebony conference table. She had assumed the interim role of CEO and fully expected to be voted into the position. Snapper took his seat to the left of his mother while Petunia sat to her right with Aconite next to her. Marigold sat next to Snapper and Gladiolus next to her.

The eighteen other board members gathered and promptly at 4pm the meeting started. The vote for the new CEO was listed as the last item on the agenda.

Confidently, Magnolia participated in all of the business and proudly stated that House of Blossom had finished the fourth quarter of 2021 with a seven percent profit increase from the third quarter.

She attributed the stability to her leadership despite her husband's murder and the subsequent ongoing police investigation.

The news media and social media had moved on from the headlines of October 31st and it seemed as if Magnolia had as well.

"Now to the last item on the agenda," announced the Board Chairman. He was a stocky fellow, with gray at his temples, but still strikingly handsome for a man of fifty-eight.

He was also Helio's best friend, Harold Gill. They met at Parsons. He had worked his way through the company starting in the design room. With every new collection, he liked to go down to the fourth floor and work with the seamstresses and tailors. He would tell them, 'Put me to work,' with a gleeful smile.

He went through the procedure that would take place for the vote. It was done by secret ballot. "Each of you have a ballot with the following names: Magnolia Blossom, Snapdragon Blossom, Petunia Blossom, Marigold Blossom, Gladiolus Blossom, and Aconite Blossom. Please consider your vote carefully. When you are ready, step behind the screen and place your ballot in the box. When everyone has voted we will count the votes to reveal our new Chief Executive Officer."

Once all twenty three votes had been cast, the ballot box was placed in front of Harold. He was the only one with a key to the box. The first three cards were votes for Magnolia, but then it changed.

"Snapdragon Blossom," Harold announced. "Snapdragon Blossom," he said again. "Aconite Blossom, Snapdragon Blossom, Marigold Blossom, Aconite Blossom, Snapdragon Blossom, Aconite Blossom…"

Magnolia's face could not hide her discontent with each pronouncement of one of her children's names. She began to sit up straighter and gripped the edge of the table. Snapdragon, on the other hand, was quite pleased. While he wanted the position, despite his outburst at the reading of the will, he knew it would piss every one of his sisters completely the fuck off if the baby of the family, little Oni, was CEO. He sat back in his chair and enjoyed the show.

Harold had announced all but one vote. "As it stands, we have three votes for Magnolia Blossom, one vote for Gladiolus Blossom, two votes for Marigold Blossom, eight votes for Aconite Blossom, and eight votes for Snapdragon Blossom. This places the last vote as either the deciding vote for between Miss Aconite Blossom or Mr. Snapdragon Blossom, or it will trigger the opening of the posthumous vote of Mr. Heliotrope Blossom that attorney Harvey has present her today.

As Harold pulled the last card from the box and unfolded it, Magnolia's eyes were burning a hole through it as if she could will it to be in her favor. She knew that she could get around Helio's vote if it wasn't for her by calling for another vote in the second quarter. She'd already worked out the details with her lawyer. The only thing she couldn't contest was a majority vote. She was completely appalled at the thought of working for, not with, one of her children. She cursed Helio's name under her breath.

"Our new CEO is Mr. Snapdragon Blossom," Harold exclaimed with a little too much enthusiasm.

Everyone stood and applauded, everyone except for Magnolia. She simply patted her hands in a dignified golf clap while all of his sisters crowded him with handshakes, hugs, and congratulations. They all truly loved their brother, but moreover, they were ecstatic that their mother wasn't CEO.

Once the round of applause ended and everyone sat back down, Magnolia finally stood to address the Board. "You have made a fine decision in electing my only son. He will serve us well and follow in the vision that his father and I have set for this company with honor and strength." With a champagne flute in hand, she raised her glass, "To Snapdragon Blossom, the future of House of Blossom."

Another rousing round of applause echoed through the room as everyone sipped their champagne and congratulated Snapper again.

Magnolia leaned over and kissed him on the cheek. "My office NOW," she demanded in his ear so as no one else could hear.

Snapper quickly thanked everyone, looked at his sisters, and walked with his mother out of the conference room.

She slammed the solid wooden door, darkened the windows of her office, and turned on the white noise soundproofing.

"What in the FUCK was THAT?" she screamed. "Why didn't you decline? Why did you not abdicate? Why didn't you do something other than sit there with that ridiculous smirk on your face? ANSWER ME!" She picked up the first thing she put her hands on from her desk, a marble paperweight, and threw it at him.

He ducked and it flew over his head, rip through her custom-made Mulberry silk walls, and plunked down beside him on the floor with a thud.

"Do you feel better, Mother?" Snapper scoffed. He was not one to test his mother, but he was feeling himself in that moment. He walked backward to the one piece of furniture in her office that was for show only. He knew he was grinding her nerves; he was testing the limits.

As he went to sit down, she screamed, "Snapdragon, I am still your mother and you will not…"

He began to snicker. "I wouldn't dare. I'm sorry Mother, I just needed to break your focus so you can hear me." He went and sat down in one of the wingchairs by the fireplace and asked her to join him. "Thank you. If I may, think about it. How would it have looked if I had refused. I would have looked weak. That is not the Blossom way; you taught me that. Don't worry, nothing has really changed.

You know I trust your judgement and I will seek your council and guidance. I have much to learn from you."

His platitudes worked and she took a deep breath. With calmness in her voice, she advised him to move into his father's office right away and to have his name on the door by morning. There didn't need to be a transition period and his taking the helm would strengthen the company's stability. She laid out a ten point plan that he needed to execute in his first one hundred days.

It was actually the plan she had created for herself to present to the board after she was elected CEO. It was a good plan and she was not about to let it go to waste. She advised him to not get it approved, to just implement it and show the Board that he was in charge from day one.

The fall collection was to be sent for final looks that Friday and model fitting adjustments were scheduled for Monday. She had always been personally involved in the decisions as she wanted fresh, natural faces. She was nothing if not progressive and she employed models of all shapes and ethnic cultures.

Her favorite tag line was that 'House of Blossom makes everyone bloom.' She was thought to be a trendsetter when the 2001 collection of ready to wear was exclusively for women of size 14 or larger and she really caused a scandal when her featured bride for the 2013 collection was a beautiful woman with vitiligo.

For all of her flaws and faults, Magnolia Blossom was ahead of her time when it came to recognizing the beauty in women the world might otherwise disregard.

"I think it would be good for you to be at these events. Put your face to the name of House of Blossom from the bottom to the top, Snapdragon."

Snapper agreed.

She also informed him that they had invited girls from around the world to be selected for the Fall New York Fashion Week. "These girls have only done local work in their areas. We have fifty coming. I pulled out all the stops this year to make them feel special, even if they don't get chosen. Fresh faces for fresh looks. Harold is extremely excited for fall. He says it will be the best summer collection we have ever put together for ready-to-wear and couture, but he *does* say that every year," she gave a hardy laugh.

Magnolia was a different person when only she and Snapper were in a room. She was slightly disarmed by her son, but she had her limits with him. As with the girls, she had no patience.

"I'm just glad it's over and decided. More importantly, who the fuck voted for Aconite? Was that a joke? She almost became CEO at seventeen. The company would have tanked in a month. Those board members see a young, fresh set of tits and simply lose their minds," Magnolia complained.

"It didn't happen, so let's not dwell. I am CEO and I will take care of everything. You won't be disappointed."

Snapper looked at his watch, "It's too late to call the decorator, but I'll phone him in the morning and go over some changes I want to make to the office before I move in."

That sounds great," she replied. "Let's go to *your* office and I'll get you up to speed on everything else. Plus, I have a few design ideas. Your father had such stuffy taste."

Chapter 5

Snapper was settling in nicely to his new position. His name was on the door, the decorator had removed the antique and dark accoutrements from the room and had created a more modern, industrial décor. The glass top desk with metal Z-shaped legs made the space feel open and bright. All of the large furnishings like sofas and chairs were light tan or light greens.

Pops of pinks, purples, blues, and yellows gave the office a softer feel that was more inviting and less intimidating than his father's oversized leather furniture and dark woods.

Unfortunately, he had not selected anything in the room except for the ergonomic swivel chair that sat behind his desk. Everything else was one-hundred percent his mother.

He didn't care. She had wonderful taste and now that his father was gone, Magnolia had planned to revamp the entire building. It was still drab and stodgy from Catkin's reign. Helio had let Magnolia redo the first floor and main lobby about ten years earlier, but even that looked dated now.

She had a grand plan to start on the first floor and completely redo the first impression. Next would be the eighteen floor, where all of their offices were located. Then she would move to the atelier. She had been creating spreadsheets, getting quotes, and designing mood boards and color palettes for over a month. She was in her element. She even spoke of possibly creating a home décor division once she was done. Snapper had put the brakes on that, for now. She'd probably get her way eventually.

As he observed her, one thing kept bothering him. He hadn't seen her grieve for her husband. There had been no tears, no breakdowns, no introspection, no reflection. She had continued on like he had not been there in the first place.

The one thing he had always thought was that she loved him, but now his doubts consumed his thoughts. It was the little things over the last year that he thought back on. How they had taken separate vacations, the usual pecks on the cheek or holding hands looked forced, they would be hold up in her office only for both of them to exit unhappy, especially Helio. Something had been happening, he just didn't know what.

Frustrated, he hadn't heard anything from the police in weeks, he phoned Detective Stone. As usual, there were no leads, none of the tips had panned out, but they were still working the case. Stone genuinely sounded defeated.

Stone knew Helio. Through the extensive work the company did with law enforcement with donations of K9 Kevlar vests, a new gym at the police academy, and hosting an annual community meet and greet BBQ to help the community and the officers bond and get to know each other, Stone had respect and admiration for Helio.

He asked Snapper once again if the family would come in for interviews. He thought that he might be able to gain some insight into who could have committed such a heinous crime to such a nice man.

"He was one of the few businesspeople in Atlanta who didn't make us regular folks feel inferior. Snapper, maybe if you came in and talked to me, your family would follow your lead. Something y'all think is nothing could be something to the investigation." Stone's pleas hit Snapper's logic and business acumen.

He agreed to come in with his attorney. He could hold a press conference and let the public know how the family was fully cooperating with authorities. As a bonus, it would be a good way to introduce himself as the new CEO.

Snapper also knew what he could do that the police couldn't, call his private investigator and really dig deep. Sam, as he liked to be called for anonymity, was a burly man. He was all muscle and had movie star good looks. He could pass as intimidating or charming depending on the situation.

When he hung up the phone with Stone, he immediately called Sam. "I want you to look into my mother and sisters for any connection to my father's murder. Someone planned this and I want to start with hopefully eliminating them. Unfortunately, I have a feeling one of them is behind this. Start with my mother. Whatever you need, just let me know."

"Got it. I'll text you the code *aubergine* when I have something," Sam replied. "Yes, I know fashion colors," he added.

A few days after contacting Stone, Snapper sat alone in the office. It was nine in the evening and everyone else had gone home. He couldn't get the nagging feeling that had crept into his brain from his conversation with Detective Stone. What was to be gained by the detective? He had to realize that he wouldn't be able to garner any information out of Mother or the girls.

Snapper's appointment was for eight the next morning. He didn't know if Stone had contacted anyone else or if he was going to wait until Snapper submitted.

It didn't escape his notice that the whole purpose might be to manipulate him into a false confession or some bullshit that was incriminating. Unfortunately for Stone, Snapper was best under pressure. They weren't going to get a word that could be used against him.

The breakfast table was quiet as the word of Snapper going to speak to the police had been confirmed. Detective Stone had called all of them and expressly told them that it would show solidarity between the Blossom's and the police if they would all follow suit.

Lydia walked into the room to refresh the coffee cups.

"This sure is good bacon today, Lydia. I like the crisp edges," Snapper complimented.

"Thank you, sir. I will continue to prepare it that way if everyone is pleased."

No one said anything but the place that had originally held thirty strips of bacon on it was currently empty. She had her answer.

"It was my grandmother's method. We couldn't figure it out and she held it close to the vest. My sister's and I got together this weekend to put our heads together to figure it out. It's not exactly like hers, but it's pretty darn close. I appreciate you all noticing the hard work."

"We do Lydia, we appreciate you." Mari said in a genuine voice.

"Oh, Miss Marigold you are going to make me cry. I'm going back to the kitchen," she giggled as she walked away.

Snapper patted Mari's hand, "That was lovely of you to say."

Mari's smile always made Snapper happy.

"What time will you ladies arrive at work today? I don't know how long my meeting will be —"

Magnolia interrupted him, "Meeting, Snapdragon Blossom, you can't possibly be that naïve. This is not a meeting, it's not a casual interview, it's an interrogation. They don't have anything so they suspect it's one of us. Seriously, son. Open your eyes. None of us wanted your father dead, but the family is always the focus." She changed the subject. "Now if they wanted to speak about releasing the monetary holdings, that is a conversation I would happily participate in with them. You really shouldn't do this," she warned. As an afterthought, she added, "You two," she pointed at Snapper and Mari, "stop fraternizing with the help. Lydia is here to do a job, not be your friend. Honestly," she sighed, "where did I go wrong?"

Ignoring the comment about Lydia, Snapper replied, "What's the worst that can happen? My attorney will advise me to not answer anything inappropriate. It'll be fine."

"I've been thinking," Aconite inserted, "I might go talk to him. Mother, they might ask questions that we haven't thought about. Don't you want to see Father's killer brought to justice?"

Magnolia scoffed, "Certainly, but I don't think that we should invite trouble. How do we know that one of us isn't a target. I could be next."

In her usually melodramatic fashion, she stood up forcefully. "None of you," she looked each one of them in the eye," should talk to the detective. Don't get involved," she commanded with a pointed look at Snapper.

With that, she walked away from the table. She was confident they would all listen and follow her instructions. She was wrong.

"Thank you for coming down Mr. Blossom. Right in here, please." Detective Stone looked haggard. He wasn't kidding when he said he was working on the case all day and night. The dark circles under his eyes and the hunch of his shoulders aged him.

He was at least forty, but he looked like he was approaching his sixties. Grey had taken over where hints of black hair remained to suggest that he had once looked so much younger. He wasn't particularly muscular, but he was in good shape. His green eyes looked dull and heavy. The weight of what he'd seen in his career was written all over his face.

They weren't in a standard interrogation room. He called it a soft room. There was basic furniture with a small sofa and a few oversized chairs placed neatly under a round table.

"I figured we'd be more comfortable in here. I'm sorry we have to do this, but any help we can get..."

Snapper interrupted, "Yes, Detective, I understand. I'm here to fully cooperate."

Stone took a deep breath and jumped right into the questions. He asked Snapper to go back through exactly what he remembered from that night. Had he seen anything suspicious, had anyone been watching or following the family, had anyone approached Helio that might be suspicious? Then he asked a question that flooded Snapper with guilt, because he had been asking the same question to himself for months.

"I hate to ask, but do you think it's possible that your mother or maybe one of your sister's took out the hit on your father?"

Snapper's face gave him away and he turned to his attorney. They had discussed the possibility and the attorney knew about the private investigator. He told Snapper that it wasn't going to hurt him to tell the detective. So, with a heavy heart he shared his concerns and that he had hired a private investigator to look into his mother's movements and communications within six months before the murder. His heart was heavy with the conflicting emotions of duty and loyalty, each pulling him in opposite directions.

"When do you meet with your PI?" Stone asked.

"I honestly don't know. He told me that he would get in touch with me when he had something. No word yet, but he is very thorough and he's not going to give it to me piecemeal. I'll share with you whatever he finds. But, Stone, this cannot leave this room. If my mother or sisters knew I was doing this, it would cause chaos to profound proportions."

I understand. No mention of it in the file."

"Thank you, Detective. May we go now, I do have a company to run and I have a class this evening as well."

"Yes, of course. I appreciate your taking the time. Your sister, Mari, contacted me to come in tomorrow. Did you know?"

"She had mentioned it. I'm glad. She's a wonderful person and I am sure she will do everything she can to help."

They all stood up and Snapper headed for the door.

"Oh, just one more thing," Stone commented, "have you checked your mother's finances or even those of the company? You know, money is a strong motivation for murder. We have been trying to access her accounts, but her army of lawyers keep blocking us."

Snapper nodded and left the room.

Chapter 6

Venus spent the next morning pulling the company financials for the last year. She had to be inconspicuous in her work. Magnolia, being CFO, kept a close watch on who accessed the files. Snapper needed his mother to be completely unaware of his covert operation to review each line of expenditures.

She enlisted help from one of the guys in accounting that she knew had a crush on her. All she had to do was unbutton one button to let a peek of her cleavage show and he was butter.

"Gary," she asked in a sweet, Southern drawl, "You know I work for Mr. Blossom and well, he's got me on a task that is larger than I can handle on my own. I was wondering, if you don't mind, if you would help me…" she paused. She didn't want to push her flirting too far, but she did what she had to do to get the job done. "no, it's too much to ask. You're such a busy man and I know how hard you work." She emphasized all of the words that she knew would get his attention.

"No, I'm not too busy," he said nervously. His pulse was racing and he couldn't stop staring at her chest. He did try to make a conscious effort to look up at her face, but she had strategically placed her breasts at eye level as she bent over and placed one hand on his shoulder.

"Really? Gary you don't know how happy that makes me. I knew you were the man for the job."

By two that afternoon, Venus had successfully procured all of the information she needed from Gary and delivered it to Snapper.

She walked into his office with four interns pushing hand trucks full of boxes. They followed her like puppies.

"Got it," she told Snapper with a smile and a wink.

Just as he began to open the first box, Marigold entered his office.

"I told her you were unavailable, "Venus said breathlessly as she rushed in behind Mari.

"It's okay, please hold all of my calls and block my calendar for the next hour."

Once the door closed, he jumped up and quickly walked over to Mari. She looked visibly upset. Mari what's going on?"

Dragon, oh Dragon, it was awful. I went to see that detective. BTW, I'm not doing that again. Anyway, He asked me all kinds of questions about father and mother, then he asked if I'd be willing to record conversations with mother."

"He did WHAT?!" Snapper yelled.

"Calm down, my attorney shut that shit down and I explained to the detective that Mother and I do not have that kind of relationship, so he relented, but still…I know you want us to help, but I don't see how that would help even if she did love me."

Snapper took a deep breath. "I know I can't convince you that she does love you, but I agree it wouldn't do any good."

Mari added, "She'd never slip or talk if she had anything to do with it. How do you feel about the possibility?"

"It doesn't sound too farfetched to me, especially after that big blow up they had about six months ago."

Mari looked perplexed.

Snapper continued, "You know, the one where they were screaming…well Mother was screaming, after Father confronted her about the missing company money."

"I don't know anything about this. What do you know?"

"Oh, I think you were in Italy when it happened. Yeah, by the time you got back it seemed to have been handled, didn't hear anything more about it. I forgot to mention it. Anyway, apparently there is, over twenty five million missing. Mother told him it wasn't missing it had been transferred into discretionary because she wanted to have access for redecorating the lobby. We all know that's bullshit. That's no more than a two or three million dollar project, but the thing is, I have looked. There have been no proposals, no bids, no vision boards, not even fabric swatches ordered. And Mari," he looked back at the door to make sure they were completely alone, "I can't find the money."

"What?"

"After the argument, I started doing some snooping. Father was right, the money just…well, vanished. I can't find a transfer that it went anywhere. That amount of money isn't easy to hide. How Father found out is a mystery to me. I don't know what it means, but if Mother isn't involved, she has let a huge fuck up happen on her watch. Come over here, Snapper requested. "These boxes are all of the company expenditures for the last year. Every invoice, note, contract, correspondence, all of it. Can you stay late tonight?"

"Yes, of course," she replied with concern and wariness in her voice.

"Good, we will go through this piece by piece and see if we can figure this out. There has to be something in these boxes to explain the missing money."

"Or it's going to give Mother a good motive for murder." Mari stated hesitantly. She walked over to Snapper and wrapped her arms around him for reassurance.

"I know, I was thinking it too," he said with a soft tone.

He walked the floors of the Blossom Building to make sure everyone was gone. Even checking the bathroom and supply closets. The coast was clear.

They started with the boxes for January 2021. They laid them out on the floor by the category of expenditure. If multiples were on the same invoice, that was its own category. It was a laborious and arduous task and they quickly realized that they would need many nights together to find what they were looking for, even if it *was* in all of the paper that was stacking high on the floor.

Once January was sorted through a first pass, they each sat in front of a stack and started reviewing, analyzing, and calculating.

"What is this?" Mari asked.

Snapper examined the document carefully. The amounts paid were too high for what was listed as the company's import of hand-painted buttons. That was a highly specialized item that House of Blossom only used in their couture collections. Stranger still was that they had a long standing contract for that item through a different company. Neither of them had heard of Ailongam Limited, but the payment was authorized by their mother.

"This is our starting point," Snapper decided, "Look for that company in all of the months. If you see anything else suspicious, sit it to the side and we'll come back to it. With Mother's hand in this one, we need to gather that information first."

Two hours later, they had found three invoices for the same company each month. It didn't look like it had started in 2021. They suspected it went back further. It must have gone back several years, if not more. The task was bigger than they thought. With thirty six invoices they had found over a million dollars.

Mari looked up the information in the company's approved vendors directory, but it did not exist. She then tried a simple internet search to find any information. That too was a dead end.

"Snapper, do you think this is a shell company? We need to follow the money. Obviously, it's not coming to the company and as far as I know we have not received 360 hand-painted buttons in the last twelve months. Although, I will check inventory logs to verify."

"It's getting late, let's take a break, go home, and get some rest. We can come back to all of this," he gestured with a sweep of his hand in the air above all of the boxes, "tomorrow. Come on, we can grab some greasy hamburgers from the diner. Mother should be asleep by now, so she won't yell at us for eating them."

"Fries too," she asked gleefully.

"Absolutely! How about we even get chocolate milkshakes?"

She nodded enthusiastically as they headed for the office door.

Snapper locked it, checked it twice, and even changed his key code. He couldn't run the risk of someone going into his office and seeing the sea of papers that littered his floor.

As the sun melted the morning fog, Snapper and Mari were already back in the office. Something had bothered him all night, to the point of obsession. He tossed and turned but got little sleep. He knew there was something about Ailongam Limited that was familiar, he just couldn't place it.

They were auditing all of the invoices and putting the pieces of the puzzle together when Snapper stood up abruptly. "Mari! You won't believe this. It's been in front of our faces the entire time. I'm embarrassed to say that it's not even clever and I completely missed it. Come look at this."

She peered over his shoulder and looked at the papers. They were the same ones that she'd now seen a dozen times and with only four hours of sleep, they didn't look any different to her.

"What am I looking at?" she asked.

"The name, the company name. It's her. Ailongam is Magnolia backwards."

Mari's eyes were wide and she began to giggle, "Well, she has always said that the best way to get one over on your competition is to hide in plain side." She paused for a moment while she paced the room. "We have proof it's her. My head is spinning and I'm starving. Waffles and bacon?" she asked.

"Waffles and bacon." Snapper agreed with a smile.

Chapter 7

The diner located just a block from the office building was bustling with patrons trying to get in a cup of coffee before work. Mari loved the fifties décor. She didn't know anything about the era, but she thought the style was unique and playful.

She thought she may do some research on the styles of the day and possibly draw up some sketches to go over with the designers for a future collection. It was popular in fashion to modernize classic garments and she liked reaching into the past for inspiration.

After ordering two coffees and two breakfasts specials, Mari didn't waste any time asking Snapper a question that had been on the tip of her tongue since they had left the office.

Choosing her approach decisively she asked, "Dragon, don't you think it would help to bring Dio into this…" she hesitated, "you know she's a genius when it comes to money and, well, I feel horrible leaving her out of this. I mean, she is my twin after all, we don't have secrets. At least we can't keep anything from each other. Trust me, I've tried." She looked up at him with her doe eyes to examine his face.

The waitress sat their coffees on the table and walked away. Snapper added a splash of creamer and took a sip.

"I'm not opposed to the idea. Her skills would be helpful, but she has a tendency to run her mouth. Nia and Oni would know everything before lunch. That would compromise our position."

She could tell that he was giving the proposal serious thought and running all of the possible scenarios in his head. Snapper had a talent for being able to assess who would be helpful and who would be a liability. His uncanny knack for finding the weak spots before they even emerged was tried and true tested.

"When we get back, I'll have Venus call her to come to my office. There will be ground rules. First on the list, do not involve Nia or Oni in any way. This needs to be contained, at least until we know more. If mother got wind, even the smallest hint of what we are doing she would…honestly, I shudder to think what she would do."

His worry went beyond the missing money, although he had not shared his dread with anyone, not even Mari. That was a suspicion that he was going to keep close to the vest.

"I'm here all great and powerful Oz," Dio announced as she sauntered into the office. Unlike her twin, Dio was incorrigible. She didn't take shit from anyone and she had a temper like a viper.

She and Mari weren't identical twins and their features were like mirror images of their parents. Dio was the spitting image of their mother and Mari's softer features echoed the kindness of their father. Despite their differences, the girls were close and just like most twins, they had what they called *twintuition*. Reading each other's minds, finishing each other's sentences, and even knowing when the other one was hurt, but most of all they knew when the other one was lying or keeping a secret.

As soon as Dio walked into the room, she made a beeline for Mari and linked arms with her.

"What are you two doing? I can tell there is something going on. Mari?"

Mari glanced at Snapper.

"Go ahead," he coaxed as he sat in his chair.

All of the details were exposed as Mari went through every suspicion and every piece of paper that she and Snapper had discovered. The floor full of papers told the story of how they had organized and categorized all of what they had found so far.

"We don't have anything concrete yet, but that's where you come in," Mari expressed to Dio.

Snapper had waited patiently to insert his one rule. "Dio, this is all confidential. Nia and Oni cannot know. While none of us are exactly fond of Mother, those two are easily broken by Mother's interrogation. It's for their own good that they not know about this, at least for now. Can you agree to that? If not, you can walk away now and consider all of this just a couple of siblings venting."

She gave Snapper a furious look. "First off, I wouldn't tell those two bobble heads anything of this magnitude. They would hedge their bets and go tattling to Mother. But, I have a question, if Mother did siphon the money, what did she do with it? What did she need it for when she has plenty of money at her disposal. Something about this makes me think that there is more to this than just missing money. There's a reason why that money is missing. We also have to consider that someone is setting Mother up to take the fall for embezzlement. I don't know, the whole thing is crude, unsophisticated…this isn't Mother's style."

Snapper looked at Mari, "She's right. The backwards name is our only possible link to Mother, but even with the hiding in plain sight theory, it doesn't track with how she conducts herself."

"Maybe, that's the point. Do something completely out of character to throw off any reasonable explanation that it would actually be her. Dio can you dissect the transactions, trace them to the source?"

"It will take some after-hours snooping, but yes, I think that can be done. But for now, I have to put a pin in this. I have a class in an hour. I need to get back to my office. You two good for now?"

"We'll start analyzing the data that we have and see how far back this goes to see what patterns we can deduce," Mari replied.

As she approached the door, Dio turned to her sister, "Mari, meet me for lunch. One o'clock at Café Lily." It wasn't a request.

Mari simply nodded and Dio disappeared into to sea of rings, buzzes, and chatter that filled the halls of House of Blossom.

After a brief moment, Snapper cut the silence, "Well, that was interesting. As much as she and I don't get along, I can admit that she is rather brilliant. I hadn't thought about someone trying to frame Mother. I mean, let's face it, she does have a laundry list of enemies."

Mari huffed, "That's ridiculous. This has Mother's name literally written all over it. I don't know what, but she's up to something. I do agree with Dio, there is more here than just the money." She clapped her hands, "Okay, let's get to work."

"Goldie, as much as I would like to make this my only task, as you can see from this stack on my desk, I have to actually run the company. I haven't even checked my emails this morning and Venus has been holding my calls all morning. We're going to have to keep this to after-work hours. First things first, we have to get all of these papers that we don't need into a filing cabinet. I'll put the important ones in my safe."

"Fuck, I have a meeting in twenty minutes," Mari exclaimed.

Snapper stood up and walked her to the door. "You go, I've got this."

Venus handed him a stack of pink missed call notes before he closed his office door to get back to work. Diligently, he returned each phone call and spent hours going over everything from the stack that had accumulated on his desk since he'd started spending so much time working on investigating his father's murder.

While his father and he were not as close as he might have liked, Snapper admired him and knew that he didn't have any enemies. Knowing that made him more worried that his mother was somehow involved. He dreaded the thought.

Every once in a while he would look over his desk at the papers on his floor. He was compelled to return to them. If for no other reason than to figure out how to prove his mother's innocence. There had to be a reasonable explanation for the fake company and the missing money.

He stood from his desk and began scanning through the documents again. As he worked he placed the innocuous ones in a file cabinet. It was an overwhelming task.

There was no pattern to the payments. Nothing to suggest that they weren't legitimate expenditures. The trail was clean on the surface, but as they had suspected, it had not just started. As he dug deeper, he realized that the Ailongam Limited Company had created fake vendors too.

Each one he looked up was not in the approved vendors list and there was no internet presence. All of their vendors were vetted and as far as he knew were established enough to have at least a website if not a complete social media presence of some kind. Nothing made sense.

He texted Sam and asked if they could meet sometime in the near future. He wanted to run this information by Sam, who was rather elusive but was damn good at his job.

Snapper had used his services for a blackmail case that had affected him personally.

Some punk, as Sam had called him, had taken pictures of Snapper at a party making out with a girl that turned out to be fifteen. Snapper had no idea. She looked like she was in her twenties. There was even a short video that had been loaded onto YouTube.

The party was at the house of one of his friends and there were hundreds of people there. It was the first legitimate party Snapper had ever been at with people his own age. Before that, his party-going had consisted of House of Blossom functions. They were very civilized and stuffy. This was not that kind of party.

He had left the house under the guise of going to a study group knowing that if he got caught it would be the ruination of his family, so he thought. He didn't care. At the time he was going through a rebellious phase and had faced his mother's wrath plenty of times before. Short of killing him, he was willing to take the risk.

When the pictures were texted to him the next day and the caption read, "Blossom likes 'em young." He knew he was in trouble.

Luckily, the pictures and video were from across the room. To the naked eye it was hard to make out that it was even Snapper.

The next text was, "$100,000 or these go public. That's when Snapper found Sam.

He'd never told anyone about it and within a day Sam had it all taken care of with a little of his own brand of persuasion. The whole thing got messy and ugly, but Sam was able to get the video taken down and the pictures destroyed, which earned Snapper's respect. That case was personal, this case was family.

Chapter 8

Mari got to the café early, very early. She practically ran out of her meeting to beat Dio there. Her twin did not suffer tardiness. If you weren't early, you were late.

Deep down, Mari was a little bit scared of Dio. She'd never admit it, but it was there, gnawing at her when her sister's face showed that 'no' was not an answer. Similar to the face she saw as Dio entered the café.

Dio's face was flawless as her jet-black, straight hair fell slightly over her shoulders. With only the accent of a red lipstick, it sometimes chilled Mari how much her twin looked like their mother. But unlike their mother, Dio had a tell when she had something on her mind. There was a small crease that formed right above her left eye. Barely noticeable to most, but Mari could spot it every time.

She sat down abruptly, but gracefully, and faced Mari. She saw the waitress heading their way and waved her off.

"Mari," she said in an exasperated tone, "what bullshit have you gotten yourself mixed up in with Snapper?"

Before Mari could open her mouth to reply, Dio continued.

"You know he is just trying to oust Mother from the company. I've heard the rumblings for years about how he wants to change the entire concept of the House. You are playing right into his hands. You are so gullible. Fuck, he probably stole the money himself to set up Mother."

"He did not!" Mari said a little too loudly. She looked around with embarrassment and mouthed 'sorry' to the couple who sat beside them. "He didn't, I'm telling you something is going on and it involves the stolen money. What that means, I don't know, but I do know that Dragon had nothing to do with it." Her tone was firm and settled.

"Okay," Dio relented, "If you think he's clean, then I believe you. I'm glad you brought me into this, even if it is a complete shitshow. I still don't believe that Mother is behind this, it's too clumsy and too easy to trace. Hell, you and Snapper did it."

"Fuck you..." Mari retorted.

Dio interrupted her, "Calm down, I'm just kidding. Honestly, I'm glad he's CEO. I didn't want Mother in that role. She'd have made all of our lives a living hell more than she already does." She paused for a moment, "You don't think one of the bobbleheads had anything to do with this, do you? Is that why Snapper doesn't want them to know?"

"No and no. He just knows they would run straight to Mother. He wasn't joking about that, he doesn't trust them," Mari replied.

"I don't blame him. They may be smart, but they are worthless when it comes to loyalty. Speaking of which, Snapper isn't so fond of me either. Why did he read me in on this?"

"I insisted." Mari left it at that. She did not need to give Dio ammunition to look down her nose at her, which she often did. Being twins aside, Dio was out for herself and she'd just a soon push Mari over a cliff than help her up from one.

"Interesting," Dio replied with a look that wasn't exactly distrust, but it wasn't trust either.

The waitress began to approach again and Dio didn't restrain her approach. They ordered and settled into lunch while they continued to mull over the details they had so far about the missing money.

After work, the three of them met in Snapper's office. It looked like nothing had ever happened. All of the files were off the floor and his stack of work was down to a manageable pile on the corner of his desk. If nothing else, Snapdragon was an impressive businessman.

With the door locked, he opened the safe and retrieved the pertinent papers. As he closed the safe, he asked, "Did everyone get Mother's text?"

The twins replied in unison, "Yes."

He looked at his watch, "That means we only have about two hours to work, then we have to head home. She'll expect us to be seated by eight."

"Yes, brother dear, we know the drill," Dio said in a mocking tone.

Ignoring her, Snapper continued, "I've organized everything into spreadsheets, created Venn Diagrams to depict overlaps and organized all that we know so far into a PowerPoint presentation. I have placed these on flash drives, so this information is not on the main server."

He walked back to his desk and pulled out a laptop. "I assume you both brought your air gapped computers. I've made each of you a copy of the flash drive." He leaned forward to hand them to the twins. "Everything is editable, so we can all access at the same time or edit or add to them on our own. I have an original backup, just in case in the safe. I'll add updated files as we go to that drive."

"Wow," Mari stated as she admired the amount of work that Snapper had already accomplished. "Dragon this is impressive. I can see all of the patterns and distributions. Wait, what is this…" she paused. "On June fifteenth of last year there is an anomaly in these withdrawals. It's fifty-thousand-dollars over any of the others and it was distributed to John Smith."

"It's obviously a fake name," stated Dio.

"Yes, I thought that as well," replied Snapper, "until I remembered that there was a janitor that was fired around that time who was oddly enough named John Smith. Personally, I don't think it's random."

"What does it mean?" asked Mari.

"That's what I'm hoping Dio can tell us. Any thoughts, Dio?"

"Was he fired or did he quit? Was he let go, that was during the time when twenty people were shifted around to other divisions of the company. Was he one of them?"

"That is a very good question. I'll pull his employ file. I don't want to do it on the company computer. Give me a minute, I'll go down to Human Resources and pull his file," Snapper replied.

As the elevator doors opened, Snapper was greeted by two sour-faced young ladies, Oni and Nia.

"You headed to Mother's dinner too?" Oni questioned.

Quick on his feet, Snapper nodded in the affirmative. He politely stepped onto the elevator and greeted his sisters with slight kisses on their cheeks. They rode down to the parking garage in silence.

As the bell dinged and the doors opened, Snapper held the door for the girls. He went to take a step out of the elevator when he patted his pockets.

"Damn, I left my phone in my office. You two go ahead, I'll meet you there."

"Fine, don't be late. I'm not in the mood to hear Mother lecture about punctuality again," Nia fussed.

"I promise, I'm right behind you, we still have plenty of time. Be safe," he remarked as he stepped back in the elevator and pushed the button for the second floor.

It occurred to him that he hadn't said his customary 'I love you' to the girls. He did love them, but he wasn't the protective brother he always thought he should be to his sisters. Mari was the only one that got that privilege.

It wasn't from a lack of trying to love them like a brother should, he just saw them as rivals instead of siblings. That was how they were all raised. To compete, not give into silly things like love.

Although it wasn't for a lack of trying on the part of his father. Helio was the light of love in the family. As overbearing and demonstrative his mother was, his father was the opposite.

As he got older, Snapper wondered what his father saw in his mother. Whatever it was, he truly adored her. His dying word was, "Magnolia."

Snapper hurried to the employee file room. As a teenager, he had worked a summer in Human Resources, so he knew exactly where to go to find the file. He plucked out John Smith's folder. In a dash, he was back to his office.

"We have to hurry; Nia and Oni were on the elevator and I pretended that I'd left my phone in here. They will get suspicious if I'm too far behind them. Here's the file." He handed it to Dio.

As she looked through it, she explained that he wasn't fired after all. He was transferred to the Charlotte division. The file noted that he requested the transfer to be closer to family to help care for his sick mother.

"That can't be right. Are you sure that *he* requested the transfer? I remember, for some reason, that he once told me that his mother had died. That was years ago. Cancer, I think," Mari commented.

"We'll have to look that up tomorrow," Snapper stated as he gathered up everything and headed for the safe. "We have to go. You know those two will tell Mother they saw me."

Hurriedly, they all got on the elevator. The last thing they needed was for Nia and Oni to invite trouble by upsetting their mother. She was volatile enough on her own.

When they got to the parking deck, they each went to their respective cars and headed to what they could only imagine was an ambush dinner with their mother.

Chapter 9

The twins and Snapper made good time as they arrived, changed clothes, and were properly seated at the dining table at ten minutes before eight.

As Magnolia walked into the room, all eyes turned to her. She was dressed in all black, which was never a good sign. She didn't even wear black to Helio's funeral. It was also disconcerting that her hair was in a slicked back ponytail instead of its usually stick straight style that flowed down her back with two perfectly placed strands over her shoulders.

Each sibling had a chill run down their spine, but they didn't show it. To show fear was weakness and there was no weakness in the Blossom household.

Snapper promptly stood as she approached the table and pulled out her chair as she took her place at the head of the table. The pork chops sat juicy while the mashed potatoes let off steam that melted the pats of butter sitting atop them and the cracked pepper and pink Himalayan salt was placed perfectly on the asparagus. But no one dared to start eating.

"Let's hold hands and say grace," Magnolia said in a sickly sweet tone.

Everyone hesitated. They hadn't done that since Helio died. He didn't push it at every meal, but every Sunday for lunch he insisted. Everyone did it at most meals anyway out of respect for him.

He grew up in the church and he had deep feelings for faith. He attributed it to all of the good things that he had in his life. Magnolia had also grown up in the church, but she turned her back on religion when the pastor couldn't answer her questions.

The one that tripped her up the most was that the gospels had been written hundreds of years after the events that they espoused and she wanted to know how these men would possibly know the events in such great detail. When the pastor told her it was from oral traditions, she scoffed and never went back to church. She was 11.

The next time she was in a church was for her wedding to Helio. She didn't go back until Helio expressed that he wanted the children to have the opportunity to make up their own minds. Magnolia couldn't argue with the logic; it was what her parents had allowed her to do.

Magnolia's prayer was awkward, "There is food in this house for those who deserve it. There is a roof above us for those who deserve it. Not everyone in this house deserves these things for betrayal is a sin. Amen."

Once the prayer was over, they all quickly released hands. They were unnerved by her words and without their father there to give a proper blessing, the girls faces gave them away that it made them long for their father. When Magnolia shot them a look, they immediately shifted their expressions.

Then her authoritative and commanding voice was unleashed. Calmly she asked, "Do you children take me for a fucking fool?"

The stare that she gave each one of them was chilling. She squared up and slowly, with no movement of her head, looked each of them in the eyes – one by one. Snapper, Dio, and Mari were nervous. Oddly, so were Nia and Oni. No one dared to look away, but there was something in each of their expressions that allowed a hint of discomfort and deception to seep through.

No one spoke. Out of fear or out of respect. It wasn't clear. For Magnolia, it was absolutely out of a hatred for repeating herself.

Snapper took the lead, "Mother, we would never. How can we reassure you?"

"Oh Snapdragon," she placed her hand on the table in front of him, "There is no reassuring me at this point. I know the answer to the question and my disappointment runs deep." Her words sounded so soft, but they landed hard. Disappointing their mother was more of a sin than murder in the Blossom house.

She let out a chuckle of sorts. It was not intended to alleviate any emotions the children felt, it was more to emphasize her point. "It astounds me how stupid you all are, thinking that you can keep anything from me. I see such brilliance in all of you. Wit, charm, decisiveness, each of you have these in spades, but none of you are cunning and that is disappointing."

They were all confused and waiting for Magnolia to give them a hint, a clue, as to what they had done to displease her. But they knew the game. She would continue to poke and lay insults at their feet as the magnificently prepared meal grew as cold as her heart. The dinner was merely a pretense to gather them for her display of discontent.

"How is it possible that I raised such irritatingly insufferable children." She paused, "I blame your father."

Oni couldn't help but to gasp at the thought.

"Hold your tongue, Aconite! I will have no outburst of grief for your father. He is gone; we move on."

One single tear escaped Nia's left eye before she could stop it. The girls were all close with their father and being left with their mother was a nightmare as far as they were concerned.

Once again Snapper spoke," Mother, we all realize that we have done something that has been well below your excellent standards. If you would let us fix whatever we have done, I can assure you it will not happen again. I will see to that personally."

"Well, that is quite the statement, Snapdragon." She let that stir in his brain. "You know, I think I will take you up on that. You need to be responsible for your sisters and make sure that each one of you is not only a steward of respectability for this family, but more importantly, a model of leadership and representation for the company."

Magnolia rang the small bell that was always placed by her plate, to summon the housekeeper. Lydia was once again on kitchen duty. The staff knew never to enter unless summoned or given permission to serve freely. That evening Lydia had been given strict instructions to stay out of the dining room until Magnolia rang.

It was demeaning and deplorable, but Lydia had three children under the age of twelve and a husband who had just gone through a knee replacement surgery. Even though Magnolia was a tyrant, she paid well, very well.

Lydia stepped out of the kitchen and without a word, Magnolia waved her in to serve. She filled up all of the glasses with water and carefully served the meal, even though it was cold. She wanted to offer to heat everything up in the oven, but she knew better. From the kitchen, she had heard the entire conversation. She wasn't about to make it worse on the children.

The dinner was met with silence as the siblings pushed food around their plates. No one was really in the mood to eat after their mother's tyrant. Each of the children repeated her words back int their heads wondering if she knew that they were investigating their father's murder. Magnolia did not elaborate and the children did not ask. Oh, the game of mindfuck she played.

Chapter 10

Once Magnolia finally left the dining table, the siblings sat there for a brief moment. Stunned, sizing each other up. Thinking, wondering. Quietly they each stood up and exited the room. Nia and Oni went to the fourth bedroom on the right down the east wing of the house. It was currently a guest room, so they were hoping for privacy and more importantly, to not get caught.

"She knows," whispered Oni.

"You don't know that. Just calm down. She could just be fishing, there's no telling with her. She loves to screw with our heads. She is the reason I'm in therapy," replied Nia while she checked the room for bugs and cameras.

"I'm telling you; she knows that we are looking into father's death." Oni sighed. "I knew we shouldn't have hired that private investigator. He probably went straight to Mother and told her. Fuck her!"

"I don't care if she knows or not. She should be the one who is looking into it. The cops aren't doing anything. I know they don't have anything to go on, but damn, someone knows something."

The girls continued to speculate on what Magnolia did or didn't know for another hour, before they both concluded that it was just conjecture. She didn't even give a hint as to who she was disappointed in, she directed it at all of them.

"What if Snapper and the twins are up to something?" I wouldn't put it past Snapper to do something and try to solve the case to be the good little mama's boy. It is sickening how he sidles up to her and kisses her ass."

"If he is, you know Mari is involved too. But there is no way that he would do anything or work with Dio. They are oil and water," said Oni.

"That's true, but if he is doing something with Mari, you know she can't stand to leave Dio out. That girl is such a plebian when it comes to her highness Gladiolus."

Nia rolled on the bed laughing. "Facts!"

"We'd better go to our rooms. Knowing Mother she's doing a bed check." As she walked to the door she requested, "Remind me again why we live here."

Um, well…"

Oni interrupted, "It was rhetorical."

"Yes, we need to meet. I need to know what you have found so far and what the next steps are in gathering information. It's been months, I will need a full report and accounting of your time."

Nia was stern with the private detective but she was worried that he'd outed her and her sister, so she had to meet with him sooner rather than later to figure out what he knew and what he'd done.

"There is a Waffle House on North McDonough Street in Decatur. No one will pay us any attention there and we can conduct business. Meet me there at 1pm."

She made the decision to go alone. Oni didn't need to know until there was something to know. From how she'd acted the night before, Nia was nervous that Oni didn't have the stomach to continue to go behind their mother's back.

The drive to the diner was long. She was used to having a driver, but she left the office with no fuss so that she could just go to her car in the parking garage.

It was nice to have a personal car available. She had bought herself a 2019 Jaguar XJR575 in cherry red a few years back. She loved that car and drove it as often as possible. So, it wasn't suspicious that she didn't call for a car since it was a beautiful day for a drive.

She told her assistant that she had a spontaneous meeting with a foreign executive that had flown in for the day and gave no more explanation than that.

Nia didn't trust her secretary much anyway. Frances was a nice enough person, but she was in the middle of the gossip circle around the office. She suspected that Frances was telling others about some negotiations that had taken place the previous year. Nia strategically fed Frances some erroneous information and sure enough it got around the office like a wildfire.

Nia took the opportunity to embarrass Frances and made an announcement to the whole office that the information was not true and she was sure that whoever had spread the misinformation was just spreading rumors which they knew nothing about. She gave Frances a sharp look and then went back into her office.

She considered firing her for it but thought that was too easy. Instead, she made her sign an NDA with a million dollar rider. Frances hadn't spoken about any of Nia's business since, but she still didn't think she was worthy of getting details or explanations.

The smell of freshly brewed coffee and syrup permeated the space as soon as she opened the door to the Waffle House. She went to the booth in the back corner away from the windows and said on the side that faced the door. She'd gotten there fifteen minutes early. She wanted to mentally prepare for whatever he had to tell her and she needed to make him understand that his business was with her and no one else.

When Rudy walked in he took up space. Standing six-foot-four-inches was enough, but he was a big man. His biceps were like boulders, his legs like tree trunks, and his belly like a keg. He had a handsome face with piercing green eyes and sandy blonde hair. Nia thought if he lost the gut he'd be a real catch for someone.

Not her, she was into guys who wore glasses and could disassemble a computer in two point two seconds. Nerds were her cup of tea. She had quite a few hacker friends who could access just about anything she needed.

One piece of information she was able to give Rudy, the private detective, was the CCTV footage from all angles the night her father had been murdered. The police said it was worthless and would not release it, but she knew that everything was valuable when it came to solving this case.

"Ma'am," Rudy said in a low, deep voice as he sat in the booth across from her.

"Thank you for meeting me, Rudy. I don't have much time; can we please get to the business at hand?"

The waitress walked over, placed a napkin with a knife, fork, and spoon by each of them and asked for their orders. Nia got coffee and a scattered, covered, and chunked hash brown while Rudy had the All-American with scrambled eggs, grits with cheese, loaded hash browns, crispy bacon, and a coffee. The thought of bacon compelled Nia to add a side of crispy bacon too.

"Miss Blossom, I have all of the reports, receipts, travel logs, and expense reports you asked for." He handed her a manilla envelope.

"I'll look at these later; what can you tell me?" she asked impatiently.

"I had my team enhance the CCTV footage. Where the cops didn't want to spend the money, we did, at your request, and we were able to break down the license plate number. We could make out four of the characters clearly, then spent days going through all of the combinations that are registered in Georgia. Unfortunately, we didn't get anything."

Are you telling me…" Nia's voice echoed as she leaned forward and began to raise her tone to Rudy.

"Now hold on," he interrupted, "I had a hunch that we needed to check the nearby states. We started with Tennessee, then Alabama, and South Carolina. We ended up with over a hundred vehicles. That took some time as we continued our efforts to make out the rest of the plate.

Nia settled back when the waitress brought over their food and coffees. Rudy immediately started shoveling food into his mouth, which irritated her to no end. She picked at her bacon and took small bites as she waited for him to devour his food. It was obvious that she wasn't getting another word from him until he was finished. She plucked the ham from the melted cheese on her hash browns as she waited.

She like the idea of the ham being mixed in with the hash browns while they cooked, but ever since she was little she'd always separated the ham before eating it.

Every once in a while, her father used to take her and her sisters to Waffle House when they were young. She loved it. Despite evidence to the contrary, Nia was the most down-to-earth of all the siblings.

With a good head on her shoulders, a brilliant mind, and beauty to boot, she was the picture of high society, but she had dreamed of leaving it all behind for a log cabin in the woods by a creek where she could watch the wildlife play all day. Unfortunately, as a Blossom, that would never happen, but it was a nice dream.

Rudy finally finished his food and gulped down the last swig of coffee before asking for a refill. He hadn't said a single word while he ate, which Nia was rather grateful. She thought his table manners were deplorable.

"Now, back to business," He stated as the waitress poured his coffee. "Where was I...oh yeah, the plate. So, we finally figured out the last number was an eight. That was the break we needed. That took hundreds down to eighteen. Long story short, it was a stolen tag from a 2008 Ford Escape out of South Carolina."

Rudy explained that he'd gone and spoken to the owner who had reported the car stolen a year prior. Nothing ever came from his report, so the insurance company just paid him blue book for it and he bought a new car.

The car was stolen in the middle of the night by two guys dressed in hoodies. He figured the car was sold or stripped. He was actually rather glad it had been stolen, it was starting to fall apart and he had put more into it than the insurance covered. Other than that, it was a dead end.

"So, where does that leave us?" Nia inquired.

"It leaves us with more work to do. We are looking into some other possibilities with the car. But ma'am, I'm telling you, this was a professional job. One shot, direct hit, instant kill. Someone was hired to take him out."

Nia's eyes became shiny as she fought tears. He had been so blunt that it took her a moment to compose herself. She had suspected all along that it was a murder for hire, she just didn't want to believe it. Hearing her suspicions confirmed made her more determined to find out who did it and why.

"Thank you Rudy, you've done good work here. Just keep using the credit card I gave you. Spend whatever you need. I also brought you some cash in case you need to pay off anyone. I had a feeling this was a purposeful assassination and that you may get to a point where you have to do some shady shit or talk to less than reputable people. If you need more, let me know. "

She handed him a package that looked like a present. It was gift wrapped beautifully in blue pinstriped paper and sported a custom 'Happy Birthday' bow. She was clever, no one would suspect that there was twenty-five thousand dollars in the little box.

"Oh, and one last thing, you are to report to me and only to me. Not Oni, not my mother, and not to any of my siblings. This is all between you and me. I hope that has been clear from the start, but just in case, it had to be said."

"Of course," he replied, "Ma'am I didn't get my reputation by double-dipping or pissing off clients. I assure you my work is with you and no one else." He paused, "But, that does remind me, there was another PI sniffing around a few weeks ago, haven't heard from or seen him since. I don't know the fella, and I assure you, I know everyone in the biz, so I don't know who he was or where he came from, but maybe someone else is looking into your father's demise too. Just a word of caution, but I'm not worried about it. If he comes around again, I'll figure him out."

Nia pondered his words and decided not to say anything, she just nodded. With their business concluded, she looked down at her watch and stated, "I've got to go." She laid a hundred dollar bill on the table.

Rudy stood first and followed her to the door. As she made her way to her car that was parked in a space away from the other cars, she couldn't help but notice that this oversized man, with a small birthday gift tucked under his arm getting into an ordinary sedan. He did not fit the profile of the television private investigators she'd seen, and she wasn't exactly confident that he hadn't spoken with her mother, but she had to trust somebody to find her father's killer.

Chapter 11

Magnolia steamed over the perceived betrayal of her children. She didn't have anything concrete, but she knew they were up to something. She had eyes and ears all over the company and it had not gone unnoticed that Snapper, Mari, and Dio had been having after-work, locked door meetings or that Nia and Oni had left work early numerous times or been to fictitious meetings over the last few months. They were all up to something and she was bound and determined to find out.

She'd set the seed so that they were all aware that she was keen to their deceptions, but none of them broke, not yet anyway. For Magnolia her anger brought out her power moves. She planned, studied, and executed her opponents one by one, even if they were her children. At that point, they were sneaky fucking ingrates as far as she was concerned.

"I blame you for this, Helio," she declared to the open space of her office. "These assholes would be loyal to me if it weren't for you and how you coddled them. I told you, 'love is weakness in family and business, especially now that Snapper is CEO…UGH!"

She couldn't even finish her sentence. The fact that her son outranked her in the company was infuriating. If she were CEO she'd have fired all of them and cut them off, which was precisely what she'd planned to do when she thought she would be elected.

She'd planned it out beautifully, they would each head to one piece of the company, a small piece that would fling them all around the world. As much as she would have like to have gotten rid of them completely from the company, her business prowess knew that each Blossom child had to be prominent within the company. Snapper to Paris, Nia to Toronto, Oni to Hong Kong, Dio and Mari to Milan, then she would finally have the company to herself not to mention the house, the money, and anything else she wanted.

Her cellphone rang. She walked to her desk. The name Darrian popped up on the screen.

"Yes, I can meet you. Let's say four this afternoon," she stated.

"Mccallan 18 neat, please." Magnolia waited at the bar of the Ritz-Carlton in downtown Atlanta for her companion to arrive. Just a quick meeting then it was back to finding out what her children were up to behind her back.

A strong figure of a man sat down beside her. He was handsomely dressed in an Armani suit over a crisp white oxford, a gorgeous blue silk tie with flecks of blush pink that was obviously from the men's luxury collection from House of Blossom, and Gucci shoes with a fresh polish.

"Michter's 25 neat, please," the man ordered.

"Expensive taste," Magnolia commented.

"If you can't have the finest in life, then what is the point?" he replied.

She raised her glass to him.

"Nice tie," she complimented.

"Thank you. A beautiful woman gave it to me."

The bartender sat the drink on the bar. The man took a slow sip.

Magnolia watched him, watched his lips as the rich, caramel color slipped past them. Her heart raced a little.

The man looked around to make sure no one was looking at them. "Maggie," he uttered as he cautiously placed his hand on her thigh.

"Darrian, not here," she scolded. "The penthouse, five minutes."

She stood up and exited the bar and headed for the elevators.

Darrian took his time with his drink. Twenty minutes later, he too headed for the elevators.

He slid a key card into the door to let himself into the House of Blossom suite. He was comfortable in the space so he didn't waste any time going straight for the bedroom. There he found Magnolia sitting on the side of the bed rolling her thigh-high stockings down her left leg. He leaned against the door frame and watched.

She ignored his voyeurism and continued with the right leg. When she stood up, he walked over. She turned her back to him and swept her long, black hair over her shoulder to reveal a zipper that went from the top to the bottom of the dress.

It was a custom made body-con blush pink, knee-length dress that went perfectly with the tie she'd given him. He slowly unzipped the dress for her and fell to his knees when he reached the bottom.

She slipped it over her shoulders and laid it on the bed while he kissed her round ass cheeks that were as plump as a twenty-year olds. She worked out every morning at five to keep her body tight and she knew she was gorgeous. With that knowledge, she used it as a weapon. She was able to easily disarm men and intimidate women.

He grabbed hold of her waist and spun her to face him. He worshiped her body and kissed every inch before he picked her up and threw her on the bed.

Slipping out of his clothes, he let them fall to the floor. He could not contain his need for her any longer. Like a panther, he stalked his prey and crawled up her body until he entered her.

With passionate thrusts, he watched her breast bounce and her face light up. She enjoyed their trysts and the way he made her body feel.

Helio had never made her feel the explosion like Darrian. He knew how to work her body into a frenzy and keep her right on the edge before she came in a blissful climax.

When they were done, there was no pillow talk, no snuggling, and absolutely no 'I love you.' Magnolia allowed him one exception to everyone else; he called her Maggie. She allowed it only because he'd asked first. She waited over a year before she agreed.

She got up from the bed, got dressed; Darrian zipped up her dress and put on his clothes as well. It wasn't a love affair; it was a matter of convenience. She had hired him twelve years earlier and had immediately set out to conquer him.

She loved Helio, dearly. He was the only person she did love, but there was something about Darrian's Italian accent and his knowledge of fabrics that intrigued her. They still did.

For ten years they'd had regular rendezvouses. Helio suspected about five years prior, but she emphatically denied it. But since his death, Darrian couldn't keep his hands off of her and Maggie approved.

She knew he was in love with her and she was fine with that, it kept him around. To her, however, he was a plaything. She only loved two things about Darrian: his eye for textiles and his dick.

"Thanks," she said in a nonchalant manner as she walked to the door. "I'll call you next week."

With that, she was out the door. Darrian waited the customary thirty minutes before he exited.

Chapter 12

Oni was anxious to find out what Nia had gathered from the private detective. She'd barely gotten any work done pacing around her office until she got Nia's text. "Be there in five."

She met Nia at the office door, "So, how did it go?"

"Sorry to say, it was uneventful, he didn't have anything new. I gave him some cash and told him to go out and get his hands dirty."

She hated lying to Oni, but it was for her own good. There really wasn't anything to tell, just little details that added up to nothing. She didn't want to get her hopes up, especially if the investigation didn't go anywhere. It was best to wait. That's how she justified her decision anyway.

She'd rehearsed what she'd say the entire drive back to the office. She thought about telling her the truth, part of the truth, but she ended up making the decision in that moment. When she saw Oni's face, she knew what she had to do. Even though all of the girls were close to their father, Oni was most effected by his death. She was broken. She still had times when she would just cry out of nowhere. Mother had always told her that she was the weakest of all the children.

Oni hated their mother, despised her, but feared her too. It was hard for Oni to be a child genius and have her mother treat her like she was stupid. Helio told her not to take it personally, it was just their mother's way of continuing to push and challenge her.

As the youngest child, she had four siblings she was constantly compared to, especially Snapdragon. None of the girls could compare to him in their mother's eyes. Oni swore that if all of the children had been boys that Magnolia would be a completely different, happy person.

They had all heard Magnolia blame Helio for the fact that they had so many girls. "You know it's one thing that I had the twins, then finally you gave me Snapdragon, but seriously Helio, two more girls?"

All of the girls felt like strangers in their own home, especially Oni.

"It's just as well that he didn't know anything yet. I really don't expect him to find the killer. It was dark, it was so fast, and no one saw a thing." She paused, "Don't get me wrong, I hope he can eventually find something, anything that will find out who did this, but you know, more than wanting to know the who, lately I have been trying to figure out the why."

Nia swallowed hard; she knew where the conversation was headed. "What do you mean?" She tried to sound casual.

"Why Father? He didn't have an enemy in the world. Maybe we are looking in the wrong direction. Perhaps, stay with me, we should be looking for the why while Rudy looks for the who."

"Oni, I don't think either one of us has the skills to do that. You're a baby genius, but —"

Oni interrupted her, "STOP calling me that!" She was mad. "I'm just smart, but we all are, we were all born with intelligence. I had all of you to set me on the right path and to help me to sharpen my skills. If I were the oldest, I would have had to learn everything on my own, but I didn't have to do that. The twins had each other, so that helped them to excel, they doted on Snapper, so he had them, and so on, so please don't call me that."

"I'm sorry, it wasn't meant as anything but a compliment." Nia looked at her sister's face and wanted to give her some kind of hope. "You know what, let's go for it. We can start our own investigation because you're right, why would anyone want Father dead."

The two girls put their heads together and began by making a list of the people who maybe, possibly, kind of, and probably secretly hated their father. It wasn't a long list.

"I think we might want to expand to people who had a motive. People might not have hated him, but there are plenty of people who would benefit from his death," Nia concluded.

The list grew and there were several people who they placed an asterisk by their names. Namely their mother. Their logic was sound. She gained the most financially from his death and before his murder, she would have had the most likely of reasons to think that Helio had left everything to her and that she would be CEO of the company. It wasn't until the reading of the will that she found out otherwise.

They decided to start with her and try to prove her innocence instead of going at it that she was guilty. As much as they hated her, they knew she loved their father and he adored her.
Oni was very methodical when it came to solving problems. She had to write everything out and have a calculated plan before she could start anything. Her items read like a detective's to do list.

- Go to crime scene
- Establish Timeline
- Canvas area
- Find out if there is a ballistics report
- Get copy of autopsy
- Establish alibis for everyone
- Examine other suspects
- Talk to the detective

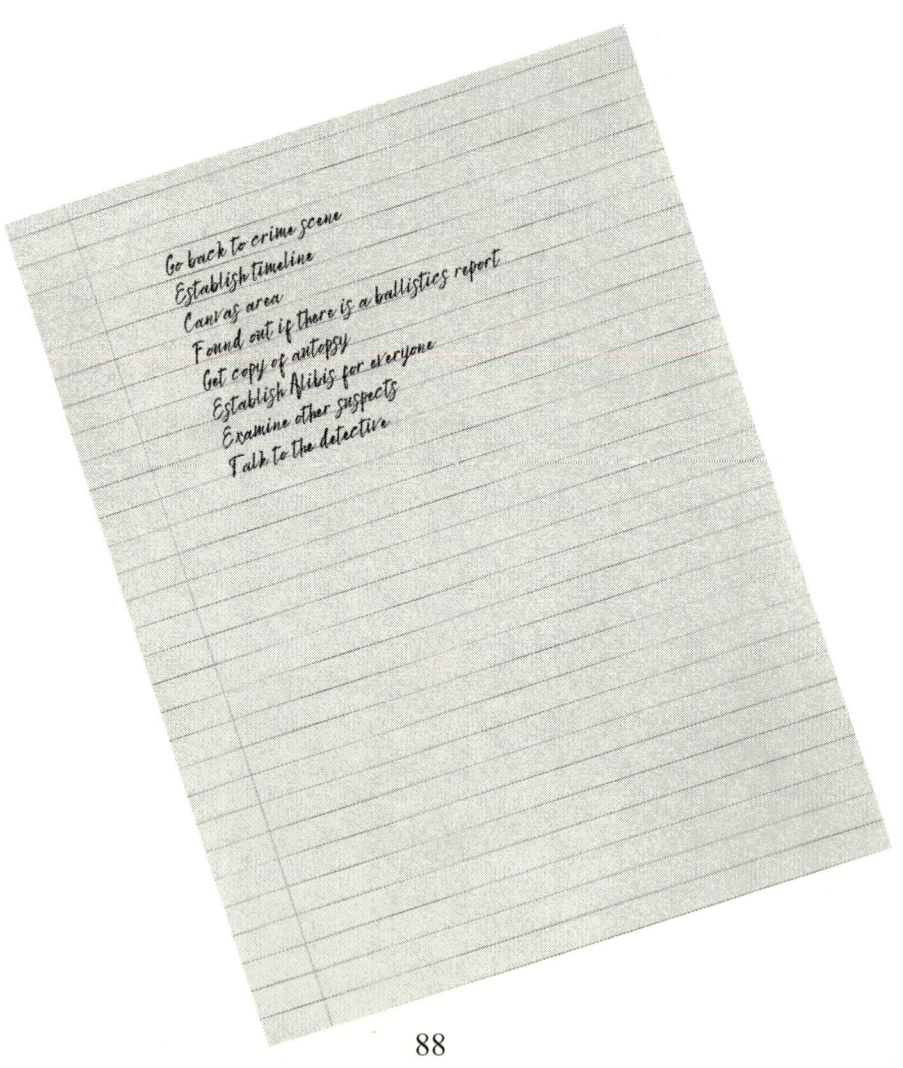

"Let's go back to the scene. I don't know that it will produce any results, but it's a place to start," stated Oni.

She felt empowered with a purpose and direction and as if it was the least she could do for her father. Someone knew something, she just had to find out who and why. She was hoping that Rudy would take care of the former and they could figure out the latter.

The crime scene looked so much different in the bright light of the day. The night of the murder, everything was so dark and felt scary. During the day it was bright and inviting. It made both of them feel uncomfortable.

They looked around, but as they suspected there was nothing to see. However, they did spot that the same doorman from that night was working.

"Hello," Nia greeted him as they approached.

He stuttered, "Aren't…Aren't you the Blossom girls? I'm so sorry about your father. He was a good man."

"Thank you. Yes, we are trying to figure out exactly what happened that night," replied Oni.

"I wish I had some information. I've talked to the police and two private investigators, but all I could say was that the car was a Ford Expedition. Looked to be a maybe a 2021, but I can't say for sure."

"Wait, I'm sorry, did you say *two* private investigators?" asked Nia.

"Yes, I don't know who they worked for, but they both asked me questions that I couldn't answer. I know that one of them talked to the hostess and the manager too. Both of them and the rest of the staff were inside the building that night, so they had no information."

He continued telling them that the manager had gotten permission from the owner to give them both the same copy of the exterior surveillance videos from the two cameras that pointed toward the doors. They were both set to wide angle, so they caught the shooting and partial views of the vehicle. He explained that he had watched it and he did not recommend that the girls do the same.

The doorman knew that both of them had canvased the entire street, at least three blocks on both sides of the street, both ways. But he didn't know if that had yielded any additional information or footage. He saw the looks on the girl's faces and realized that they were perplexed by something.

"Did I say something wrong?" he asked.

"No sir, not at all," Oni quickly replied. "We are curious as to the other PI. We hired one, but we have no idea who would have hired another one."

Nia pondered the implications of an additional PI trying to find out information. Was it there mother who hired him to make sure she had covered her tracks, was it the person who killed him, or was it possibly an insurance matter? She couldn't' come to a reasonable conclusion as to why someone else would also be looking into the matter. Was it possible that it was Snapper or the twins? She'd have to think on that one too.

As they left the doorman with a fifty dollar tip for his time, he yelled after them, "Miss, I do remember one name, one of the investigators, his name was Sam."

Nia nodded her head in recognition of his additional information. Her guy was Rudy, so who in the hell was Sam?

Chapter 13

Snapper wasn't much for sitting around. He did have a company to run, classes to take, and a murder to solve. He was more convinced than ever that his mother had been the one to hire someone to kill his father and he felt like the money discrepancies he'd found would be more than enough to trace all of it back to her.

His private detective, Sam, finally got back to him, but it was a phone call, not a meeting as Snapper had requested. Snapper filled him in on the information he and the twins had discovered in the invoices and how they thought that the missing money from the House was going into a fake company called Ailongam Limited.

He didn't have any concrete connections, but he shared with Sam that he truly believed in his mother's guilt. Nothing else made sense to him.

With the new information, Sam assured Snapper that he was on the job and that he may have already uncovered some information that he was still looking into, that involved Magnolia's financials.

Where the police had failed, thanks to Magnolia's lawyers, Sam was able to find that Magnolia had withdrawn two million dollars just six months before Helio was murdered. He couldn't find where the funds had gone and from what he could tell no purchases were made by Magnolia with the money.

Sam also told him he would look into the fake company and try to dig up some dirt there too. He speculated that the withdrawal may have ended up there. Ailongam sounded too important to ignore and Sam had a gut feeling that Ailongam was going to be pertinent to the case in some way.

Snapper was not exactly happy with the no news is good news concept, but he was becoming more convinced that his mother had the financial expertise as CFO to manipulate payments, invoices, transactions, and to create fake companies. As far as he was concerned, the clues were stacking higher and higher against Magnolia.

Snapper wondered about the two million dollars and finding the link propelled his resolve. While he loved his mother, he hated her for killing Helio. He was more convinced of it than ever and he needed to read Mari and Dio into the conversation to see what they had been able to collect.

He sent them each an encrypted text. After Magnolia's magnificent display at dinner earlier in the week, they had all gotten burner phones and installed encryption apps on them. None of them were taking any chances.

They no longer met after work in his office. He knew his mother had spies everywhere not to mention the cameras on every hallway, it wasn't too hard to figure out why she was suspicious. It would only take one person to casually mention that they had seen the three of them together in his office after work for his mother to conclude that they were up to something. Although, he was curious why she hadn't just called them out.

Instead, she was placid and cold toward all of them. No one escaped her wrath that evening. What could Nia and Oni have possibly done to incur the glares and disappointment? Not that his mother needed a reason, but her usual approach was the call out the bane of her existence and humiliate them. But it wasn't out of character for her to just despise all of them collectively.

He knew that the twins were on campus for class so he couldn't call them. He had a microeconomics class in half an hour so he decided to text them to meet him at the bookstore at two. He knew that was the one place where they could have some privacy and that there wasn't anyone to spy on them for their mother.

Magnolia never came to campus. She said it was full of oversexed, undereducated young people. Definitely, not her scene. She had not been thrilled when Helio had insisted that the children attend. But their MBA program was ranked among the best in the country and it was close enough where she could still keep a watch over them.

Being the oldest, Dio didn't like being shuffled around by her little brother. She took the two minutes and forty-eight seconds that separated her birth from Mari's seriously. She lorded it over every one of the children that she was not only born first, but also that her birthday was the day *before* Mari's. In those mere minutes the calendar flipped from August twelfth to August thirteenth. It was just one more thing that made Mari feel inferior to her sister.

The disfunction was palpable between the siblings, but for the good of their father's memory they had joined forces. Snapper was smug when he walked into the bookstore fifteen minutes early, only to quickly drop his face to see that his sisters were already there.

"You're late," Dio announced.

"Fuck you, Gladiolus," he replied only half joking. "I don't have time for idle chit-chat, did either of you find out anything?"

Mari began to open her mouth to speak, but she didn't get the chance.

"I was able to dig into the files of the janitor more closely. He's not the best of people. He was in jail when he was twenty for killing a guy in a bar fight. He was charged with involuntary manslaughter. Apparently, he punched him after the guy grabbed his girlfriend's ass. It was only one blow, but it was bad enough that the victim fell so hard he cracked his head open on the concrete. He was in jail for that offense for five years."

"What do you mean *that* offense?" Snapper asked.

"After that he had several more charges. Assault, having a weapon while on parole, and that same girlfriend he defended, he ended up smacking her around after she waited for him to get out of jail. How romantic." The disgust in Dio's voice was evident.

"I'm not sure how he made it through Human Resources to even work at the House. We never hire violent offenders," Mari added. "His file doesn't mention any of this information. He checked no on his application about being arrested. There was no background check to be found in his file either. It was like they just rolled out the red carpet for him and skipped about twenty procedures," she continued.

"Sounds like nepotism to me," stated Snapper. "Find out who worked in HR when he was hired. Better yet, find out if he has any connections to anyone in the company. He still works for us, but that's about to change."

"You can't fire him," Dio exclaimed.

"The hell I can't. One phone call and he's gone."

"You're an idiot! If you fire him and he is involved, it will take away our leverage." Dio explained. "Dumbass," she added.

"Then what do you suggest?"

Mari was standing as the third point to the sibling triangle, but she could barely get a word into the conversation. "I have…"

Dio interrupted, or rather ignored her, "I think we should go back through his background and maybe even find his ex-girlfriend. She's probably got some stories to tell."

"That's a…" Mari tried again.

"You call me an idiot? That's the worst idea ever," Snapper retorted.

"I think we should…"

"Mari what are you saying? You keep interrupting me," Dio snapped.

"I have an idea if the two of you would listen."

"I'm sorry Mari," Snapper genuinely apologized. "What's your idea?"

"I know someone at the facility where he works. I trust her and I could discreetly ask some questions. If I think she can be trusted I could get her to keep an eye on him, maybe even talk to him. I would make it out like it's her idea, of course."

Dio rolled her eyes but conceited that it was the best idea they had.

With the next phase of the plan decided, Snapper filled them in on what Sam had discovered and his emphatic belief that their mother had in fact paid someone to kill their father.

It didn't take much convincing to have the twins thinking the same way. They had known all along that money was the key to finding out what happened and with this new information, all roads led right to their mother. They weren't exactly surprised, expected really, but deep down they had hoped. Hoped for a different outcome, a different understanding, a different person.

"I'm going for a walk," Dio announced.

"I'll go with you," Mari suggested.

"No!" Dio calmed herself. "I'm sorry, but I want to be alone, please." She walked away without waiting for a reply.

Snapper and Mari stood there, in shock. Not about their mother, but about Dio.

Mari turned to Snapper after the door closed behind Dio and she walked out of sight. "Dragon," she paused, "Did Dio just apologize…to me?"

"Shocked the hell out of me too. I don't think I've ever heard that word come out of her mouth. Not even when she caused the cake to topple to the floor at her best friend's wedding because she was on the phone telling someone that the bride was a whore and the only reason she'd come to the wedding was the promise of Usher singing at the reception."

"Needless to say, that friendship ended rather quickly. But in Dio's defense, the bride was a whore. She'd slept with the best man the night before the wedding," Mari added.

"True. It still makes me laugh that the band for the reception was that local band Crusher. Remember, the bride and groom were secretly into heavy metal and the drummer was the groom's friend from college?"

"Well at least the name was apropos. The groom did *crush her* when he sued her for breach of contract and the cost of the lavish, no refund honeymoon."

"He snatched the engagement ring right off her hand in open court." Snapper laughed.

Chapter 14

Oni's office door was open when Magnolia passed by and noticed that no one was around. She walked in and had originally planned to leave Oni a note that the fabric's from Milan had been ruined in transit and that a press release would need to be issued.

She wanted no mention of the disaster and instead wanted it to be worded that House of Blossom was creating a limited edition of something for ready-to-wear for summer. Oni and Dio could work out the details with Mari based on what fabrics were available for a small four or five piece collection. If possible Nia, could sell it internationally.

Magnolia wanted to get home early. It had been a long day and she knew she needed to lie down before dealing with her children. Such dregs. They were an anchor around her neck and she had already started her plans to get them all out of the house.

As she approached the desk, she saw the notepad. Just as she went to flip the page, the writing caught her attention. She mumbled to herself, "Crime scene, canvas, autopsy. What in the fucking hell is this?" she said aloud. "Ungrateful child, I knew they were up to something."

She grabbed up the pad, stuffed it into her bag, and grabbed her phone. She was absolutely fuming. So much for getting a rest before seeing the children. She was going to get to the bottom of what was going on. She'd hoped that she'd put the fear of God in them, but apparently not. She'd been too subtle. Well, there was nothing subtle about what she was going to say now.

It took her three attempts to type a message that conveyed the urgency she felt. Three times to express her anger. Three times to get their attention. "Come to my office NOW!"

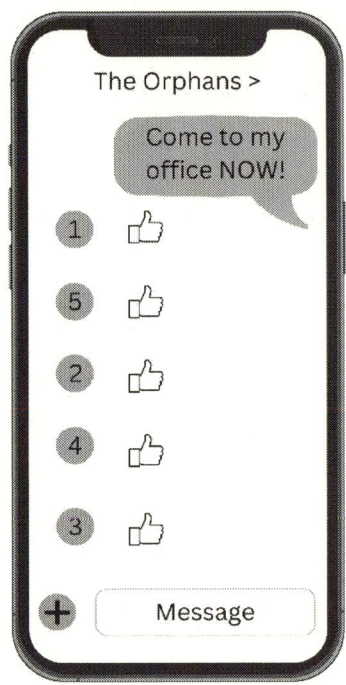

Within a minute the first ping came through from Dio otherwise known as one on Magnolia's cell phone. The children were merely the number of their birth order in her phone. A minute later Oni and Mari chimed in. Impatiently, she waited for the last two responses as she stomped back to her office to wait for their appearances. She was relishing the looks that would be on their faces. Finally, another minute later the last two gave a thumbs up.

Magnolia didn't like text messages and she despised reading them even more. The children had been instructed to only use a thumbs up to her messages. Nothing more, nothing less.

They were all scattered around the House of Blossom headquarters so the text between them started immediately as each made their way to their mother's office. Their group chat was titled the orphans.

Oni started it after Helio was murdered. To them, they didn't have a parent in their mother. As a collective, they felt like orphans who had to live with this person who had brought them into the world and would just as soon take them out. That sentiment was feeling more real every day for all of them.

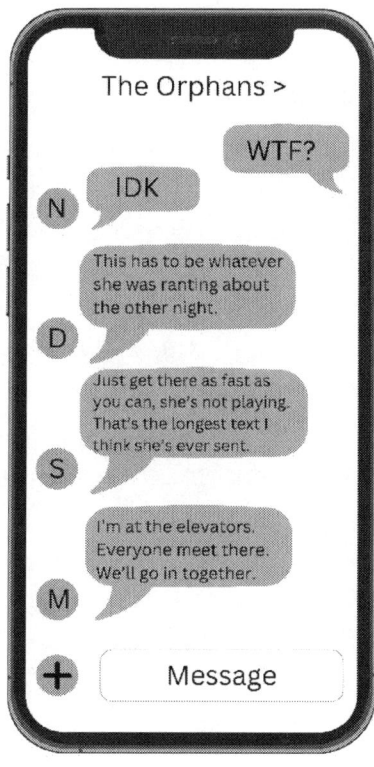

Once everyone was at the elevator, they went to their mother's office with their heads high and with poise and a bit of disdain. They were not children they were adults with important jobs. Snapper was mentally kicking himself for encouraging them to go. Once he saw his mother's face, he wished that he'd told them to ignore her. Neither option was a good one.

Magnolia glared at each of them as they walked into the room. She was sitting at the head of her eight chaired, Italian marble conference table. Most people thought that it was ironic that she'd buy such a cold, rigid item to gather around, but it matched her personality perfectly.

One by one they took a seat. Snapper of course sat by his mother while the girls opted to leave a few chairs between themselves and Magnolia. The move did not go unnoticed by their mother and she huffed at the sentiment.

She did not say a word, she simply slid the notepad down the table toward Oni. Magnolia watched her carefully. As suspected, Oni's face dropped as soon as she saw her handwriting. She knew what it was and what it meant.

Snapper, Dio, or Mari knew what it was, but they too saw Oni's reaction. Her little hand stretched over and completed the pad's descent toward her. She couldn't speak, she knew the risk she had taken even looking into the matter. She knew because she had approached her mother a week after the funeral and asked her about doing exactly what she was doing – investigating to find her father's killer.

"Mother, I have the resources to help the investigation. The police can't spend that kind of money, but I can. Don't you want to know what happened to Father?" Oni pleaded with her mother with tears in her eyes when they finally had the house to themselves after all of the funerary traditions had been exhausted.

"Let it go Aconite, it's for your own good. Your father was murdered in the darkness of night, there's nothing to investigate. Besides you're a child and you need to concentrate on your studies and your job. That is what your father would have wanted. Carry on his legacy and put away these silly notions."

At the time, Magnolia's words didn't mean anything but another day of being belittled, but as much as she wanted to prove her mother's innocence, she started to wonder if there was anything to prove as those words swirled through her mind.

"Oni, can you explain this?" Magnolia asked sternly.

There it was, the beginning of the humiliation. Only this time, Oni didn't take the bait.

She stood up, "Is this what you called us all up here for? Some scribblings on a notepad? I was just jotting down things I wanted to ask the detective about Father's case. I know it's a '*silly notion*,' but I still want to find out who murdered our father and who ordered the hit."

"Sit down young lady!," Magnolia demanded. "You are not to talk to me like that ever. I don't know who you think you are, but you," she paused and lowered her tone, "no one ever speaks to me like that, much less my youngest child. And another thing, you are *not* to talk to the detective. I thought I had made that clear months ago. In fact, I will make sure that he doesn't speak to any of you. I knew you were up to something, but this...it's beneath even you."

Nia bravely spoke up to defend her sister, "She's not the only one who wants to know what happened."

"You too, Petunia, this is all nonsense. Your father was the victim of a drive by shooting. There is nothing else to know. I honestly thought that all of you were planning something, but this is ridiculous." She began to laugh as she waved her hand toward them all. "Carry on with your day, this is too trivial for my time. I have plans. You are dismissed."

As they all stood up and stepped toward the door, Magnolia gave them one more thing to think about before the evening was over.

"By the way, I want you all out of the house by the end of the month."

Chapter 15

"Everyone to my office," Snapper insisted. None of the girls opposed his request. They all needed to talk.

He asked them to give him a minute to speak to Venus, so they all went and waited in his office.

"Here are your messages, sir, and the reports you requested from all departments. Do you need anything before your meeting?" she asked in a less than professional way. She could see that he was exasperated and that usually meant that he needed to release some tension.

"Yes, in fact, can you wait until my meeting is over. I don't know how long we will be, but I do need to meet with you afterwards," he replied.

"I'll be right here, sir."

Snapper let out a sigh, straightened his shoulders, and walked into his office. Shutting the door behind him.

He walked over and sat at his desk. Oni and Nia were sitting in the two chairs in front of it while Mari and Dio opted for the loveseat against the wall. Everyone was quiet which created an awkward silence that Oni just couldn't handle.

"Just say it Snapper, I fucked up and I shouldn't be talking to the detective." She was sticking to the story she'd told their mother.

"Is that what is really going on here, Oni…Nia?"

"What are you implying," Nia asked with a tone of anger.

"Calm down, I'm just trying to figure out what is going on. Mother is already fucking crazy, none of us need to add to that. If you're just talking to the detective, that's fine, but I think that's over now. I can probably convince her to let me talk to him, but I can't promise."

"Oh, yeah, the favorite can absolutely get her to do anything," Nia stated as she rolled her eyes. "No thank you, we can handle this all on our own, we don't need your help or Mother's permission."

Dio chimed in, "Umm, excuse me, but don't we have a more pressing matter to discuss? What in the fuck was that about us all having to move out by the end of the month. I don't know about any of you, but I'm not going anywhere."

"I second that," agreed Mari.

"So, Snapper, how are you going to fix that with Mother?" Nia asked sarcastically. "She's said a lot of tragic things but she's never tried to kick us out."

You're right, Dio, that *is* the priority. Let's figure it out," Snapper calmly replied.

For the next two hours the five of them yelled, argued, and finally talked through the situation. None of them wanted to leave the house, but they decided that they were either going to call their mother's bluff or they would be out before the end of the month.

Snapper called a friend who was a real estate agent and asked him to join a Zoom with them. They had decided that they would put in offers on several houses. The twins, Snapper, and Nia would each purchase a house. Unfortunately, Oni was not old enough to purchase a house in her name, so Snapper gave her some options.

She could either move in with any of them, stay at the house or he would buy a house in his name, but put the title in her name. She didn't want her own house, she didn't want to be away from any of them, but Nia stepped up and asked her to live with her, to which she agreed.

The agent, Rod, was excellent at his job. Within an hour he had houses for each of them, but then he found a property in Buckhead that he thought would solve all of their problems. It was a compound on eighteen acres. The house was huge with ten bedrooms, an infinity pool with a pool house, and multiple guest houses on the property. Two of which were over two-thousand square feet. It also had a horse paddock and stables, and a duck pond that was fully stocked with fish.

It was pricey, of course, but if they pooled their money, they could all stay together and have plenty of room to have privacy.

While the twins loved the idea of some independence, they did hate to be on their own. The dysfunction in the Blossom family was real. They hated each other, but they didn't know how to be anywhere but all under the same roof.

Nia and Oni were on board immediately. They hated the thought of having to manage a household. But, Snapper was the voice of reason before they all made a decision.

He pointed out that it wouldn't just be buying a compound, there would need to be a full staff for both the house and the grounds. He had each of them take time to figure out their financial liquidity because he wanted to make sure that each one of them was equally responsible.

Snapper did a few rough calculations of how much they would need to buy it outright and approximately what it would take for a staff. He wrote the number and told them that if they couldn't meet at least that comfortably in less than thirty days then the compound was not an option. It was the fairest way.

They all checked their portfolios to see where they were at for cash flow and one by one they gave their totals to Snapper.

The price of the compound was $23 million. Between them they could liquidate $62 million within fifteen days minus around $10 million in penalties.

When he told his sisters that they had enough, they were ready to put in an offer. Oni was more relieved than happy. It was more than obvious that they all were honestly putting aside their differences for her. She needed stability and she needed her siblings to take care of her.

With that, Rod started the paperwork. "I'll email it over and send the selling agent a text. I'll get with her in the morning. I just need to ask, are you all sure about this? I can tell you this property has been on the market for over twenty days. Sellers start getting nervous around the thirty day mark and usually take it off the market."

They all agreed that it was the best solution, even sight unseen. The pictures were gorgeous and that was all they needed. They all thought of it as an investment.

If Magnolia was bluffing, they could use the property in a variety of ways for the company so none of them were worried about not getting a return on the investment.

Dio was already talking about selling off ten acres to a developer she knew to get a ten percent return on the purchase within the year.

"So, it's settled. Rod I'll send you my attorney's information so you can contact him tomorrow as well to set up a fast closing."

"Ladies, are you all ready to sign the docs?" Rod asked.

With their confirmation, he emailed them over.

"Now let's see who Mother thinks is a child," Oni professed.

Snapper had asked the girls to go ahead when all of their business was concluded. "I'll be home for dinner, but I have to look over these reports. Don't be surprised if there are some cuts in your departments. The projections showed us down two percent. I'm hoping the reports prove that to be untrue."

He walked them all to the elevator and promised again that he would be to the house soon, stating that he wouldn't miss it for the world. Once the doors closed, his pace quickened to get back to his office, to Venus.

With a simple nod, Venus followed Snapper into his office and locked the door behind her. Neither of them spoke as they undressed. With barely a second to breathe, Snapper scooped her up and put her on the loveseat. He kissed her, hard. Like a man filled with passion, but instead it was rage. Rage for all that he had to deal with and for all that he knew to be true. He was pent up and Venus was his release.

There was no foreplay, no silly giggles, no words before he entered her. He was powerful and too focused for niceties. He needed the release as he drove deeper and faster into her. Over and over he drilled into Venus like a man with only one mission.

This wasn't about her and she was fine with that. He'd given her more than her share of orgasms; this was all for him and she knew how to get him there. With one word she knew he would explode into her.

"Faster," she purred.

Snapper saw it as a challenge and permission. He obliged. Faster, deeper, harder until there was no restraining or holding back. He flowed into her with such vigor and prowess that when he finished he had no strength to be anything but sated.

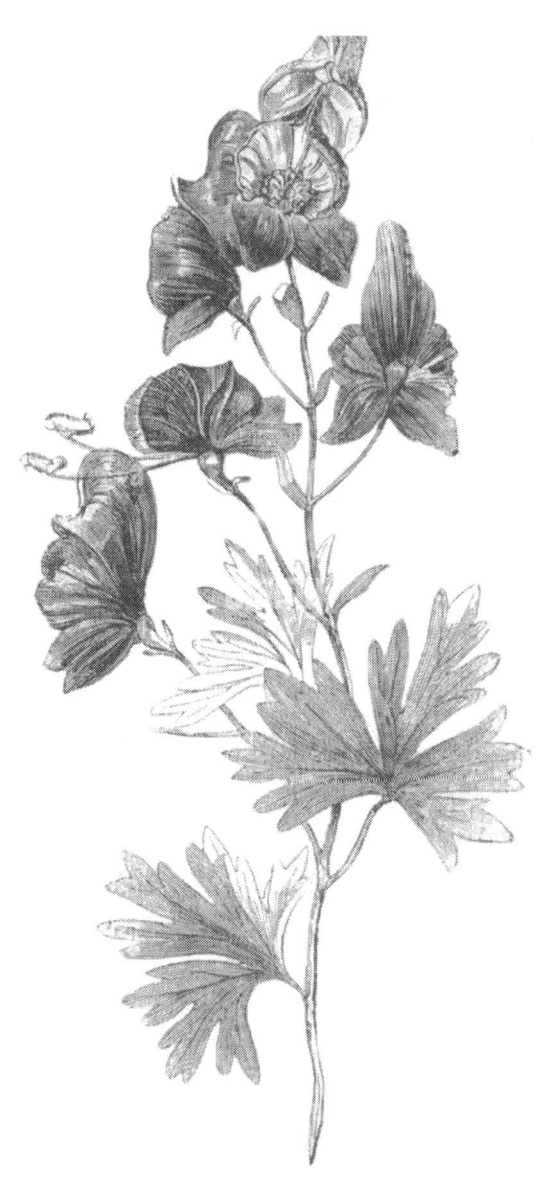

Chapter 16

With rather smug looks on their faces, the siblings entered the dining room. They knew that the one bullet that Magnolia had loaded into her gun was now gone. They felt a sense of bravery - the fear that was usually a permanent guest at the table, vanquished. They had a newfound independence that irritated Magnolia to know end.

"What are you children up to now?" she asked.

"Mother," Snapper spoke, "We heard you today and we understand that it is time that we all venture out on our own. So, to that end, we have placed a bid on a house that keeps us all together. You are, of course, welcome to visit anytime. There is plenty of room."

"What?! Let me get this straight, you fools found a house in a day that can house all of your egos and idiocy. Why in God's name would you all live together? The whole point of my declaration was to get you all to grow up and take responsibility for yourselves. You are spoiled and that needs to stop. Living together changes nothing. You all are truly fucking stupid."

No one replied. But Dio was feeling herself and she was starving. She had no intention of letting the food get cold. Without permission, she ladled out some mashed potatoes onto her plate and passed the bowl to Mari. With that all of the children started eating the fried chicken, green beans, rice and gravy, and homemade sour dough bread - one of Lydia's specialties.

Magnolia was so angry, she instructed Lydia to make her a plate and have it sent to her room. She refused to eat with ungrateful, heathen children.

As for the siblings, they were happy to eat in peace. They even asked Lydia to join them. It was a feast that had never tasted so good.

The next month was tense within the house. No one was willing to back down and there was optimal silence from Magnolia toward the siblings both in the house and at the House. Snapper was surprised to find out how little he needed to interact with her for business. It was cordial and professional, but the attention she had lavished him with compared to his sisters had vanished.

She'd started something that she refused to stop, even though for one of the rare times in her life, she was feeling small, minuscule prickles of guilt and a sprinkle of sadness. Although, it was quickly covered by resentment and elation.

Everyone had been moving their items out of the house as their new compound had closed the week before. The purchase was almost thwarted when Magnolia decided to find the property in which the children had placed a bid. She had placed an offer that was ten-million dollars higher than theirs, but she didn't know the contracts had been signed the morning after the bid. Plus, Rod had warned the selling agent that Magnolia might try to tank the deal.

When her efforts were useless, she had no option but to let the children go. In truth, she had options, but she refused to exercise them, or at least the one that would have halted all of the consequences of her words. She didn't want the siblings in the house anymore, but she didn't want them to leave either. She had to decide which she wanted more. Her decision – they had to go.

The movers were just about done with the bulk of the items, but Oni still had some special items that she wanted to handle herself, as they were gifts from her father.

When she went up the stairs she heard noises, but she wasn't sure where they were coming from or what they were. The house was supposed to be empty, but she thought that maybe the movers were still working so she scurried up the stairs to gather her trinkets as not to get in the way.

As she walked down the hallway the sounds were louder and closer. Moans, grunts, a scream.

Oni realized the sounds were coming from her mother's room. She rushed in to find her mother and Darrian in the throws of sex.

Oni screamed, Magnolia screamed, Darrian, just smiled with Magnolia straddling him as she jerked the bedsheet to cover her breasts that had moments before been bouncing as she rode Darrian's cock.

Frozen, Oni wasn't sure what to do. She closed her eyes tightly and stood there.

"Get the FUCK out!" Magnolia screamed.

With her eyes still closed, she turned around toward the door and whispered, "Sorry."

"No worries, love, Maggie and I were just having some rigorous love making," replied Darrian.

"Maggie?" Oni said to herself as she walked out and slammed the door behind her, "Fucking the Italian, really? No wonder she wanted us out of the house."

She texted the orphans that they needed a family meeting at the compound as soon as possible and that it was extremely important.

Being the kind girl she was, she added that everything was fine, she just had information that everyone needed to know.

Even though purchasing the compound and moving away from their mother had been a bonding experience for the siblings, they still had not told each other what they were doing to find out about their father's murder. Secrets were still running rampant with the Blossom's, but one secret was about to be completely exposed, more than it already had been.

Only moments after Oni's text, Magnolia had texted the children to come to the house immediately as she kicked Darrian out and threatened him within an inch of his life if he said a word. She tried calling number five while she got dressed, but Oni did not answer.

Frustrated, she texted her, no reply. For that matter, none of the children had replied to her previous text. She went downstairs, poured a glass of wine, and waited. But no pings or rings permeated from her phone. It was a bit disconcerting to Magnolia that her children were silent, but it did not escape her as to why.

Everyone had ignored their mother but were sure that Oni's 'extremely important' information must have something to do with her since Magnolia's text pinged immediately after Oni's. They each texted back to Oni about how long it would take them to get to the compound, but that they were on the way.

Since it was a beautiful Saturday, they were all out running errands or shopping for the compound. They still needed to give it a name. Calling it 'the compound' sounded weird to them. Purchasing items to give their new home an air of personality, they hoped it would spark their creativity for a suitable name.

Within an hour everyone was present and accounted for in the living room. They were surrounded by boxes, but once the decorators came, the main house would be picture perfect. They had paid an extra twenty thousand dollars to get the perfection started the following week.

Everyone was focused on Oni, who was grinning from ear to ear like a coy fox with a big secret. She stood up and cleared her throat.

"I have an announcement to make," she started very professionally. "Mother is," she paused for dramatic effect, "fucking the Italian!" she yelled. Then fell back into her chair laughing.

She didn't notice that no one was laughing with her. Instead, they all sat there stunned, looking at each other to confirm they had heard her correctly.

Nia tapped her on the shoulder. "Care to explain?"

When Oni realized that no one was laughing with her, she apologized and explained what had happened.

"...and that's how I unfortunately found out that she is fucking the Italian in the bed she shared with our father. Oh, and he was right proud of the fact. Real smug. I hate that asshole," Oni continued.

There were more questions than answers. Oni's combination of genius level brilliance and youthful innocence did not allow her to comprehend the consequences or ramifications of having this knowledge. It was deadly.

Snapper felt like he had no choice but to tell her his suspicions about their mother's involvement in Helio's death. If she could have Helio killed she wouldn't hesitate to kill Oni to keep her secret from being public knowledge. But he couldn't make the decision alone. He asked the twins to follow him to the backyard.

"We have to tell her. She has no idea the danger this has placed her in with Mother," Snapper started.

"I agree," Mari stated.

"Of course you do," Dio rolled her eyes. "We need to think. Mother wouldn't go after Oni because she knows that the first thing Oni did was tell us. Remember, we ignored her text. Come to think of it, *why* did *you* ignore her, Snapper?"

"Seriously," he huffed, "I might as well be one of you girls now. Mother wants nothing to do with me. I took your side over hers. If anyone should be dead right now, it's probably me."

"She would never kill her pride and joy. I'm actually surprised you've lasted this long without the hand pats and loving words of affirmation."

"Shut up, Dio, that is not what we are talking about here. Oni's in trouble and she thinks this is funny. Are we going to tell her or not?"

"I don't think so," said Mari in a voice that lingered with I'm sorry behind it.

"What, the boy wonder's pet now disagrees with him," mocked Dio.

"What? Why?" Snapper asked with confusion.

"Dragon, I think Dio is right," she threw Dio a *not so fast look*, "partially," she added. "I don't see anything happening to Oni because it would be too obvious. But, honestly, my main reason is that it would spoil her innocence. She doesn't suspect Mother and if she did, I think it would break her even more. I don't want to be responsible for shattering her world."

Snapper relented, "Okay Goldie. I hear you. We won't tell her. But if any of us get a hint of anything that would bring her harm, then we settle it right here that we will immediately tell her. Agreed?"

In unison, they both agreed.

Chapter 17

Not only did Snapper and the twins not know that Oni suspected their mother, but they also had no idea that she too was looking into why their father was killed. She was making significant headway on the matter.

She and Nia had talked to all of the businesses up and down Peachtree Road and had gained a few tidbits of information. Nothing of any significance yet, but they were of the mind that every little bit helped.

One of Nia's hacker friends had been able to secure the CCTV footage from the restaurant. The doorman was right. Her friend, Troy, would not let them watch the footage. The camera had a direct view of their father getting shot and falling backwards on the sidewalk. It was in color, so the bullet hole in his head and the pool of blood that followed were like a technicolor film. He had nightmares about it for weeks.

The autopsy report didn't reveal anything they didn't already know, but they were able to talk to Detective Stone, after much assurance that they no longer lived with their mother.

He told them that the gun used was a rare Russian Glock-T Pistol. The ballistics analyst had only seen one in his twenty-seven year career. The 9mm bullet that was recovered was a partial matched to a ballistics report out of Charlotte, North Carolina.

The gun had been reportedly used in an altercation of road rage a few years back. The victim reported the driver and had written down the license plate. The gun was test fired to match it to the bullet that went through the victim's car.

Unfortunately, when the analyst requested to compare the gun with the bullet the coroner retrieved, the gun was not in evidence. It had mistakenly been given back to the owner.

Detective Stone would not give them the name of the owner. He assured them that even though the gun was rare, it was not unique. Even the analyst had told the detective that it was a long shot, but he wanted to at least compare it if it had been available.

Meanwhile, Snapper and the twins were making leaps in their investigation as well. All of the twenty-five million that Helio had confronted Magnolia about had been found through erroneous transactions. Along with the couture buttons, there had been fabrics, and leathers, and other items that were all from Italy. Yet, none of the actual items could be accounted for within the company's inventory.

Mari had spoken to her friend, Cindy, who worked in Charlotte about John Smith. She said he was a nice enough person who kept to himself and did a good job. She didn't know him, but she'd seen him around and she noticed him when he first got transferred.

Cindy told her that there was a rumor that he'd gotten fired from Atlanta but that he caused a big stink and threatened to sue because all of his performance reviews were excellent, so even though it's a right to work state, there was no just cause.

Mari assured her that none of that was true and that he had actually requested the transfer to be close to family.

"Not that I'm all up in his business or anything," Cindy said, "but I did talk to him a few times back when my mama was so sick, you remember, and he mentioned that he knew how that was because his mama had lingered with cancer and had passed away years back."

"I knew it," Mari said out loud instead of in her head.

"Knew what, Sugar?" Cindy asked.

"Sorry. It's nothing. I just remembered something. How have you been doing since your mother passed? I know that the two of you were very close. Did you decide to keep the house or did your brother and his wife stay since they were living there while she was ill?" Mari changed the subject quickly to distract Cindy from her ill-timed outburst.

"I sold it to them for a dollar. They were already settled in there and you know he hurt his back while he was caring for Mama, so moving was just going to be too hard on him. Plus, honestly, I didn't have the heart to just sell it to some stranger. I'd rather they be in there. Anyway, back to this John Smith guy. Is there something up with him?" Cindy asked.

"Oh no, I just like to know how transfers go, to make sure everything is smooth and that people are a good fit. It's been six months and since I know I can trust your judgement, I wanted to talk to you before I spoke with his supervisor. You know how it is; they don't say anything bad unless it's really not working."

"Well, Sugar, that means a lot. You know you should come up here sometime. We can paint the town. Maybe get John to go out with us so you can see for yourself how he's doing up here." She laughed at herself.

"The coming to see *you* part sounds great. I'll do that soon. I'm in the middle of the fall collection sketches right now. But I say we leave Mr. Smith right where he is, you know, since we don't know him. I never really got to talk to him when he worked here," Mari replied.

"Very true. Stranger danger. Maybe I should keep an eye on him and make sure he really is doing a good job. I could even ask around and let you know. Anyway, I'd jabber on with you all day if we could, but I'm going to let you go, so quit talking my ear off and get back to work. And don't worry, John Smith won't get away with anything on my watch." Her infectious laugh abruptly ended.

Mari looked at her phone. Cindy had hung up, but the seed had been planted. Cindy would keep an eye on Mr. Smith.

The problem that the trio of siblings had was that they nor Sam could connect Magnolia to the money, not directly anyway. Snapper had posed the question to the twins if they thought it was possible that someone else had accessed the accounts. Was it possible that their mother was being set up? It didn't seem likely.

Sam had been able to connect Ailongam to an account in the Cayman Islands. He'd used the information that Snapper had sent him to find out that the account had withdrawals in the same amounts within a month of each deposit.

With the dates he was able to narrow down when he thought the withdrawals were being made. Accessing the CCTV footage from the bank, he had a grainy black and white photo of the person who was making the withdrawals. A little more digging got him a name, John Smith.

Sam couldn't tell from the photo if the person matched the description of John Smith. The person was wearing an exorbitant amount of clothing, a hat, and sunglasses. For a place like the Caymans, someone should have noticed that he looked extremely out of place.

But Mari had called his supervisor in Charlotte under the guise of checking on the transition and she found out that John Smith had been to work every day and hadn't taken a single day off. So, whoever was taking out the money wasn't *their* guy. He was the fall guy.

Chapter 18

Oni's 18th birthday was in three days. She was more excited about it than she'd been about anything in the last seven months. She woke up like she had every morning for the last 15 days of May with excitement and joy.

Her siblings had decided that it was the twenty one days of Oni. Starting on May first, they made all of her favorite breakfast items. For the first time, in their new home, they sat down together and had a meal together. It would be the first of many to come.

Usually, it was grab a cup of coffee or a bagel while running out the door for everyone, but they all got up extra early to start the celebration.

On day two she was given a pair of gorgeous diamond earrings, on day three she was given three days at the Four Seasons with full pampering at the spa. They all divided her work schedule so she could lay around and do nothing. Days four through eighteen were filled with more gifts that were all of her favorite things. She was particularly loving the eighteen dozen roses that now filled their entire home from the day before. She couldn't wait to see what was waiting for her on day nineteen.

No one was waiting for her downstairs, but the dining room table was filled with nineteen wrapped boxes. Like a kid at Christmas, she had to shake each one. They were all the same size and wrapped in identical bright red paper with black ribbons.

She took a video and posted it on her Instagram like she'd done each day. She'd had over a million followers before May, but as she posted the videos of all of her presents her account had blown up to over two million. Everyone anticipated the next day with her.

She sat down to open the first box. It was a pair of bright pink Louboutin heels. With that she knew. She had nineteen new pairs of shoes. She was ecstatic and ripped into all of them in record time.

She did a try on video for her followers of all the shoes. The likes rolled in and her following went up another two hundred thousand. With the help of her followers, she decided to wear the bright pink ones to work and show them off.

When she got to work she had an unwelcome visitor waiting for her in her office. Her mother.

Oni walked in and ignored her by going to her desk, turning on her computer, and buzzing her secretary for a latte.

Magnolia cleared her throat.

Oni continued to ignore her. Instead, she began typing an email to all of her siblings to let them know that their mother was in her office.

Magnolia spoke. "I will not be ignored, child. We need to talk about what you saw. You have been avoiding me, not returning my calls, and I even resorted to texting you multiple times, but you didn't have the decency to reply. I will not be trifled with, young lady."

Oni continued with her business on the computer once she received replies from Snapper and Nia that they were on their way.

"What do you want Mother?" Oni asked in a dismissive tone and without looking up at her.

She had gained self-respect and confidence in the short amount of time that she had been away from her mother. She no longer feared her and after what she saw, what little respect she had for her went right out the window.

" I want you to act like a woman who is about to turn into an adult and have a conversation with me about how you barged into my room the other day."

Oni didn't flinch.

Magnolia continued, "I have changed all of the locks on the house and installed a new alarm and security system. None of you are welcome at the house without my permission."

Nonchalantly, Oni acknowledged her mother's obvious attempt to get under her skin. "That's fine, Mother. None of us care to come back to the...I mean *your* house. We have Freedom Flowers Estate now."

"You have what?" Magnolia scoffed.

"We named our compound. We're having a stone column made to go out by the road and everything, just like Flora Fields. We figured we'd keep the tradition, even if we aren't a traditional family."

"Let me guess," she crossed her legs and leaned forward slightly, "you all have your freedom now, is that it? So clever. So juvenile. I wouldn't expect anything better, more creative, or original from the lot of you."

Oni finally looked up at her mother. Exasperated she asked with a sigh, "Can you please tell me why you are waiting for me and interrupting my morning? I saw you getting it on with the Italian, so what. You're grown. You can fuck him or anyone else. Father is gone, you're allowed." She paused and tilted her head just an inch to the left, "It just seems distasteful that it hasn't even been a year and that you are doing it in the bed you shared with Father, but I wouldn't expect anything better, more creative, or original from you."

Just then Snapper walked in. "Mother, how can we help you?" His professional, dry approach and Oni's dig at using her words back on her, caused Magnolia to lose her composure.

She stood up and leaned over the desk with both of her hands firmly planted on the desk to get right in Oni's face. "You'd better watch your back, Aconite, because I can promise you that karma is a bitch and her name is Magnolia Blossom."

She stood to walk out and ran smack into Nia at the door. "Get the fuck out of my way, Petunia." She pushed Nia aside and walked out.

"Okay Oni, what was that all about?" Snapper demanded.

"Oh, nothing. Mother being Mother. You know the drill. Threats, intimidation, the usual menu.

"She threatened you?" Nia screeched.

"Pretty much. It's nothing. She's just pissed that we aren't under her control anymore. She's also furious that I called her on her bullshit with the Italian. I don't care about any of it. I'm almost eighteen, I'm smarter than she will ever be, and I'm happy. Honestly, I didn't think the latter would ever happen. But here I am, loving life and amazed that I stood my ground with her. It was...," she wanted to think of just the right word, "exhilarating."

"I'm just glad you're okay. When I got your email I was worried." Snapper hesitated. "Oni, there's something you need to know."

He ran the conversation he'd had with the twins through his mind. They had all agreed that if Oni was in danger that they would tell her. She had to know what their mother had done. He wanted her to be cautious, alert, and aware.

"Did the twins reply to your email?" he asked.

"Yes. They are in a meeting and said they would be here as soon as possible." Oni replied.

"Good, there's something we all need to talk about and the twins need to be here for it.

"Sounds serious, Nia injected.

"It is," stated Snapper in a low tone.

The twins arrived about fifteen minutes later and Oni filled them in on what had transpired with their mother. She brushed it off, as she had earlier, but the twins agreed that she needed to know what they and Snapper had been doing.

Hesitantly and carefully, they told her and Nia everything. They conveyed the information they had learned from Sam and all that they had learned about the twenty-five million dollars that their father had discovered was missing the year prior.

Oni and Nia listened patiently as the trio recounted their months of investigation and evidence they felt like pointed straight to their mother. When they were finished, they thought that Oni would break down and be terribly upset. They had prepared mentally to comfort her and to tell her that they would keep her safe. That was not what happened.

Her first question wasn't about the investigation or their mother. "So, Sam is *your* guy?" she asked in a way that surprised them. Like she knew him or at least *of* him.

"Umm, yeah. He works for us. Do you know Sam?" Dio asked.

"No," she giggled, "But I've heard the name."

Nia began to explain that she and Oni had also been investigating and had come to realize that the person with the most obvious motive was their mother. They too suspected her, or at least her involvement.

Relieved, Snapper asked for the details they had about the case. To which they happily obliged. It was a weight off of Nia and Oni to share with their siblings. They had information that the others hadn't even thought to look into and together they all had more than enough to set up a meeting with Detective Stone.

Each time their mother threw down the gauntlet, the siblings got stronger and closer. They were all on the same page, the same team to prove that their mother had killed their father.

They met with the detective the next morning and laid out all the evidence they had against their mother. They were confident that somewhere in all of it Detective Stone would be able to make a case against her and finally have justice for their father.

"I appreciate all of this hard work," Stone started after hearing their entire presentation, "but, unfortunately, it's all circumstantial. None of this gets us to your mother. Yes, it does point in her direction but take her out of the equation and it could point at anyone and the list of other possible suspects. Like you said, Miss Blossom, you had the fleeting thought that maybe someone was setting your mother up to take the fall for your father's murder. If we look at it that way, it could be possible."

The siblings were disappointed, but not surprised. When they were putting everything together, Dio had pointed out the possibility of someone else trying to take down their mother. She did have a laundry list of enemies.

"Let me have some time with all of this and I promise I will get back to you," Detective Stone stated.

With that, the siblings had to let it go…for now. The next day, Saturday, was Oni's birthday and nothing was going to stop them from making it special for her.

None of them had gotten a birthday party growing up so they were all looking forward to the celebration. It was a new tradition they decided to start in the Blossom family. Instead of getting nothing for their birthday, since Magnolia always said that the days of their births should be a celebration of her, not them, they would embrace each of their birthdays and make it all about that person. Gifts and parties would replace whatever it was that their mother did – mostly didn't do for their birthdays.

Most of the birthdays would pass without a word from their mother, but Helio had always gotten them some small gift, a trinket, small enough to hide in their room. Softly, he would sing "Happy Birthday" when Magnolia wasn't around.

If he'd had his way, there would have been pony rides, cake, ice cream, and all of the trappings of a traditional birthday party. The children still wondered why their father had given in to so many of Magnolia's demands, considering where it had gotten him.

Chapter 19

Oni's life had been cloaked in the shadows of duty and responsibility; a reality forged by the demands of her family's legacy. But that night, the stars had aligned, and her siblings were ready to unveil a spectacle unlike any other.

All of her guest had walked the red carpet amidst the rotating spotlights, paparazzi, and on lookers. It was a veritable who's who that were invited to the Southern Exchange Ballrooms for Oni's party.

When she stepped out of the stretch limousine on the arm of her brother, she dazzled in a vintage 2004 House of Blossom couture black and silver sequined gown from the vault.

She stood poised at the threshold, a melody of wonder and disbelief swirling inside her. Beautiful ebony locks framed her face and cascaded like a waterfall at midnight down her back as they carried whispers of her lineage – a legacy that was stitched into the very fabric of her being and the stunning gown that was reminiscent of celestial radiance she wore. Exuding a tranquil grace that veiled the sea of emotions that were welling up inside her, she couldn't help but to take a moment to catch her breath and survey the scene.

The grand ballroom boasted soaring ceilings with crystal chandeliers that cast a warm, shimmering glow over the marble floors below. The sequins from Oni's dress looked like diamonds as they sparkled. Elaborate and elegant floral arrangements in shades of blush and lavender adorned every surface giving a fragrant warmth to the space.

Silk fabrics billowed as they draped down from the ceiling and wrapped around each column. The iridescent sheen reflected twinkling fairy lights that had been carefully placed to stream down behind the silk. The walls were adorned with ornate gilt-framed mirrors, reflecting the beauty of the space, and created an illusion of infinite grandeur. Plush velvet curtains in rich jewel tones framed the windows, their luxurious folds cascading to the floor in elegant waves.

Tables were draped in sumptuous silk linens and featured towering centerpieces of overflowing blooms, interspersed between the stems of crystal candelabras. At the other end of the ballroom, a lavish buffet stretched the length of the room with a feast fit for royalty. From decadent caviar and oysters on the half shell to gourmet delicacies from around the world, no expense had been spared in creating a culinary experience that would delight the senses and tantalize the taste buds.

With her siblings surrounding her, she practically squealed as she spotted celebrities, friends, and loved ones, mostly from her father's family.

Her siblings had even put out the call on social media for ten of Oni's followers to win an invitation to the party. They crowded her as she walked in and stole her away for selfies and autographs. Oni was charming and endearing, which made her fans love her even more.

She walked around with them and greeted the other guests, making sure to introduce her fans, for whom she was a quick study at remembering all of their names. Once she had made the rounds she found her way back to her siblings one by one.

"Snapper, this is amazing. I didn't know birthdays could be so much fun. Thank you."

"Tonight, my dear, the evening is yours." He placed his arm around her shoulder and stooped down a little. "See that man over there by the bar? The one who is standing there with the tea towel over his arm. He is here for one reason. You. If you want or need anything, you tell him and I can guarantee he will get it, find it, or do it. Have fun, Oni, and happy birthday!" He waved her toward the dance floor where hundreds of people were dancing.

She bounced away to join them. She couldn't remember the last time she had danced. She'd taken ballet as a child, they all had, but to be able to just dance freely, she didn't think she'd ever done that.

Mari, Dio, and Nia were already on the dance floor and the four of them formed a circle together. The bass from the music vibrated the floor and pulsed through their bodies.

The ballroom swayed with vitality as the rhythm of the music coursed through the air while their laughter harmonized with the heartbeat of the music. Each movement was a testament to the intoxicating allure of the night. As she danced with her siblings, they laughed and twirled, lost in the moment, their worries and cares melted away beneath the spell of the music.

With each step, she moved with a joy that was infectious, her spirit soaring. Oni's laughter resonated through the space and with every graceful step, she danced with a contagious delight, her essence abound. In that moment, her burdens and troubles dissolved beneath the enchantment. There was only the music and her bond with her sisters.

They made their way off the dance floor to catch their breath and get something to drink. They found Snapper at the bar.

"Snapper!" Nia exclaimed, her voice a melodic lilt that cut through the din of the crowd. "Fancy seeing you here."

Snapper turned at the sound of her voice, his grin widening as he caught sight of his siblings approaching. "Well, well, well," he chuckled, his words tinged with amusement. "If it isn't the enigmatic Blossom sisters," he teased. He lowered his face to Oni, "Are you having fun?" he asked.

"Fun? Snapper, I don't think there is a word in my vocabulary for this one. Fun doesn't cover it."

"Wow, that's saying something, because you have an impressive vocabulary. I just hope it's everything you could have wished for, my beautiful sister."

"I couldn't have wished for this, Snapper. I didn't even know *this* existed."

"Five glasses of the 1990 Dom Perignon that is chilling for the birthday girl, please," Snapper requested from the bartender.

All of the sudden the lights went out and the music stopped. Everyone gasped and looked around to see a silver cart being wheeled out with a scrumptious looking birthday cake topped with sparklers and the numbers one and eight in six inch high candles dotted elegantly within each of the eighteen frosting roses. The gasps changed to awes as everyone gathered around Oni and her siblings.

The ordering of the champagne was the signal and everything was timed perfectly. The bartender sat their glasses on the bar and Nia was the first to speak.

"This is a magical night for a magical woman. She is our baby sister but she outshines us all. Happy Birthday Oni."

A rousing, "Here, here," came from the entire ballroom.

"This night is a celebration of you, your future, and all of the possibilities that may come. Happy Birthday," Dio announced.

Finally, Mari spoke, "Oni, I know we all," she gestured toward her siblings, "don't say this enough, but I love you."

With that, Oni held back her hair and blew out the candles. Everyone clapped and cheered. Soon a wave through the crowd chanted, "Speech, speech, speech."

Oni giggled and stepped forward. "I cannot thank you all enough for being here tonight to celebrate with me. I am truly honored that you would take the time to be here. Some of you flew halfway around the world and I will gladly return the favor. This has been a magical night and it's not over yet. So please continue to enjoy yourselves. Oh, and one more thing I've always wanted to say. Hey, DJ, Spin that shit!"

A second later the music was thumping again and the lights were back on as if she had commanded the world to dance.

Snapper raised his glass, "To Oni!" The twins and Nia followed suit and the five of them clinked their glasses together in the air.

Chapter 20

After lazing around on Sunday morning, mostly sleeping off their hangovers, the siblings decided to float around in the pool while the chef made them hamburgers and hot dogs on the grill. It was Oni's only request for her birthday. Their mother had never let them have hamburgers or hot dogs, although, their father had taken them a few times without her knowledge.

The staff they had hired was working out nicely. They had a household manager that governed over two housekeepers, a butler, a chef, a maintenance contractor, a gardener, two horsemen, two stable hands, and a landscaper. They needed a few more people, but for now they were doing well.

To them, feeling the tranquility of life without their mother underfoot was worth every penny they had placed into their home, the décor, and the staff. For them, money could buy happiness, but more importantly, it bought them freedom.

Now that they had shared all of the information with Detective Stone, they felt like they could start to regain their focus at work and school.

Everything was going well. Then the phone rang.

"Sir, "the butler called out to Snapper, "the phone is for you. It's a Detective Stone. He says it's urgent."

Snapper exited the pool and dried off just enough to take the phone.

"Yes, I understand. We'll be on the first plane there. Thank you."

The girls clamored around him as they dripped pool water on the deck.

"What was that all about?" asked Mari.

"There's been an incident. John Smith attacked a woman at work. He's in jail and she's in the hospital. Mari, I'm sorry, but it's Cindy."

Dio called the pilot. "The jet can be ready by four," she stated. "I suggest we eat because once we are there, none of us will eat until we have answers."

"I think she's right," Nia replied.

"You're probably right and the chef is almost done. I'll call Venus and arrange for all of your departments to have supervision and coverage. Excuse me."

Snapper walked into the house and went to his bedroom to call Venus while he started packing his bag.

"It's bad, Venus. He broke her jaw and three ribs. Apparently, she was watching him work and he got freaked out. He confronted her, she coward to his yelling at her, then he punched her. She hit the ground and he kicked her. Then he just walked away like nothing had happened even though there were multiple witnesses to the whole thing. I knew I should have fired him," he said with regret.

"I'll take care of everything. Y'all just be safe and let me know if there is anything else I can do from here."

He went back down to join his sisters. They were sitting at the outdoor table nibbling on their food. What was meant to be a lazy Sunday had quickly retreated to their usual chaos.

"There's one more phone call you need to make," stated Dio.

"I know. I need to call Mother." The thought of it filled him with dread. "I'll call her on the way to the airport. That way she can't try to come with us or something outrageous."

Nia verbalized the one thing that everyone was thinking. "Is it possible that Mother was set up or framed? Could we all be wrong about her having Father murdered.?" This attack made the possibility a thought that none of them could escape. Maybe John Smith was violent enough to have had their father murder for some unknown reason.

The flight from tarmac to tarmac was only an hour. They split up. Oni went to see the crime scene and to speak with the supervisor, while Snapper and Nia went to meet Stone at the Charlotte police station. Mari and Dio went to the hospital.

The hospital corridors were a maze of sterile white walls as Mari and Dio made their way to ICU. The smell of antiseptic hung heavy in the air. Mari and Dio navigated the labyrinth of hallways with measured steps, their hearts heavy with concern for their friend. As they approached Cindy's room, a sense of dread settled over them.

Pushing open the door, they were met with the stark reality of Cindy's condition. The room was bathed in the soft glow of overhead lights. Machines beeped and hummed in a contorted symphony.

Cindy laid upon the hospital bed, her body a canvas of bruises and bandages. Her face was swollen and bruised; her features distorted by the pain of her injuries. Tubes and wires snaked from her body, tethering her to machines that monitored her every breath.

Mari's heart clenched at the sight of her friend's suffering; a knot of anguish tightened in her chest. She crossed the room in hurried steps, her hands trembling as she reached out to grasp Cindy's uninjured hand.

"Cindy," she whispered, her voice an echo in the sterile silence. "We're here and we are going to take care of everything."

Dio stood beside Mari, her expression a mask of stoic resolve. Her eyes, pools of liquid steel, surveyed the scene with a steely determination. Though her heart ached at the sight of Cindy's pain, she knew that now was not the time for weakness.

Cindy stirred at the sound of their voices, her eyes fluttering open, but the pain was etched in lines upon her forehead as she attempted to speak, her words a whisper lost amidst the beeps and clicks of the room.

Mari leaned in closer, her heart breaking at the sight of her friend's suffering.

"Don't try to speak," she urged, her voice a gentle murmur. "Just rest."

Dio nodded in agreement, her gaze softened with empathy as Cindy drifted back into unconsciousness, her breathing steady and shallow. Mari and Dio remained by her side, their silent vigil a testament to the strength of their friendship. They felt helpless but in the silence they both knew what the other was thinking. There was no way that John Smith was going to get away with hurting their friend.

Dio stepped out into the hallway and made the needed phone calls to get the company lawyers up to speed on the case. She demanded that they prosecute him to the fullest and that as much compensation be awarded to Cindy. She wanted them to find a way to circumvent the company insurance plan and for them to use the emergency relief fund that their father had set up for employees to be used to pay her deductible immediately so that everything else was paid in full by the insurance.

Cindy didn't have the money for what all she was going to have to endure. Dio also requested that home health and physical therapy be arranged at the best facilities as soon as the doctor gave the orders. Anything else would be handled as it surfaced.

She quietly reentered the room. "It's all taken care of," she told Mari.

Oni spoke with everyone who had witnessed the event. As Chief Information Officer, part of her job was to keep incidents like this out of the press for as long as possible. She needed to have everyone sign NDAs and she handed all of them cards with the company's legal team's information. She instructed everyone to contact the lawyer before speaking to anyone, including the police.

Unfortunately, she found out that she was too late on that one. The police had come and gone. Everyone had already been asked brief questions and had appointments to go in and speak at length with the officers the next day.

"I don't know what to tell you Miss Blossom. The guy has been a fine worker. He's here every day on time, does his work, doesn't bother anyone. He came to me last week and told me that 'some woman,' his words, not mine, was following him. He didn't like it, but he didn't know who she was, so I couldn't follow up on the complaint.

Next thing I know, he's cleaning the johns on the fifth floor and she apparently went in there. It startled him, he panicked, punched her and she crawled out enough where everyone saw him kick her while she was down and then just walk off."

Oni thanked him for his time and asked him to please convey the information he knew to the company lawyers and to only speak through them.

"If you find out anything else that I might need to know here is my card too," she stated before exiting his office.

She noted that she needed to speak with Snapper. The facility had many violations that needed to be addressed. Someone needed to be held accountable for the gross negligence that she saw in just a cursory glance around the facility.

Nia and Snapper arrived at the police station as Detective Stone was pulling into the parking lot.

"Stone what is going on with this John Smith guy?"

"Let's talk inside," Stone replied.

He led them to the police station's version of the soft room back in Atlanta in which he had used when he talked to Snapper after the murder. To a decerning eye like Snapper's the room looked like a child's playroom with what looked to be donated furniture and mismatched accoutrements, but in reality it was a space that housed plush couches and comfortable chairs that would make the average person feel more relaxed. It had the opposite effect on Nia and Snapper.

Stone explained that since John worked for House of Blossom he was legally allowed to give them a few details, but he made no promises for answers to their questions.

Nia had only one question, "Did John Smith kill our father."

"No, we don't think so, but we are interrogating him and questions about the murder will be posed to him. He may be a piece of the puzzle or he may know a direction we can go in order to find some new information. It's too early to tell at this point. More than anything, I wanted you all to know that I am still working this case." He paused. "I liked your father. He was good to the department. By the way, Nia, thank you for the canine training facility you're having built. The five dogs we rescued from your shelters have turned into true assets to the unit. The little beagle is a hell of a tracker and the German Shepard mix is a natural at chasing down criminals who run. Two of the other ones are in training to be drug dogs, and the last one, the Mastiff, is going to be a great search and rescue dog. When the new place is finished, we can add another ten dogs to the training program thanks to you."

"I'm just glad I could help. Our father respected law enforcement and we hope to continue all of the traditions he has in place. We are currently working with your chief for the summer fun day we sponsor each July fourth for the department. We hope to see you there."

After all of their business was concluded, the siblings met back up at the airport to go home. They were all mentally drained and as predicted, had not eaten a single thing during their time in Charlotte. They all took a nap on the jet and when they got home they each went their separate ways.

Even though they were under the same roof, they felt more divided than ever about who had their father killed.

Chapter 21

With the arrest of John Smith, the siblings weren't sure how to think. Oni, Mari, and Dio were convinced that their mother had hired Smith to kill their father, but Snapper and Nia were not so sure.

He was a terrible person, that was for sure, but Snapper couldn't figure out a connection between his mother and Smith now that he had more facts. Nia couldn't fathom her mother associating with him, even for something as heinous as committing murder, much less of her own husband. Both Snapper and Nia had gone over what Stone had said backwards and forwards, but their sisters had their own conclusions.

A week after they were in Charlotte, they were still divided. Snapper had called a family meeting because the tension in their home had become unbearable. Everyone met in the living room and it was obvious who was with who. Snapper's heart clinched a bit when Mari didn't sit by him on the sofa.

"You didn't see her, Dragon. Cindy is fighting for her life because of him. It was cold and unprovoked, just like father. What possible motive would Smith have had to kill father without mother's involvement. Besides, it was his gun, how do you explain *that*?"

Mari's words hit right in the middle of Snapper's chest. His favorite was against him and he didn't have it in him to be intolerant to her assessment of the situation.

"Goldie, I'm so sorry about your friend. We will take care of her, but I don't see how this leads us back to Mother. Trust me, I want her to be guilty. Yes, I know that's horrible to say, but I can't condemn her through John Smith. I haven't abandoned the possibility, but I'm not as sure as I once was about her guilt."

"I'm going to look into his employment record again," Dio stated. "I know I've missed something. I don't care what his supervisor said, there was a day, somewhere that he was off and he figured out a way to kill Father. There's no other explanation."

"Besides, I don't care how rare that gun is, it's rare enough that it can't be a coincidence that the exact gun he owned just so happened to be a partial ballistics match," argued Oni.

"All of you need to stop," Nia cut in as tempers were about to reach a boiling point and voices were getting louder. "We won't stop looking into Mother, but we do need to start thinking about other people who could have done this to Father. The more I think about it, the more this looks professional. Smith is not a professional; he's a thug. If Mother is involved she would have hired someone with a reputation as a hitman, not a felon janitor."

"She's right. He doesn't fit the profile. Mother is sophisticated and cunning. She would have been methodical and meticulous in her planning. Stone said that the loquacious Mr. Smith bragged about punching Cindy but swore that he didn't know anything about Father. Don't you find that strange?" asked Snapper.

"Did anyone find a connection between Smith and anyone else in the company?" Oni asked.

"I searched through all of the HR files for potential relatives, girlfriends, high school friends, everything, but I couldn't find it.

When he checked no to all of the legal questions, for whatever reason he was not given a background check. I have spoken to the HR supervisor and all of the personnel in that department are to be retrained about exact policies and procedures," Dio replied.

"So, what is the solution? We can't continue like this, not talking, keeping secrets. I can't go back to that," Oni said.

"I think we need to combine all of the theories. Mother and Smith, Mother and a hitman, and the possibility of an unknown variant that we haven't figured out yet," stated Mari. "That's how we stay on the same path together."

"Oni's right about the gun. That's the key," pondered Snapper.

He suggested that they find out what happened to it. Smith told Detective Stone that he'd sold it to a friend. But when the friend was questioned, he said that he gave it to his father-in-law as a gift. Unfortunately, the father-in-law passed away shortly after and when the family inventoried his gun collection, the Glock T was missing.

They figured he'd left it at their mountain cabin the last time he'd gone up there thinking that he'd go back. The family didn't realize any of that until after they had sold the cabin. The new owner was also questioned, but he signed a statement that he never saw it.

The siblings wanted to establish a solid timeline for all of the details as they felt like something was getting lost. Oni suggested they go to the war room they had constructed by repurposing one of the guest houses on the property. As they walked out, Mari linked her arm in Snapper's. He smiled down at her.

"Glad to have you back, Goldie."

"Oh Dragon, you're so sappy," she giggled.

The war room was a meticulously organized space designed to facilitate the investigation process. The space was brightly lit, with walls of light green. There were no windows as to not allow glare and to create an atmosphere of focus and concentration.

At the center of the room was a large glass table, strewn with various documents, financial records, and notes. A corkboard hung the length of one wall, covered in photographs of potential suspects and key locations. Color-coded markers connected different images, forming a plethora of possibilities.

Opposite the corkboard was a series of whiteboards covering the entire wall. Each whiteboard was divided into sections, with headings like "Theory 1," "Suspect List," and "Timeline of Events." Sticky notes adorned the boards, providing visual cues and reminders for the siblings.

In one corner of the room stood a safe that was disguised as a filing cabinet. A large map of the city hung on one end of the cork board with marks for every business and person in which they had talked.

Nia and Mari started back at the beginning - Motive. Who had it, what it was, and why. Just like a college study group, they split the work. This had been Oni's comfort zone from the start. She began with a fresh list of suspects.

Dio went back through the financials. There was still something bothering her about the missing twenty-five million. She'd found all of it, but she felt like she was missing the origin of the payments, who was the man in the bank surveillance, and how was the money actually used.

One of Nia's hacker friends had been able to get Magnolia's phone records, so Snapper logged the calls on a spreadsheet and created a formula to detect duplicates. They were still trying to clone her phone to get to her text messages, but with the self-inflected estrangement, she was radio silent except for brief moments at House of Blossom.

Oni went through all of the social media accounts for the potential suspects to search for anything that might be telling or to see if anyone had been doing any lavish spending. With each person she checked off her list, she became more and more disheartened. There was nothing that suggested any of them had a single issue with her father or that they had come into any substantial amount of money.

They spent hours combing through and poring over documents. A sense of urgency hung in the air, as Snapper, Nia, Oni, Dio, and Mari worked tirelessly to solve the murder and bring the perpetrator to justice no matter who it might be – even their mother.

Chapter 22

With the children out of the house, Magnolia wasted no time moving her boyfriend, Darrian, into the house with her. She knew how to be discreet and he was still under the threat of castration if he told anyone. He wasn't completely living at Flora Fields, but he spent enough time there that he had his own room, which for Magnolia that was a magnanimous gesture.

Darrian had protested and their relationship was nearly broken because he was insistent that he be allowed to stay in the room with her. She was having none of it so her "compromise" was she put him in the room that was across the hall from hers.

There were ground rules, of course. He was not allowed to stay overnight except for on Saturday. He could not enter her room without permission, and if she didn't want him in the house, then he was not allowed to be on the property until she called. The rules were installed after he tried to surprise her by being naked in her bed with rose petals leading from the door to the bedroom.

"What in the literal FUCK are you doing? Get your ass out of my bed!" Magnolia had already had a rough day at work. It was the same day in which she had confronted Oni.

Darrian had heard about the incident, it was the talk of the company, so he thought she would appreciate the surprise. He should have known better. He had tried surprising her only once before about six years earlier. It was what had caused Helio to suspect that she was having an affair. That surprise hadn't gone over well either. She didn't speak to him for a month.

This surprise went over like a lead balloon. She stomped over to his bedroom, flung the window open and started throwing all of his shit out.

"Get out! Get the fuck out of my house, off my property, and if you ever try this again, you will be out of my company. I don't care how much business you bring in, your dick isn't worth all that. Oh, and that generous allowance I have been giving you for years, that fucking shit is over! Ailongam is closed – both ways!"

Darrian had nothing to say. He just pulled on his pants, grabbed up the rest of his clothes and like a child left the house pouting. He didn't even try to get any of the items she'd thrown out of the window, he just got into his Lamborghini Veneno and sped off down the winding drive that was lined with sturdy live oaks that danced in the wind like they were waving goodbye to Darrian.

He thought about flying to Italy for a respite from her, but his love for Magnolia kept him in her orbit. Plus, he knew if he went back to Italy, he would most likely have to stay. His family owned a vineyard and going back meant working there.

He was the black sheep of the family. The one who left the family business to be in fashion. It was one thing when he worked for Versace, but when he decided to move to the States to work for House of Blossom, they cut him off. That was where Magnolia's allowance came into play. She'd been giving him money for years through the discretionary funds, but when Helio realized that twenty-five million was missing, he confronted Magnolia.

She'd set up a shelf company and Darrian had the, at the time, funny notion to name it Ailongam – Magnolia backwards, because her favorite position was being taken from behind.

Now she found it crude and distasteful, but it was something that she couldn't undo easily. She had exposure and even if she had paid the money back, which she could have easily done, she would most likely get caught. As the CFO, her reputation would have been ruined.

As it was, the account was untraceable back to her, except for the shelf company literally being her name. It was not her finest hour when she went along with it, but she was trying, one of the few times in her life, to make him happy.

That was not to be confused with love. It was his attributes she was after, not him. She paid him a handsome salary and he was worth every penny, but in the beginning he had come to her and Helio with nothing but his name and a recommendation letter from Versace himself.

Magnolia had plans for him the moment she saw him. She knew his work and she knew why the children called him 'the Italian.' Not only did he have a reputation for a keen eye for fabrics and design, but he also had a reputation for being promiscuous with both men and women. He loved love and he made no secret of his ability to please his companions.

But when he saw Magnolia, it was true love at first sight. He'd never seen such beauty and her confidence was sexy. She was wild and headstrong. She was a challenge.

It was his latter reputation that caused Magnolia to make him wait for two years before they started having an affair.

Originally, his allowance did come out of the discretionary fund as a legitimate payment for services so that he could get settled in the States. But once the affair started and he was well established, she changed the process because Helio asked, frequently, why Darrian was still getting an allowance. Magnolia wanted to give him the money.

In her logic, it made their relationship more of an arrangement. It was transactional. She insisted that he take the money, even though several times over the years he'd asked her to stop paying him. When she wouldn't, he invested it in real estate.

He had houses all over the country and around the world that were all paid for with House of Blossom money. He had tried to pay the money back to her multiple times, but she said that it would cause more problems than it would solve.

That night he wondered if she had finally had enough and really would figure out a way to dissolve the fake company. That was what he'd wanted for years and she knew that. He considered it an empty threat since she had refused to do it so many times.

She eventually let him back in the house, but the rules were in writing, signed, and stored in a safe. She was the only one with the combination. She would never admit it, but she wanted him around despite all that it had cost her.

Lydia did not understand the relationship between Magnolia and Darrian. He was Helio's exact opposite, which Lydia hated. He invaded her space in the kitchen, he got his own coffee and helped himself to the liquor cabinet. To her, he was brash and rude.

She'd known about the affair and there was more than one occasion in which she thought about telling Helio the truth. But she thought better of it thinking she'd never find another job that paid so well.

Snapper had offered her to come run the Freedom Flowers Estate. He'd offered her a huge raise but despite how she felt about

Magnolia, she'd been with her for years and she didn't feel right leaving. Loyal to a fault.

All of that changed a few months after Magnolia had let Darrian back into the house. When she kicked him out, Lydia was pleased and secretly said goodbye to the rubbish. The house was calmer and quieter. She could do her work in peace and not have to worry about the middle of the night screeches and howls she could hear through the vents.

Unfortunately, his return just made her life even more miserable than from when he was there the first go round. As a proud English woman, she didn't suffer the likes of Darrian's type of Italian. All of the Italian's she knew were loving, family-oriented people who tried to help others. That was not Darrian. He was loud, obnoxious, and brutish.

"I'm telling you Lydia," Darrian said one morning while he stood against the counter in the kitchen in nothing but his boxer shorts eating a bagel and making a mess with crumbs, "I'm going to be the next Mr. Blossom." He took another bite, "I mean, I can't expect her to take my last name. She's too important." He brushed the crumbs off his chest onto the floor. "Don't get me wrong, Maggie Conti would be fabulous, but I don't see her doing that. Don't you think it's time we get wed?"

Lydia cringed. She tried to be as proper as possible. "Sir, I do not believe that a respectable amount of time has passed since the demise of poor Mr. Blossom."

She turned and went to the pantry to retrieve the broom. When she returned, he was licking the cream cheese off of his fingers. She began to sweep up his crumbs from the floor and accidentally, deliberately poked him with the bristles of the broom.

"I'm so sorry, sir. If you wouldn't mind vacating the kitchen, I can have all of this cleaned up in a jiff."

Darrian scoffed, threw his napkin on the counter, and walked out. Under his breath he said, just loud enough for her to hear him, "She's got to go."

Right then Lydia knew what she had to do. Talk to the children.

When she left work that day, she did not take the interstate exit to the right like she usually took to take her home. That evening, she went one more block, under the bridge, and turned left.

She spoke with her husband through the Bluetooth in her car and asked him to check their children's homework and get them to bed. She had never missed tucking them into bed, but that night was too important and she had to make an exception. She had to warn the siblings about what Darrian had said to her. She felt that she owed them at least that much.

She'd taken care of them, fed them, and watched them grow into fine adults, despite their mother's influence. This was too egregious even for Magnolia, she thought, as she drove toward Freedom Flowers Estate.

Lydia had called Snapper to let him know she needed to speak with him and his sisters immediately. He texted his sisters to drop everything and come home.

Once everyone had arrived, Lydia nervously began to tell them about Darrian and the hidden secret she had kept for eleven years. She recounted all of the trips, the afternoon meetings that were actually at the house, and the late night returns to the office Magnolia had done during her marriage to Helio just to have time with Darrian.

She wept as she spoke with the stunned faces of the Blossom siblings hanging on her every word. She was embarrassed and felt so much shame and guilt that the words poured out of her like an open spigot. She had years of anguish built up and she felt relief as they unraveled. An hour later she finally got to that evening and what Darrian had said to her in the kitchen.

"Marriage?" Dio screeched. "He has lost his marbles if he thinks that Mother would marry him. If she's kept him on a string this long, then that is where he is going to stay."

"Has he really moved in?" Oni asked quietly as silent tears rolled down her cheeks for the years of disrespect her mother had given her father.

"I'm afraid so. After their fight, I thought he was gone for good. But when she allowed him back it seemed that he was even more emboldened," replied Lydia.

Snapper sat back in his chair. He was calm. He hadn't said a word. He was processing all of Lydia's words and revelations. He wasn't sure what to think, but he knew that there was no way the Italian was going to stay at House of Blossom.

Chapter 23

Snapper met with Nia the next morning in his office to discuss the Italian issue. He had barely slept, but he was angry and filled with one purpose. Get rid of Darrian Conti.

"Nia I need you to discreetly put out feelers to our international contacts and find me someone who is better than Conti. I want someone young, with a few years of textile and design experience but who hasn't broken into the industry completely. I don't want someone from the other Houses. Get me someone fresh, unknown. Look into small collections, someone who is talented as hell, but just needs a break."

"I can make that happen. What is your plan?" Nia asked.

"My plan?" he paused, "My plan is to kick that fucking asshole back to Italy. I don't care how talented and knowledgeable he is, he just rehashes our old designs and puts a modern spin on them. I don't think he has an original thought in his brain."

"Venus," Snapper called from his desk, "Can you get Mari up here?"

Nia rolled her eyes. She was often jealous of the relationship Snapper had with Mari.

"Don't be a dick, Nia. I need her input. She's the Chief Design Officer, remember?" It was a rhetorical question. "If it makes you happy, I won't tell her what I'm doing. There, another Blossom secret."

"Hi Dragon." Mari bounced into the office with a grand smile for her brother as she walked over and kissed his cheek. She turned to see Nia. "Oh, I'm sorry. Good morning, Nia."

"Mari," he paused. For a split second he almost told her his plan, but he did want her unbiased input, so he would wait until later to fill her in on Operation Kick His Ass to the Curb. "I'm thinking we need a fresh designer for the House. I've asked Nia to look into who is out there that isn't working for one of the other Houses. What would you suggest as our target?"

"Oh, this is interesting. I'd love to have some fresh ideas in the designs. I mean our designs are timeless, but it would be nice for next summer's collection to have more color and sizzle. I've seen some designs out of Asia that are creative and vibrant."

"Sounds intriguing. Nia, thoughts?"

"I agree. I have seen the same and my last trip to Asia I went to Vietnam, Singapore, and Seoul. All of which have extremely talented designers."

"Dragon, I have an idea." She smiled and went to his phone and dialed a number. "Hey, can you come to Snapper's office for a minute?"

"Goldie, what are you up too?"

"Just trust me Dragon, this will take House of Blossom to another level."

A few moments later, Oni walked through the door. Snapper was worried that his plan had just eroded and Mari was planning something big. He was right.

Mari filled Oni in on Snapper's idea and what she wanted from a new designer, then she put *her* plan into action.

"Oni, can you put together a designer contest? Nia can promote it internationally, but I think that it needs a social media angle. Something like having designers enter to win an opportunity to submit a video of their best designs. They could post it to Instagram and we could have the public vote for our top ten with likes. We could fly in those ten and give them a month to create four designs – couture, ready-to-wear, business, and formal…" she trailed off as she spun ideas in her mind.

"This would be fantastic," squealed Oni. I can start working on this today. It would be a real boon for the House to get someone fresh and new. We need to expand into more social media events and this would be the perfect introduction for House of Blossom into the 21st century." She backpedaled, "Don't get me wrong, our sales are great, but we are still designing for women over thirty. We need to tap into the eighteen to twenty-nine demographics. This would do it."

The girls all put their heads together and started making plans while Snapper just sat at his desk slack jawed. This was the complete opposite of what he wanted. He expected a few low key phone calls or emails that were strategically sent to the appropriate people who could keep the search under wraps. Now he could hear them talking about competitions, press releases, and photo spreads in People Magazine.

He had created this mess. Nia was right, he hated to admit, when she objected to Mari's involvement. But his sisters were excited and he couldn't take that away from them, not after the blow they had all been dealt the night before. This was the plan now, which was an amazing plan, he conceded.

Darrian wouldn't know it had anything to do with him and Snapper could start looking into him while it all played out. He needed to know Mari's thoughts on him. She worked with him every day and would have the most insight into how he works and what makes him tick.

As his sisters wrapped up their brainstorming session, they didn't even acknowledge Snapper as they left his office to get started on the social media blitz.

Two months after the campaign launched the ten finalists had been found from all over the world. The Instagram competition had been a rousing success. House of Blossom was on the cover of every fashion magazine and was featured several times in the business section. More importantly, celebrities got involved and the second quarter profits went up sixteen percent.

Everyone was thrilled, except for Magnolia. She had wanted Snapper to fail as CEO so that the board would have no choice but to replace him with her.

She'd been methodically working behind the scenes to sabotage his position. She had called suppliers and deliberately changed orders; she had directed Darrian to manipulate the designs for the September fall collection launch so that they didn't all get done in time. She'd hired and fired multiple models at the last minute so they didn't know if or when to show.

Being CFO, she had a lot of control and with her many contacts she made sure that most of the business went through her to circumvent Snapper. Unfortunately for her, her efforts were in vain. The siblings were all on the watch for any miscalculations, erroneous invoices, and supplier complaints. They were able to fix most of what she broke, so when the internet campaign hit the streets Magnolia was furious.

She had not been consulted, which meant she couldn't do anything to stop it. She instructed her assistant to try buying followers to get them to leave rude and nasty comments on the designers pages so that they would drop out, but it was too late. The campaign went viral within an hour thanks to Oni's own following of three million followers.

None of the schemes worked and the fact that she tried them just infuriated the siblings and bonded them against their mother even more.

The finalist were flown into Atlanta from Idaho, Kentucky, Hoi An, Vietnam, Dongdaemun, South Korea, Melbourne, Australia, Oslo, Norway, Paranaque City, Philippines, Bibury, Cotswold Valley, England, Dedham, Essex, England, and Lorong Buangkok, Singapore.

They were given one of the guest houses on Freedom Flowers Estate that had been converted for them into ten small bedrooms and five large workspaces where two designers would work in each space. The girls, especially, wanted to keep up with the designs and creations. Mari was their mentor and worked at least two hours a day going over their designs and textiles.

The siblings were anxious to add the four pieces from the winner to the summer collection that would be presented in September in New York Fashion week. House of Blossom always had a premium venue and slot and it would either make or break the House. A lot was riding on this experiment.

No one was going to be a loser, per se. The ones who were not selected would be offered a one-year internship in Mari's design department. But everyone wanted the top spot. To work side-by-side with House of Blossom designers like Darrian Conti was a dream for all of them.

Little did they know that the winner would actually replace him. Nia and Snapper had still kept that fact to themselves and no one was none the wiser.

The models had been hired and the reveal day came on August twenty-sixth. It was to be a three day event at the Waldorf Astoria garden courtyard in Atlanta. Only a small, very selective group of press were invited to the events. The intimate nature was to give an air of exclusivity, but it was going to be live streamed on the House of Blossom Instagram.

Ten designers, each with their own unique vision and flair, converged behind the scenes of the bridge runway that stood above the reflective pool in the courtyard. Their creations were draped delicately over the models like works of art, but nerves crackled like static electricity, mingling with the scent of freshly steamed fabric and the hum of clamoring conversations.

As the competition commenced, the runway became a stage upon which dreams and aspirations collided. Each designer poured their heart and soul into their creations, stitching together fragments of inspiration to form garments that transcended mere fabric and thread.

The siblings watched with discerning eyes and impeccable taste, observing intently from their front row seats, their expressions inscrutable as they assessed each design with a critical gaze.

The air was heavy with anticipation as the final moments of the competition drew near on that third evening. In a flurry of whispers and murmurs, Snapper, Mari, Dio, Nia, and Oni conferred amongst themselves, deliberating the merits of each design with meticulous precision. Finally, with a solemn nod and a sweep of their pens, they rendered their decision.

The designers hearts raced in harmonious rhythms as they awaited the verdict, trembling with anxiety. Isabelle from the Philippines was announced as the newest designer to join the ranks of House of Blossom.

Tears of joy streamed down her cheeks as she embraced her fellow competitors, their shared journey forged bonds that would last a lifetime. For Isabelle, this was not merely a victory, but a validation of her talent and dedication to her craft.

For in that moment, she realized that the true beauty of fashion lay not in the garments themselves, but in the stories they told and the dreams they inspired. And in the hallowed halls of House of Blossom, her story was just beginning.

Little did she know that it would be the end of another designer's story. For in the months leading up to the event, Snapper had secured Darrian a position at House of Blossom's Milan headquarters. He would even get a promotion to Head Designer. It even came with a handsome raise. Snapper couldn't wait to tell him Monday morning.

Chapter 24

"This is bullshit, you can't do this to me," shouted Darrian after Snapper told him the *good* news.

"Honestly, Darrian, I am shocked by your protest. This is a highly prestigious position for you; your reputation will skyrocket," retorted Snapper as he fained shock and masked his delight.

"This is because I'm sleeping with your mother, isn't it. I knew that bitch of a sister would tell you. I'm going to —"

Snapper stood up forcefully from his desk, "I'm warning you right now. Say another word and you're fired." He gritted his teeth together, "This is the only time I will say this. You have two options, take the job, or get fired. Which will it be? Oh, and before you answer, whichever way you choose, you are to pack up your things immediately and get out of my House."

Darrian relented. In a much softer tone he replied, "I'll take the job." He walked out with his tail between his legs and once out of Snapper's view, he marched straight over to Magnolia's office.

He didn't even pretend to care if she was busy. He stomped in. "Did you know about this? Is this some kind of punishment?"

Magnolia was completely taken aback. "I don't know what the fuck you are talking about, but you'd better watch your tone and remember who you are speaking to right now."

"I know exactly who I'm talking to; the woman I'm sleeping with who doesn't give two shits about me. Seriously, Milan? How could you?"

"Again," she clenched her jaw, "no, I will not repeat myself. You can either clarify your exasperation or get the fuck out of my office."

He told her what had just happened with Snapper. The job, the move, the threats, the options.

"I would be ruined if I were fired. I have to go to the new job, unless…" he paused in hopes that Magnolia would save him. She did not.

"If Snapper has arranged this, I highly doubt that it has anything to do with us. He just hired that new designer. Don't worry, I have no doubt that the kid will fall flat in September. When that happens, Snapper and the girls will come to see what a horrible mistake they made and you'll be back on the next flight. You really do worry too much."

"I assume you have a plan?" he asked with a hint of doubt that whatever she tried would fail, although he would never say that.

She ignored the hint and looked up at him from her desk, "I always do. Now go do what you need to do to prepare for your trip. It's a prestigious promotion. This could cement your career as a legendary designer. That's what you've always wanted. Especially when Snapper has to beg you to come back here."

He paced the room. He didn't care what she said, if his family got wind of him being back in Italy, they would trash his name if he didn't come back to the family business. He did not think that his reputation would be cemented, instead, it would be ruined.

Continuing his turn around the room he stated nervously, "He knows what he's doing. He's not sending me to Paris, no Milan! Milan of all places!" He threw up his hands in exasperation. "Maggie," he said as if he'd had a thought. He quickly approached her desk and silently demanded her attention as he stood there.

She finally relented and looked up at him from her laptop.

"Come with me," he requested with hope in his voice.

She rolled her eyes and continued working.

"Maggie!"

"Know your place, Darrian," she bristled.

She finally acknowledged his request, sort of, "Don't even entertain such a thought. That will *never* happen. My place is here. That is the end of this conversation."

She did not speak to him anymore. He sat in one of the chairs in front of her desk for another fifteen minutes, but she was deep in her work and he knew that was her way of dismissing him. He stood up and quietly slunk out of her office.

When he finally left, Magnolia called Snapper and requested a meeting. She was fuming at the insult that Snapper had just laid at her feet. It was one thing to mess with the family, it was another to mess with the business, but now he was messing with her and that would not stand.

An hour later, he was escorted into Magnolia's office by her assistant. Before she could say a word, Snapper asked, "Have you heard the good news?"

"Why no, Snapdragon, I haven't," she said calmly as if she didn't know anything, "pray tell what good news do you speak of on this fine day?" She was mocking him in a pious tone.

"Conti has been promoted to head designer. It's a grand day for House of Blossom." He conveniently and deliberately left out the part about the promotion being in Milan. He hoped that she would tip her hand. She didn't.

"This is indeed a banner day for the House. Will your new designer be working with him?" she inquired.

"No, her merits stand on their own. She has ideas that the House has not seen in fifty years. She doesn't need to work under anyone. Oh, that reminds me, I have added her to the New York Fashion Week lineup."

"You've done what? Fuck no, she's an unknown. She needs at least five years to selectively place her garments in a show under the tutelage of an established designer. The fashion world will not stand for it. We will be considered with the likes of…" she could barely get the words out, "big box superstores. We might as well hang a sign out that says get your discount clothes here."

"Mother, the fashion industry needs a little shake. Isabelle is ready to make some noise. Her color choices sing and her style is modern, sleek, and bold. The last collection we had like that was in the sixties. It's time. She is right on schedule for a shock to the summer collection."

"I will not stand for this. Don't force my hand Snapdragon, I will cancel our venue."

"So, let me get this straight. You'd rather see the House burn and fall to the ground, that is what you are proposing, than give Isabelle a chance to skyrocket us to the top?"

"You are so melodramatic. No, I'm saying she is the gasoline that will be poured all over us and the fashion industry will light the match."

"Now who's being melodramatic?"

"It is truly exhausting to have a conversation with you. Circles, that's all this has accomplished, going around in circles." She tried again to get Snapper to admit what he'd done. "You expect Conti to place his designs next to an amateur?"

"Absolutely not. His collection will launch in Milan, where he is head of design. Didn't I mention that part?" He knew she was baiting him, but he was enjoying her discontentment too much not to let her reel him.

"There it is. The real reason why you've done all of this. Oh, one fact is true, I have taught you well. Kudos on playing the long game. You are sending Darrian away simply to get back at me."

"Mother, if I wanted to get back at you, there are a hundred different ways in which I could accomplish that. This is simply a good business decision that the CEO of House of Blossom has made to give an unknown, as you called her, a chance to shine, and a seasoned designer the opportunity to have a larger market. His designs are wasted here in America."

"You spin it anyway that helps you sleep at night, but I know you and I know that as soon as your sister told you about seeing him with me," she shuttered at the thought of Oni barging in on them, "you put this plan in motion."

"You're wrong, Mother. One hundred percent wrong." That was the truth. He was shocked, but not surprised by the two of them having a tryst. It was all of the information from Lydia that had solidified his decision to do something about it. "Mother, I have work to do. If there's nothing else, I'd like to exit this circle and get back to work."

Without waiting for a reply, he turned and walked out of her office. As he walked back to his office he texted his sisters, "It's done."

Mari replied, "He's packed up and I personally walked him to the front door. You know, to give my heartfelt warmest wishes for a safe trip and much success in Milan," with a winking face emoji at the end.

Dio and Oni gave a thumbs up and Nia replied that she hoped it was the end of their mother's nonsense. Oni sent another reply that expressed her disgust of Darrian, "Thanks for taking out the trash, Snapper."

Chapter 25

Now that Darrian was out of the way, the siblings wanted to get back to the business of finding their father's killer. They all had so much on their plates with work, getting ready for Fashion Week, school, taking care of their home, it was hard for them to find time, but they all dedicated their weekends to the hunt.

The war room was well utilized as their central command. On that Saturday, Sam and Rudy were with them to give updates. Since the siblings cleared the air, their PIs had been working together to work more angles of the investigation.

They had all decided that Stone, while a dedicated detective, had newer cases that pulled at his attention. It had been nine months since Helio had died and with the case going colder by the day, he had to devote less and less time and resources to the case. It was understandable. The city needed him.

Sam was making some headway on following the money trail. "I'm telling you; the money all leads to a shelf corporation with a ton of real estate holdings."

"What is a shelf corporation," Rudy asked.

All at once everyone in the room began to answer, but they deferred to Nia's voice as it broke through the noise to answer the question.

"A shelf corporation, known by various names such as a ready-made company, blank check company, or aged company, occupies a unique position within the legal domain. Imagine a company formally established and registered under the law, yet dormant, devoid of any operational activity. This encapsulates the essence of a shelf corporation, existing merely on paper and in name.

The term "shelf" fittingly characterizes its state - placed on a figurative shelf, left to mature, and gather dust until its intended use arises. This concept prompts an exploration of its practicality and significance."

Rudy still looked a bit confused, so Snapper chimed in. "The appeal lies in the convenience it provides. By creating a shelf corporation, one can circumvent the arduous and time-consuming process of starting a new business from scratch."

"Why not just start a business when you need it?" Rudy asked.

Oni took over the explanation, "Consider the time and energy saved by bypassing bureaucratic obstacles and administrative duties. Acquiring a shelf corporation enables a person to promptly initiate entrepreneurial ventures, leveraging the established legal structure of the acquired entity. The prospect of immediate access to a pre-registered entity proves enticing, particularly in industries where timing is critical, offering a shortcut."

"Like the fashion industry," Rudy concluded.

"Exactly," Sam added. "Wow guys, that education is really paying off. When I got my MBA I could rattle all of those facts off like a textbook, but I've been out of the game for so long, that I only remember the basics these days."

"You have an MBA," Dio asked with curiosity and bewilderment.

"Yes. I was a corporate raider back in the day, but I gave up the stress to be a private investigator. The money was great, but after two heart attacks, I had to make changes. I kind of fell into this PI game."

Dio was intrigued. "We'll talk," she stated to Sam with a lift of her eyebrow.

Sam nodded to her and continued to explain that the shelf company had been active for years and had installed over ten real estate holdings in just the past year. They had appeared out of nowhere. The addresses of the properties were redacted from the files he was able to get, but what he found even more interesting was that the financial holdings totaled over thirty million dollars.

His theory was that someone had been stockpiling monies in accounts around the world and when they activated the corporation they deposited the funds to make the holdings look even more legitimate. It wasn't a complicated plan, but he was sure that the person who created it knew the benefits of the long game.

Rudy had a few updates that were going to change or at least add to the trajectory of the investigation.. His team had been able to get enhanced footage of the car. There were two people in the SUV. This was completely new information. It had always been thought that the execution was a solo job. There was a reflection in the passenger rearview mirror of another person that no one had noticed because it all happened so quickly.

Another thing they were able to analyze was that the SUV had been parked a block from the restaurant for fifty-six minutes before the shooting. As soon as Helio exited the building, the van started up and the hit was made. It left no doubt that he was the target.

One of his military sources told him that from a high position, in a moving car, while driving, took precise skill and training. His bet was that the person was a sharpshooter. He'd put out some feelers to research ex-military who were taking hired gun jobs.

They all felt a little defeated. With a new person in the mix, they weren't sure if they had ever been on the right path. Maybe it was an enemy or a rival. The fashion industry was a deadly game sometimes and when you were at the top of your game there were plenty of people who wanted to take you down. The siblings might not have known of anyone, but that doesn't mean that no one existed who wanted their father dead.

Even their mother wasn't that cold, they had come to believe. Despite troubles that seemed to have been brewing in their marriage, there was no proof of that either. Couples fight and from what they knew there was rarely a cross word said between them. One bad, overheard spat did not a murder make they concluded when they collectively decided to take the focus off of Magnolia.

They had no suspects, no motives, no leads.

Chapter 26

Amidst the whirlwind of excitement and anticipation that enveloped New York Fashion Week, House of Blossom stood as a beacon of creativity and elegance. The renowned fashion house was prepared to unveil its latest collection to the world.

Behind the scenes, the atmosphere crackled with energy as designers, seamstresses, and stylists worked tirelessly to bring their vision to life. In the heart of the studio, Isabelle, the newest addition to House of Blossom, meticulously crafted her designs with a deft hand and a keen eye for detail.

Isabelle's aesthetic was bold and uncompromising, characterized by vibrant colors, strong forms, and decisive lines. Her garments spoke of confidence and empowerment, each piece a testament to her unwavering vision.

As the models prepared to showcase the collection on the runway, the backstage area buzzed with activity. Makeup artists and hairstylists hurriedly worked their magic, transforming the models into ethereal beings fit for the spotlight.

Meanwhile, Isabelle made final adjustments to her creations, ensuring that each garment draped flawlessly over the models' frames.

Her fingers moved with practiced precision, sewing seams, and fastening closures with the skill of a seasoned artisan.

Outside, the streets teemed with fashion enthusiasts and industry insiders, eagerly awaiting the unveiling of House of Blossom's latest masterpiece. Cameras flashed and reporters jostled for position, capturing every moment of the spectacle unfolding before them.

As the lights dimmed and the music swelled, the models took to the runway, their confident strides echoing through the cavernous space with each beat of the music. Isabelle's designs shimmered and glowed under the spotlight, commanding attention with their boldness and grace.

With each passing moment, the audience was captivated by the beauty and artistry on display. Isabelle's collection transcended mere fashion, evoking emotion, and inspiration in equal measure.

As the final look made its way down the runway, a wedding gown in a blush hue of lavender, a hush fell over the crowd, punctuated only by the sound of applause that erupted moments later. House of Blossom had once again cemented its place at the forefront of the fashion world, thanks in no small part to the bold vision of its newest designer, Isabelle.

The show was a spectacular success much to the chagrin of Magnolia. In public, she was thrilled, of course, but she had placed strategic calls throughout her fashion contacts and to the press that the collection was incomplete or not to expect much.

Once again, her plan had backfired. The buzz that the show was going to be a disaster and could spell the end of House of Blossom made everyone clamor for invitations and to press space. No one wanted to miss what was rumored to be the dumpster fire of the season.

When Magnolia slid through the crowd to congratulate Isabelle, the young designer was overwhelmed by all of the attention and while she was thrilled with the respect she'd earned; she had not been coached on the craziness that came after the show.

As the applause reverberated through the venue and with the presence of Magnolia Blossom in front of her, Isabelle felt a wave of unease wash over her.

Despite the outward appearance of confidence, a knot of anxiety tightened in her chest, threatening to suffocate her. The weight of expectations bore down upon her as each breath became more labored than the last.

In the chaos backstage, Isabelle's composure began to crumble. Panic clawed at her skin, causing her thoughts to feel disjointed. With a sudden surge of desperation, she broke free from the throngs of people surrounding her, her heart pounding in her chest. Ignoring the bewildered stares of those around her, she made a beeline for the nearest exit, her vision blurred with tears of frustration and fear.

Outside, the cool night air provided little solace as Isabelle stumbled blindly towards the waiting limousine parked at the curb. With trembling hands, she yanked open the door and tumbled inside, her breath coming in ragged gasps as she collapsed onto the plush leather seats.

For a moment, the world seemed to spin around her in a dizzying whirl. All she could focus on was the relentless pounding of her heart, each beat echoing in her ears.

The driver looked back at her, "Miss, are you okay?"

Isabelle waved her hand toward him and through staccato breaths she got out the words, "Just drive."

As the limousine pulled away from the curb, Isabelle clung to the faint hope that she could outrun her fears, if only for a fleeting moment. But deep down, she knew that the shadows of doubt would continue to haunt her, lurking just beyond the edges of her consciousness.

In that moment of vulnerability, as she hurtled through the darkness towards an uncertain destination and as the lights of the city blurred past her window, she couldn't help picturing Magnolia's face.

Isabelle realized that her panic started when the word, 'Congratulations' was spoken. The word was correct, but Magnolia's face, there was something. It didn't match the word. It almost looked contorted, like the word was painful for her to say. It wasn't sincere, it was forced.

In the midst of all the jubilation, Magnolia looked out of place. There was a sinister tone in her voice, but Isabelle couldn't conceive of a reason why Mrs. Blossom would not be happy with the rousing success of the show.

She had been pleased when she popped into the design studio to check on the progress. She'd complimented the color combinations and the Filipino influences that Isabelle had infused into the garments. They were fresh and innovative.

Magnolia had given her advice to make sure that the designs were inclusive because the models who had been hired were from size two to size twenty-two. It was part of the vision of House of Blossom to make every woman feel beautiful. Being a size sixteen herself, Isabelle was thrilled to have the green light to incorporate larger sizes.

The local designer she'd worked for in the Philippines didn't want anything above size six. She had felt like a fraud working for him and after three years she decided to go independent. She had a successful plus-sized swimsuit collection on her online store, which House of Blossom had acquired the rights to after Isabelle was hired. They added her existing designs to their ready-to-wear that went out to Bloomingdale's with an exclusivity rider for a year.

She had distracted herself enough to where her breaths were back to normal. She asked the driver to take her back to the House of Blossom New York building where she had been working for the last two weeks getting ready for Fashion Week. She wanted to be in the solitude of the design studio. That was where she felt the most comfortable and she knew that touching the fabrics would calm her brain.

She scolded herself for thinking badly about Mrs. Blossom. It was her, not Magnolia, that was speaking in a sinister tone. She caused her own panic attack and tried to place the blame on the person who had made her feel like her designs mattered. She should have stuck with her first instinct.

In the peaceful and empty studio, Isabelle was completely calm until she heard a faint, slow clap coming from a dark corner of the space. The sound began to move closer and Isabelle positioned herself behind one of the tables to give her cover. She picked up a pair of scissors, but they trembled in her hands.

Her heart leapt into her throat, pounding against her ribs. She scanned the shadows, her breath catching in her chest as the sound drew nearer.

As the slow, deliberate clapping drew closer, Isabelle's mind raced with a thousand questions. Who could it be? What did they want? And why here, in the dead of night, when the world outside slumbered in blissful ignorance?

The darkness seemed to swallow her whole as the sound reached a crescendo, echoing off the walls of the studio. Every nerve in Isabelle's body screamed for her to flee, but she stood her ground, her resolve steeling against the encroaching fear.

And then, just as suddenly as it had begun, the clapping ceased, leaving behind an eerie silence that hung heavy in the air until she heard footsteps falling away from her.

For a long moment, she remained frozen in place, her senses on high alert for any sign of danger. But when none came, she dared to peek out from behind the table, her eyes wide with apprehension.

In the dim light of the studio, she saw nothing but shadows, but she knew someone was there, or at least had been, but she had no idea who would do something so cruel.

She crouched down on the floor and for the second time that night she had to calm her breathing. She just hoped that her hotel room was more secure and safe. She took off her shoes and quietly exited, looking over her shoulder, watching the shadows, and still holding the scissors as she headed for the waiting limousine.

Chapter 27

As soon as she arrived back in Atlanta, Isabelle went to Mari about what had happened and her encounter with Magnolia. She explained how she felt when Magnolia approached her and the slow clapping in the studio. She didn't think it was Magnolia. The footsteps that descended from her sounded heavy, like a man's stride.

Mari immediately texted Rudy to get the surveillance footage and find out who was in the studio. She kept her calm and nurturing nature with Isabelle.

"Look, it's not a secret that there is no love lost between my mother and I, so I wouldn't put anything past her, but I don't want to change your perception of her. If she has been supportive of you, then I would say continue to soak up all of the knowledge you can from her, but my best advice is watch your back. She wasn't on board with hiring a new designer and Conti being transferred to Milan, so I can't honestly tell you what her motivations are toward you."

"I appreciate the honesty. I've heard horrible things about your mother and I always get worried when she just shows up in the studio, but she has been helpful. The collection was better because of her. I think I was just freaking out, but I will keep my eyes open and be cautious. I have been warned about her. She likes to play the long game with people before she pounces, or that's what I've heard," she trailed off sheepishly.

"You can speak freely with me," Mari reassured her.

They walked the studio and inspected the textiles that had come in that morning. Isabelle had been sketching on the plane on the way back for the fall collection. She was a workaholic and wanted to make House of Blossom proud.

Snapper had told Mari that he wanted to expand the bathing suit line they had acquired from Isabelle because it was already selling out faster than the garments could be made. They were going to hire in new seamstresses to keep up with demand. It was a good problem to have.

The sale of Belle, the swimwear collection, had netted Isabelle over eight-hundred-thousand dollars and she retained twenty-five percent ownership. She had creative control over the designs and she negotiated an increase in sizes up to twenty-four for all designs. She believed that every woman should feel sexy and comfortable in a swimsuit. They were still talking about adding an accessory line, like wraps and cover ups, but that would have to be placed on hold until after the February collection for fall 2023 was finalized.

Great things were happening for House of Blossom, so when Snapper got a call from Sam to call him immediately, he knew that the proverbial shit was about to hit the fan.

"Rudy called me. He knows who was in the studio. It was that designer you fired or transferred, whatever you did, he's back in the states. Darrian Conti."

The news infuriated Snapper. "How is that possible?"

"I did some digging. He didn't finish the collection for the Milan House of Blossom, so instead of sucking it up, he took a leave of absence. I'm looking into when he arrived, but I figure he came in for

Fashion Week. I think he was trying to scare the new designer after the success of her show. He got in through an unlocked door on the loading dock."

"Someone is getting fired for leaving a door unlocked. Sounds like he knew it would be open," Snapper commented.

"I'll find him and keep an eye on him. Rudy's going to try to figure out some more information on him. What he did was cruel at best. You could go after him for trespassing, the footage is as clear as if he were standing here. There's no doubt that it's him," Sam continued.

"I agree. It's high time there be some consequences for his actions. I'll get with Detective Stone. Can you send me the footage?" Snapper asked.

"It'll be to you within the hour," Sam replied. As he was about to hang up, he added one piece of advice. "For what it's worth, I think this guy is dangerous. A person doesn't just wake up one morning and decide to be evil to a kid who's just had the best night of her life. It feels like he's playing some sort of game."

With that he exited and left Snapper to ponder the warning.

The siblings didn't meet that Saturday to continue their quest for justice, instead, they had a conference with the mayor and their mother to finalize plans for the one year anniversary of Helio's death. It was fast approaching. The city, with donated funds from the Blossom's, was unveiling a statue that had been built in his honor. It would be placed on the grounds of the police station in remembrance of all he contributed to the city and community.

Seeing their mother outside of the context of work was going to be awkward, but they all knew that she would be on her best behavior.

She and the mayor were close and she always poured on the charm for him.

"Children," she said when she entered the room. Her voice dripped with a fake sweetness as if she were elated to see them.

Snapper and the mayor stood. Snapper pulled out the chair at the head of the table for her. He did not kiss her cheek as he once had when he performed this task.

As the grieving widow, she was to be the focus, so the mayor and Snapper flanked her on either side of the table. The girls were in the same order as they were when the family used to have dinners together. In their new home at Freedom Flowers Estate, they had opted for a round dining table.

In unison they replied, "Mother."

The mayor took her hand and expressed his deepest condolences again. His kind words fell on deaf ears. She was a widow, but she was hardly grieving.

The mayor jumped right in as not to prolong the process for Mrs. Blossom. "We have secured the choir from your church to sing at the ceremony. Of course, the chief of police and I will speak. Snapper, last we spoke, you would be speaking on behalf of the family. Is that still the case?"

Before he could reply, Magnolia interjected. "I will take over the duties of speaking for the family. When I made that decision, I was still in a deep mourning. With time for reflection, I believe that the community deserves to hear from me and I want to personally thank them for all of their love and support during this year without Helio."

"Mrs. Blossom, that is a stupendous idea. I know that everyone would adore seeing you. The strength you have astounds me," the mayor complimented.

It took all of the poise and training the siblings had not to snicker at her words. Instead, they were respectful and the epitome of composure. Snapper did not get a chance to speak. Actually, none of the children said a word as Magnolia dominated the meeting and the mayor hung on her every word. Beauty, charm – weapons.

An hour later, Magnolia had approved the arrangements and the children had simply nodded in agreement whenever she would address them with, "Don't you agree, children?"

In the parking garage, the siblings walked to one limousine while Magnolia went to another. It didn't matter that they were all going back to House of Blossom.

Before she entered the car, she called out to Snapper. "Snapdragon, I've spoken with Milan. Conti wasn't happy there, so I have contacted Human Resources to start his transfer paperwork. I hope you don't mind." She gave a faint smile.

With a coy look, he bent down and winked at his sisters then stood back straight. "Unfortunately, Mother, that will not be happening." Snapper looked at his watch, "Right about now, Darrian Conti is getting arrested."

Magnolia's mouth fell open, but before she could say a word, Snapper disappeared into the car and it drove away.

Snapper had coordinated with Detective Stone to execute the arrest warrant during their meeting with the mayor. He knew that his mother always put her phone on silent during meetings, which worked to his advantage. No one would be able to contact her or give her a heads up about the arrest.

Detective Stone was one of the few in the police department who was not enamored by Magnolia Blossom. With her influence from City Hall to the station, she knew about anything that related to House of Blossom before it ever happened. What she didn't know was that Snapper had invited the mayor out for drinks a week before the meeting and was able to lay the groundwork for a finalization meeting for that day and time.

The schedule took precise planning. Venus had covertly conversed with Magnolia's assistant under the guise of setting up a meeting with Snapper. She was able to get a look at Magnolia's calendar to find out when she was open. With that, Venus asked for that block of time. But when the mayor called, Magnolia told her assistant to cancel the meeting with Snapper. It worked out perfectly.

As they drove away, the siblings couldn't help themselves. They had to look back at their mother as she stood there in shock. The expression on her face went from shocked to furious in two point two seconds. She entered the car and directed the driver to take her to the police station. She was going to talk to the chief and find out what was going on and why Darrian was arrested.

She didn't have to wait that long. When she turned her phone back on, the messages were buzzing. There were two missed calls from the chief and a dozen texts from different officers trying to notify her.

But the worst messages were from a journalist from Vanity Fair and Phillip Griffin from the Atlanta Journal Constitution. They wanted confirmation that Darrian Conti had been arrested.

She called Dawn, the House of Blossom publicist. "Yes, Mrs. Blossom, I am writing a press release as we speak. No, ma'am, I don't have the details…yes, I know I should have known about this…Yes…I'm working on it ma'am." Magnolia hung up on her and turned her phone back on silent.

Chapter 28

"Mrs. Blossom," Chief Fryer stood up nervously as Magnolia walked quickly into his office. She had ignored all of the officers she had passed on her way to confront him.

"Stanley, I don't have time for pleasantries. I was in a meeting with the mayor, but I should have had a heads up on this situation before it was ever executed. How did this get past you? Do you know what a shit show this is going to be for House of Blossom?" It was a rhetorical question.

"Please, Mrs. Blossom, have a seat."

She looked at the green, plastic upholstery on the two standard heavy metal chairs, "I won't be here long enough to sit. What are the charges?"

"Trespassing," he replied.

"Are you fucking kidding me? That's a misdemeanor. Where?"

"Mrs. Blossom, please have a seat. This is more complicated than a simple trespassing charge."

She relented and begrudgingly sat.

"Thank you. He sat back down too. This isn't an Atlanta charge, it's from New York. We are just holding him until they come to pick him up."

"New York! Why would they even hunt him down for a trespassing charge? Can you please start from the beginning?"

Chief Fryer explained that Darrian had trespassed through an open loading dock door at the House of Blossom New York offices with the intent of intimidating a Miss… he flipped through the file to find her name, Miss Isabelle Tan. He detailed that according to the report, Conti had stayed in the shadows and slowly clapped at her to scare her.

Magnolia couldn't contain her amusement. She laughed. A boisterous laugh that came from deep in her throat. It took a few moments for her to contain herself before she could ask how they knew it was him.

Fryer explained that the CCTV footage was extremely clear with the state-of-the-art security system along with the other cameras in the area that also pointed in that direction. They were able to get his car, license plate, and an unmistakable recognition of the suspect.

"Let me guess, my son identified him," she said annoyed.

"That's correct. He made a statement to Detective Stone."

"Stone?" She questioned loudly. "That son of a bitch can't solve my husband's murder, but he can arrest an employee of my company for entering a building of said company?"

Fryer took offense to her allegation. He was protective of his officers and detectives. Stone had been on the job for twenty-two years and he was a damn fine detective. However, Fryer, for all of his power, didn't have the backbone to say those words to Magnolia.

"Unfortunately, it's not that simple. You know House of Blossom has very strict protocols for entering the buildings. His nefarious entry through the loading dock is considered trespassing. It's a class D felony. If that were all he did, it would most likely have not been escalated, but since Miss Tan felt threatened and trapped, the prosecutor is adding kidnapping to the charges. I don't think that charge will stick, but he could get up to seven years for the trespassing. They take that shit seriously up there."

Magnolia knew immediately that Snapper had arranged the whole arrest. She couldn't help but to be a little proud. It was something she would have done. In the wake of the John Smith debacle, no felons could work for House of Blossom. Darrian would be ruined and that would be that. She couldn't associate with him after something that egregious.

She stood up and turned on the charm. Gone was the angry, frustrated Magnolia. She was now the polished, professional, and charming version of herself. "Thank you for your time Chief Fryer. As always it has been a pleasure to see you. I hope that next time is under much more pleasant circumstances." She extended her perfectly manicured hand to him.

Taking it gently, he added, "Yes, if I don't see you before, we will speak again at the ceremony for your husband.

For a brief moment she had forgotten about Helio's statue dedication. Here she was fighting for the man she was sleeping with just minutes after she'd planned a celebration for her dead husband. The irony of the situation was not lost on her.

When she re-entered the limousine, she told the driver to take her to House of Blossom. Turning her phone on once again, there was only one new message. It was from Darrian. He'd used his one phone call to call her. He wanted her help. His message was pleading and unapologetic. Of course, he said he didn't know he was trespassing and that he would do anything. She found him pathetic and desperate. Two qualities she hated.

When she returned to the House, she went straight to Snapper's office. He was at his desk working when she arrived. Venus didn't even try to stop her. She had expected Magnolia to stomp in at some point that day.

"Snapdragon, I would just like to thank you for taking such care and attention to the matter with Darrian. I plan to put in a call to the New York District Attorney and offer him my personal guarantee of cooperation from House of Blossom and myself. You have not been derelict in your duties as CEO and in less than a year you have introduced the company to a new demographic of clientele."

The high praise was foreign to Snapper. Yes, she had given him affirmations of good will and favored him over the girls, but to outright state that he had done a good job was unheard of in the Blossom family. He felt like it was a trick, a scheme, some kind of backhanded compliment, but he couldn't find it.

"Thank you, Mother, but whatever it is that you are up to, I want no part of it," he replied in a dismissive and suspicious tone.

"I realize that I usually have a motive when I address you in such a casual manner," she walked slowly around his office, inspecting every detail that she had designed. "But I assure you I come in peace. Darrian was such a bore anyway, I'm glad to be rid of him. He was getting too emotional for my liking," she approached his desk, "Honestly, you've done me a favor by making sure that he pays for his crimes. I am curious though," she continued, "what is this I hear about kidnapping?"

Snapper rolled his eyes.

She slapped him across the face with her open palm.

"Don't you ever do that again toward me. I am your mother and I will be respected."

With a bright red handprint on his cheek, he stood up. "Mother, I am going to say this as *respectfully* as I can. That is the last time you will strike me. I will press assault charges on you if it happens again. Now, *respectfully*, get out of my office."

He sat back down, turned his eyes to his computer screen and did not look back at her until she was past the threshold of his office. He pressed the speaker button on the phone to speak to Venus. He knew his mother would hear his command.

"Venus, if Mrs. Blossom comes to my office again without an appointment, do not let her enter."

"Of course, sir," Venus replied. She looked up at Magnolia who was staring down at the phone. "Mrs. Blossom, would you like to set up an appointment with Mr. Blossom?" she asked in a condescending tone.

Magnolia stomped away. She had been genuine in her praise since it got Darrian out of her life, but she knew her words felt wrong when she said them. Despite her intensions, she hated Snapper for manipulating her. He did not deserve her compliments. However, he did deserve the slap. How dare he roll his eyes at her, she thought. His insolence was intolerable to Magnolia. She concluded that without her daily guidance he might as well be one of the girls.

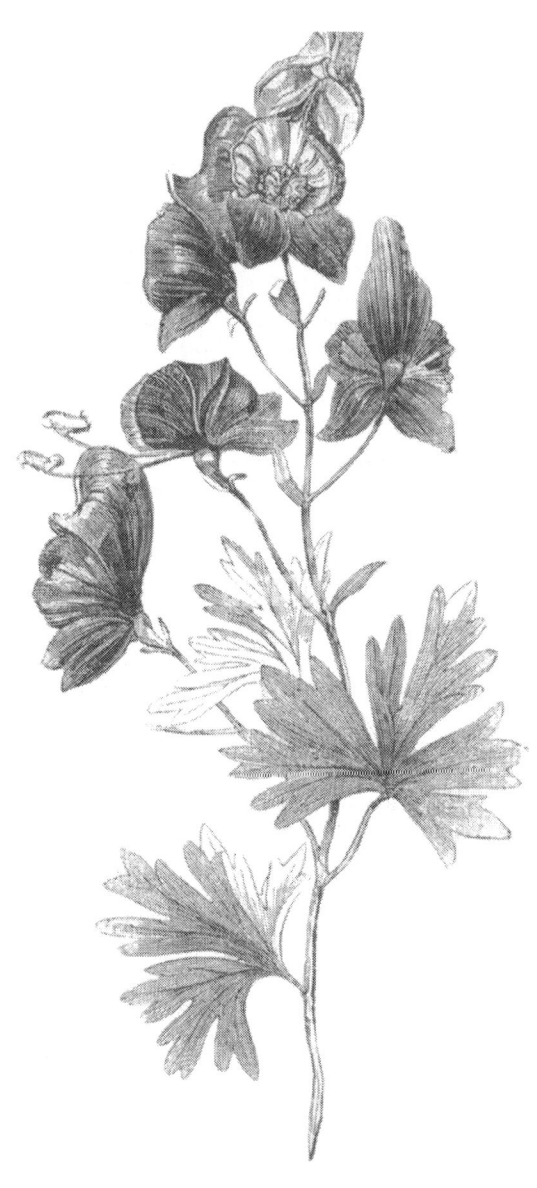

Chapter 29

The day of the ceremony was upon them and the siblings were in a desperate state. They wanted Snapper to speak for Helio's children and they regretted not saying something when they had met with the mayor. While they didn't know what their mother's prepared words were, they knew that they would not include them, at least not in any meaningful way.

Snapper wasn't sure how, but he was going to let the community know that Helio's children were the ones who were truly suffering because the murder had not been solved and their father's guidance and quiet dignity was no longer a part of their lives. He wanted to assure them that their father's legacy was strong within his children and that they would continue all of the programs that he had put in place.

Three blocks that surrounded the police station had been cordoned off and metal bleachers had been erected by the sidewalks to accommodate the hundreds of people who were expected to attend the solemn event.

There was an elevated stage placed a few feet away from a silk drape of fabric with the Blossom crest embroidered on it that covered a ten-foot-tall statue of Heliotrope Blossom. Magnolia had insisted that she be the last to address the community and to be the one who unveiled the remembrance. She had also insisted that the children be seated behind her, not with her, although she didn't put it that way. She wanted them to be present as tribute to Helio's memory.

Chief Fryer, the mayor, and Magnolia were seated in the front row of the stage and would each take the podium in that order. The stage was set.

As the crowd gathered beneath the shadow of the imposing police station, a sense of reverence hung heavy in the air. Among the assembled throng were members of the community, dignitaries, and representatives from the police force, all united in their desire to honor the memory of a man who had touched so many lives.

Chief Fryer stepped up to the podium, his gaze steady and unwavering as he surveyed the sea of faces before him. Though his heart weighed heavy with the burden of an unsolved murder, his demeanor remained resolute, a beacon of strength in the midst of uncertainty.

"My fellow Atlantans," he began, his voice steady despite the turmoil rolling within him. "Today, as we gather to honor the memory of Helio Blossom, we are reminded not only of the man he was, but of the legacy he leaves behind. For years, Helio Blossom was not just a pillar of the business community, but a steadfast ally in our ongoing quest for justice and security." Chief Fryer continued, his words ringing out with a quiet authority. "Together, we worked tirelessly to make Atlanta a safer, more harmonious place for all who call it home."

A flicker of emotion passed across Chief Fryer's face as he recalled the countless hours he had spent alongside Helio over the years. Their shared commitment to the city forged a bond that transcended mere professional obligations.

A murmur of agreement rippled through the crowd, a tangible reassurance that they stood united in their determination to see justice served.

"So let us honor Helio Blossom not only with our words, but with our actions," Chief Fryer concluded, his gaze sweeping over the faces of those gathered before him. "Let us pledge ourselves anew to the pursuit of truth and justice, knowing that together, we can overcome any obstacle that stands in our way."

With a final nod of solemn resolve, Chief Fryer stepped back from the podium, his heart heavy yet buoyed by the unwavering support of the community he served.

The mayor's speech echoed the sentiments of the Chief and he vowed that the work of the community was not over, it was just hitting its stride. With that, he looked back at Magnolia. But, before she could stand, Snapper squeezed through the small space between the chairs and went straight to the microphone.

Magnolia was livid, but she couldn't show it. Snapper knew as much and he took the opportunity to be ready to ambush her. His confidence was high and he was not scared of any consequences his mother tried to invoke.

She had tried for months to do her worst to him, but he had thwarted her at each turn. He was strong and the fact that he was powerful as CEO of House of Blossom emboldened him.

His words were heartfelt and steadfast. Plus, he knew how to put his mother in her place – as the *fake* grieving wife.

Ladies and gentlemen, esteemed members of the Atlanta community,

As I stand before you today, representing not only myself but my four sisters, I am filled with a profound sense of pride and gratitude.

For we are the children of Helio Blossom, a man whose legacy of compassion, generosity, and unwavering dedication to this city will forever echo in our hearts.

My sisters and I have been blessed to witness firsthand the indelible impact that our father has had on the fabric of this community. From his tireless efforts to improve the lives of those less fortunate, to his unwavering commitment to creating a safer and more harmonious Atlanta for all its residents, his legacy is one of boundless love and selflessness.

And so, it is with the utmost humility and determination that I stand before you today, vowing to carry on his legacy with the same passion and dedication that defined his life. We will honor his memory by ensuring that all of the community projects he held dear remain in place, and by embarking on new endeavors that continue to uplift and empower those in need.

But our commitment to this city extends beyond mere words and promises. We stand with you in the pursuit of justice for our beloved father. In the face of adversity, let us come together as a community, united in our resolve to uphold the values that Helio held dear. The legacy of Helio Blossom will live on, a beacon of hope and inspiration for generations to come. And together, we will ensure that his spirit continues to shine brightly in the hearts of all who knew and loved him. None more that his children. Thank you. Now I would like to welcome my mother, Mrs. Magnolia Blossom, to do the honors of unveiling this magnificent tribute to my father, her husband, Heliotrope Blossom.

Magnolia, ever the beauty, gracefully accepted a kiss on the cheek from her son, that made her blood boil.

She thanked her son and addressed the crowd not with the words she had prepared, but with platitudes and basic repeats from the three speeches that had come before hers. Her self-important words were professional, not heartfelt or comforting. She knew she couldn't promise more than Snapper had, especially since she had secretly planned to cut the funding for most of the programs and significantly reduce the company's charitable contributions and donations. She'd always thought that Helio gave too much. She wanted just enough for it to be a meaningful tax write off.

She did get to do the big reveal. The statue stood large as she read the words that were chiseled into the marble base of the bronze statue.

The ceremony ended with a solemn rendition of "Amazing Grace" from the church choir.

Chapter 30

The Saturday after the ceremony, Sam called for an emergency meeting with everyone. They all met in the war room, as usual. Sam was amped up that he had pertinent information.

"I used some of that cash you gave me Snapper and put the word out that I was looking for a job to be done. I specifically said I was looking for someone who could get the job done clean with no trace."

Everyone was completely transfixed by his words.

He continued, "I'm pretty sure I have found our shooter. He's, as suspected, ex-military. I don't have a name, but I have a meet with him in two weeks. He's out of South Carolina and that is honestly all I have on him. He is elusive and keeps a very low profile. But there is a hitch…" he trailed off.

Six sets of eyes looked at him pleading to tell them what they needed to do. Oni was completely overwhelmed; tears began to form in her eyes. She fought them.

"He won't meet without a one million dollar wire transfer to this account number." He slid a piece of paper onto the table that he had been clinching in his fist. He didn't want to get their hopes up. "and the money has to be untraceable."

The siblings were all in when he said it was just money, but untraceable money was harder to get.

Snapper had a suggestion. "Do you think he'd take crypto? I've got a few million in Bitcoin. That's untraceable and completely anonymous."

"I don't know. I never would have thought about it to ask my contact. But I can put the word out and see if he'll bite." He changed his tone to a word of warning. "Listen, there is no guarantee that this is the guy or if you do send him the money that he won't just take off with it."

"We understand all of that," Dio replied. "Anyone here worried about the money?" she asked.

Only Rudy and Sam raised their hands.

"We all knew this would come down to money to find out information. We're fine with that. We'll pay whatever it takes to find out who murdered our father," added Mari.

"Asking about the crypto is either going to solidify the meeting or scare him off. It needs to be a unanimous decision. Who is not comfortable with the risk level?" Dio asked.

This time no one raised their hand.

"Sam, when can you make this happen?" Snapper asked.

I can get with my contact tomorrow. He's the kind of person who is unscrupulous and reclusive, but he knows every shady character in the Southeast," he replied. :"I forgot to mention, his information isn't free. That twenty-five grand you gave Rudy, " he looked at Nia, "he is now the proud owner."

"That's not a problem since that's exactly why I gave it to you. I knew it was going to take cash to get people to talk. Sounds like you may have found the right person," replied Nia.

Sam continued to give them a few more minor details and Rudy let them know that he had taken over the leads on who owns the shelf corporation.

He was able to get a few of the real estate holdings addresses, but they were all in the name of another erroneous company - DIC Unlimited, which is under the parent company Ailongam Limited.

"Wait, we found all of that money, well found might not be the right word, but we traced it all back and with information we got from our former housekeeper, we know that Mother was giving Darrian an allowance out of a company discretionary fund. She's been doing it for over ten years. I think she still is, or *was* until he got arrested," stated Dio.

The siblings had thought that Ailongam was a singular company with a singular account to launder Darrian's allowance. Now there was a company attached to it. It was making their heads spin as they were all back to questioning if their mother was in fact involved in their father's murder.

"That still doesn't make sense," Oni injected. "We know that Mother set up the company, but all of the money went to Darrian. If real estate was bought with that money, it had to have been him making all of those deals. The money – " she paused to collect her thoughts, "the account has to be his because Mother wouldn't have had access to the funds once they were in his hands. Ailongam was Mother's account, but what if we missed something because we weren't looking for it?" she proposed.

They all looked perplexed. They knew she was headed somewhere with her logic, but they weren't following. Instead of asking, Snapper and Dio immediately pulled out all of the financial files they had for Ailongam. They tore through the papers, looking for that needle in a haystack, of which they had no clue what it was, but they were looking. Mari grabbed up a stack and started looking through the papers with them.

Finally, Nia asked, "Oni can you please tell them what they are looking for before they ruin all of the work that we have done organizing all of these files?"

"We need to look for ownership. Who owns the DIC company? We know that Mother owns Ailongam, but does anyone else have privileges to use that account, to attach assets to it, to use it in any way?" Oni replied.

Everyone took a file and they went through every month methodically. There had to be some way to prove that Darrian at least had access to the company and its accounts.

After hours of looking, they had nothing. Darrian's name wasn't on any document and he hadn't signed for anything. Everything was laundered through the company and into the account in the Caymans.

"That's it," Sam announced. "The account in the islands. The male figure I saw on the CCTV footage going in and withdrawing money. That had to have been Darrian, right?"

"Nia, do you think your hacker friends…"

Nia interrupted Mari, "On it," she replied as she dialed the phone.

Meanwhile, Darrian sat in a New York jail feeling defeated and regretful. His emotions weren't for his actions, instead, they were for the fact that he got caught. He knew there were cameras everywhere at the New York House, but he wasn't thinking. He just wanted to intimidate Isabelle. When he saw the dock worker exit without locking the door, he saw his chance.

He hadn't been able to finish his collection. He blamed her and Snapper. He had been standing in the wings of the backstage crowd that had surrounded her at the end of her show at New York Fashion Week. He wore the disguise of a mustache and dark sunglasses. Even he was surprised that it worked.

When he saw Magnolia come up to Isabelle and congratulate her, he completely saw red. His perception of the situation and Isabelle's were different. She saw insincerity while he saw acceptance.

He'd been arraigned, which didn't go the way he had planned. He thought his money and notoriety would serve him well. He had expected bail and to be release on his own recognizance. Instead, they sent him back to jail, but his lawyer was fighting it.

Orange was not his color and he thought back to the only orange dress he had ever designed. It was a light orange with a white outline trim. It was part of his 1968 summer collection. He hadn't had an aversion to orange, he just didn't think that it looked good on most people. His suspicions were confirmed when he looked around and saw that no one in the jail was sporting their orange jumpsuit in a flattering way. It was just cloth that covered their body. Darrian was miserable.

He had tried to call Magnolia several times, but each time the recording came on to ask if she would accept a call she would hang up. His attorney had reached out to her, but she ignored the letters that asked for her to meet with him.

Darrian had disclosed to her about the shelf corporation he had created and that he had activated it with properties and monies.

"I created it for us," he declared one day the summer prior. "You and I both know that your marriage isn't going to last much longer. What if Helio divorces you?"

"You are out of your mind. He would never, and my marriage is just fine. Trust me, Helio would drop dead before he would divorce me."

Chapter 31

It took some time, but Nia's hacker friends were able to get some incriminating information. The Ailongam company was only in Magnolia's name as far as anyone could find, but there were multiple accounts associated with the company; however, only two of them had activity – the one they knew about and one that had been depleted over a year earlier.

They weren't able to find who was authorized on the accounts, but the depleted one did have a code, RBJ. They were still trying to find what that meant. The signature cards for the accounts were highly encrypted so they had not been able to crack those yet. The work continued.

Sam was making some headway with his contact and the ex-military hitman, but it was slow going. When they all met, he told the siblings that the guy had been flown to Russia for a job according to his contact. He wasn't sure when the hitman would be back in the country so the meet would have to wait.

The one piece of good news they had was that he had accepted the idea of crypto. Snapper had hoped he would, so he had prepared for that to take place by placing the funds into a hold just waiting for the transfer.

It was a good plan, but they had missed their first window for the information, that was if the guy was legitimate. Snapper wasn't willing to do that again. He was more anxious than ever to find his father's killer after finding out about the depleted account. He had a gut feeling that it was important.

Unfortunately, with the holidays fast approaching, the hunt would have to be put on hold for the siblings. While Rudy and Sam continued to work in the background, the Blossom children had a grand New Year's Eve party to prepare. They had planned an extravaganza to ring in the new year at Freedom Flowers Estate.

"5…4…3…2…1, Happy New Year!" the crowd shouted in unison as they rang in 2023 together with the siblings. Anyone who was anyone in Atlanta was there, except Magnolia. She was put on a watch and do not enter list by security on the explicit instructions of Snapper.

When the children were growing up, holidays were either nonexistent or celebrated with House of Blossom employees. The only exception was Christmas. Helio had always insisted that it was only family at the house. The tradition was carried on by the children at their new home.

There was a twelve-foot-tall live tree in the living room with stacks and stacks of presents. They had splurged and spoiled each other just a week prior to the celebration they were giving for New Year's Eve. As their guests reveled in the possibilities of what would be in their future, the siblings mingled and joined their friends on the dance floor.

They had hired a local band, Jensen, to perform. They were a hot and upcoming group with a female lead singer who formed the band when she was a teenager. They knew all of the latest songs as well as the popular classics. There wasn't a request that was asked of them that they couldn't execute. Snapper even thought about trying to help them get a record deal.

He knew a record producer in Atlanta that he thought would be a perfect match for their talent and tenacity. When they auditioned, the lead singer, Jensen, said they were willing to play for free in exchange for the exposure. When word got back to Snapper, he was impressed by her fortitude to make a name for herself. He immediately instructed the planner to hire the band after hearing their demo. Of course, he offered to pay them, but she refused.

As the party goers exchanged the traditional kisses and well wishes, a blaze of fireworks and cheers ushered in the new year with all the pomp and splendor befitting such a momentous occasion for the siblings. The sky erupted in a dazzling display of color and light, casting a magical glow over the revelers below.

After midnight, the celebration at Freedom Flowers Estate reached its peak. The live band continued to play, their music pulsating through the air and keeping the energy high on the dance floor while groups of friends laughed and toasted to the new year with glasses of champagne in hand.

Around the estate, colorful lights illuminated the pathways and gardens, creating a festive ambiance. Some guests wandered to enjoy the cool night air, while others gathered around crackling fire pits, sharing stories and laughter as they warmed themselves against the slight chill.

At the outdoor bar, bartenders expertly mixed cocktails and poured drinks, ensuring that no glass remained empty for long. Meanwhile, a team of servers circulated through the crowd, offering trays of hors d'oeuvres and delectable treats to satisfy late-night cravings.

Laughter and chatter filled the air, mingling with the sound of clinking glasses and the occasional burst of applause as guests cheered on impromptu dance-offs or shared heartfelt toasts to the year ahead.

Throughout it all, the Blossom siblings moved gracefully among the crowd, their smiles bright and their spirits infectious. They greeted guests with warmth and enthusiasm, ensuring that everyone felt welcome and included in the festivities.

As the guests began to wind down and head for home, the first signs of sunrise broke through the clouds. Some guests opted to stay in the well-appointed guest houses while others took advantage of the bank of town cars that the siblings had hired for the event.

Beyond making sure that everyone had a great time, they wanted all of them to get home safely. Extra drivers were hired to follow anyone who had driven to the event so that they could wake up to their cars being at their respective homes. Every detail had been thought of to ensure that 2023 started out with happiness and joy for all of their friends.

Chapter 32

As the new year progressed, so did Dio's interest in Sam. They had met for coffee a few times at her request under the guise of talking about the investigation, at first, but this time, there was no talk of bogus companies, mysterious accounts, her mother, or murder.

She was intrigued with his intelligence and how he had gone from being a corporate raider to a private detective. His journey had been fascinating to her and she asked questions about him while they sipped their coffees.

"With all of the jobs out there, why be a private detective?" she asked.

"I had torn things apart for so long without knowing who it effected and honestly not caring, that I wanted something that was more personal. In this job I can get to know who needs my services and I can make them whole through my work. I'm selective as to who I take on as a client. I don't take revenge or pity cases."

"Which of your cases has been the most rewarding?" she inquired.

"That's easy. I helped a mother and her two children out of a horrible situation. I can't disclose details, but just understand that I had to do some shady shit to get dirt on her husband. He was good and methodical. No one outside of the four of them knew that anything was wrong. When she came to me she was broke and desperate. I didn't charge her a dime. I can happily say she and her children have a good life now out West."

"I've never done anything so altruistic in my life. Sure, we give money, start programs, and help out where we can, but to get into someone's life up close and personal, I have never experienced anything like that. I can only imagine that the feeling to literally change someone's life is…" she paused, "I'm not sure I have a word for it," she confessed.

"Are you up for an adventure?" he asked with a coy smile.

She couldn't resist. Her curiosity was immediately piqued. She looked at her watch. "Can we do it within the hour?"

"Give me thirty minutes and I will change your view of the world," he replied.

Two blocks and around the corner from the expensive coffee house they had just been at was a small, blue building with a simple hand-painted sign that read, "Salvation House."

Dio was rethinking her decision to trust Sam, but when he took her hand, her hesitations vanished. She let him lead her up the three brick steps and he opened a plain white door for her.

As soon as they entered there was a wooden desk with an older, white-haired man sitting behind it.

"Sam," he greeted with a big grin. "I was wondering when you would stop by this week. We have a new guy. He just joined us yesterday. He hasn't spoken much. Just walked in the door around noon and said he needed help. We haven't been able to find out anything about him. Not even sure how he found us, but you stopping by today might be just the medicine he needs to open up."

"I'll give it a try, Jerry. By the way, this is my friend, Dio Blo - "

Dio interrupted him. "Hi, I'm Dio, very nice to meet you. She extended her hand to Jerry.

She knew that her name came with expectations and she wanted to just be there as herself without the influence of her last name.

"You know, Sam, if she doesn't mind, she might be able to help you with our new guy."

"Exactly what I was thinking, Jerry. Where can I find him?"

"Second room on the left up the stairs."

"Ready?" Sam asked Dio.

She nodded.

Sam knocked on the door, but no one answered. They waited for a moment and knocked again. A click of the door lock let them know that someone was at the door, but that was all they heard. Slowly, Sam turned the doorknob and carefully opened the door. He looked back at Dio and nodded when he spotted a thin, disheveled man sitting on the bed.

Slowly. They walked into the room, but left the door cracked just in case the gentleman wanted them to leave. Sam spoke softly when he introduced Dio to him. Then he told him his name. The man was silent. Although, he did make eye contact, he quickly lowered his eyes.

He wiped his hands over the top of his shirt and pants like he was trying to brush down the wrinkles for his guests. He ran his fingers through his hair making one last attempt to look presentable. He was barefooted. Sam surveyed the room and didn't see any shoes.

He wondered if the man had walked there without shoes and made a mental note to ask Jerry. Sam did not approach the man, as not to spook him or make him feel uncomfortable. Since no one knew anything about the man, Sam wasn't going to take any chances, especially with Dio in the room.

After a few moments, Dio quietly addressed the man. "Hello. I was wondering if you might want to talk?"

The man glanced up from under his eyelashes at her and a faint smile crossed his face.

Dio was encouraged. "Wonderful. I would like to know your name if that would be okay."

She was met with silence and the man looked back down. But a few minutes later, without looking up, he said, "Carnell."

"Hi Carnell. It is really nice to meet you. Do you mind if I sit in this chair?"

There was a metal folding chair in the corner of the room adjacent to the bed.

Carnell shrugged.

Dio sat down and allowed him a minute to get used to her being at eye level with him. She was usually a bully, but she found herself wanting to be calm and find out more about Carnell. She didn't know what the purpose of the Salvation House was or how Carnell had found himself there, but none of that mattered. To her, Carnell was all that deserved her focus.

"Do you have any gum?" Carnell asked.

Dio softly giggled and told him that she had never had a piece of gum before in her life.

Carnell found this strange and tilted his head to the side as he looked up at her, making full eye contact again with her. "So, no gum," he chuckled.

"Can you tell me your favor gum," she asked.

"Big Red," he replied.

"What does that taste like," she inquired.

"Hot cinnamon."

Dio was thrilled that Carnell was talking to her. She was never nervous in dealing with people and she didn't care if they liked her or not, but she wanted Carnell to like her and she had to force herself not to ask a million questions.

"That actually sounds interesting. If you'd like, I can visit again and bring you some Big Red."

Carnell was thrilled at the prospect of another visit from the beautiful and kind Dio. The Big Red would be a bonus.

Sam stood behind Dio and just watched in amazement how she was able to get Carnell to open up. She was a natural with people.

"What is your favorite food, Carnell," she asked.

He thought for a minute. "I had a steak once."

Dio's heart clenched. She had steak for dinner just the night before. Carefully she asked him more simple questions about himself and she was able to find out that he was homeless and that the soles of his shoes had come apart somewhere outside of Atlanta.

He had been living in a homeless camp in the woods somewhere outside of the city and another person had told him about Salvation House. He'd been told the people were nice and didn't ask too many questions. She felt like she had blown up that last one. But Carnell didn't seem to mind.

The thirty minutes she had allotted turned into ninety and before she knew it she had to go. She had felt her phone vibrating the entire time from the pocket of her purse.

"Carnell do you mind if I ask what size shoe you wear? With your permission I would like to get you a new pair since you have been so kind and hospitable with me today. I know we interrupted your day."

Carnell felt respected by Dio and didn't think of her offer as charity, which he wasn't too proud to take, but he liked it better that it was a gift. "Ma'am I'm a nine, if that's okay."

She smiled, "That's wonderful. What kind of shoes do you like?"

"Slippers," he said quickly, then backtracked, "no, sneakers. Yes, sneakers." He smiled.

"Excellent! A pair of size nine sneakers. That I can do. I'll bring them by this evening. If you're not up for a visit, I can leave them with Jerry."

Carnell nodded.

She stood and extended her hand to him. Carnell looked down at his own hands. They were dirty and he was embarrassed. Dio felt that it was important for him to know that she didn't care. It was more important for him to feel like a respected man. When she did not take her hand back, he wiped his palms hard on his faded jeans and shook her hand.

"Until we meet again, Carnell. Thank you for inviting us into your home."

Carnell couldn't stop smiling. After Sam and Dio left, he walked downstairs and asked Jerry if he could take a shower.

Chapter 33

Snapper had asked Jensen, the singer, to meet with him a few weeks after the New Year's Eve party. He'd had inquiries about her from those who wanted to hire her band as well as by a record producer friend of his who had attended the party.

When she arrived at House of Blossom, she frowned. She had tried to get out of the meeting, at least at the behemoth building that was the House, but Snapper didn't have any time to be away from the office with the fall fashion week preparations being in full swing for February. The building was intimidating to Jensen and she felt completely out of place there.

Isabelle was hard at work incorporating her flare for color into warm, cozy garments. Her forte was summer, so she had been relying on Magnolia's tutelage. Surprisingly, Magnolia had taken a shine to Isabelle. With the success of the September New York Fashion Week and a small, slight, minuscule, almost imperceptible pang of guilt over Darrian's antics, Magnolia had taken on Isabelle as her latest project.

That suited Snapper just fine. He didn't want his mother to know that he was doing anything that wasn't fashion related. Snapper was a businessman, but he had thought for a while that fashion wasn't his only option.

After hearing Jensen and her band, Snapper called his friend, Axel Garnet, and told him that he wanted to talk about sponsoring them for some studio time.

Jensen was careful to watch who she saw when she exited the elevator on the executive floor. She was nervous and quickened her steps to Snapper's office.

Venus greeted her and asked if she would like a beverage, to which Jensen declined, before announcing her arrival to Snapper.

Snapper introduced Jensen to Axel and they all gathered at a round glass top table located by a bank of floor to ceiling windows that overlooked Downtown Atlanta.

The meeting started with Snapper telling her about his friends who had inquired about hiring her and gave her their contact information. If exposure was what she wanted from performing at his party, she absolutely got it. With the clients he'd given her, she could easily be booked for the next six months.

"Jensen, I wanted to make a proposal that you have absolutely no obligation to take. I was just so impressed with you and your band; I thought that it might be possible for me to help.

I hope I am not being presumptuous, but I listened to your demo, which was great, but I could tell it was recorded with less than professional equipment. Please no offense. I admire your hard work and commitment."

Jensen was getting a little annoyed. She felt like his words said one thing but his intentions were condescending. She came in with a chip on her shoulder. She had no use for rich people.

She had grown up poor with a single mother in Decatur. Her father had abandoned them before she was born, so she had a deep seeded hatred for men too. She felt like men with money were self-serving and that she only wanted to associate with them long enough to perform with her band and take their payment for a job well done.

Her mother had played the piano, guitar, and banjo, so Jensen grew up in a house filled with music. Her mother had a short-lived career as a singer in local bars and small venues, but when she got throat cancer from smoking too much for many years, her career was over by the time she turned forty. She'd suffered for years and finally succumb to it in April of 2021 when she contracted COVID.

So, while Snapper's intentions were pure, Jensen didn't see them that way. She was there for the clients he'd mentioned on the phone. He hadn't told her that she would be ambushed with a record producer that she, of course, knew of through his reputation in the music business.

She couldn't control her contempt. "Mr. Blossom, I'm confused. What are you talking about. I have band practice in an hour. Could you please just stop with the platitudes and lay it out straight?"

"Yes, of course. Axel here is a good friend of mine and I have spoken to him about a proposition that would be beneficial for both of you. I would like to sponsor you for some studio time so your band can have professionally recorded demos."

Jensen was floored. That was completely unexpected and a little creepy that he wanted to just give money for her band after one gig. She thought, "*Oh yeah, bored rich guy.*"

She stood up. "Mr. Garnet it was an honor meeting you. Your work is legendary, but," she faced Snapper, "Mr. Blossom, I don't take charity. I work for what I get. It's the way I was raised." She took one step to move away from the table.

Axel requested, "Ms. Jensen, please don't leave. I was at the party and I think you are very talented. I would at least like to discuss some possibilities."

With his request, she returned to the table. She wasn't about to piss off Axel Garnet. She was fan girling a little inside but kept her composure.

"You've proven your talent, this isn't about the money, this is so you can improve your chances of taking that talent to whatever level you envision. If you just need a demo to get more local gigs, that's great. However, this could be your one chance to have a demo that could advance your career."

Jensen listened to the words, but all she could think was that Blossom wanted to own her. There had to be a catch.

"That all sounds great, but I'm waiting for it," she replied.

Both Snapper and Axel looked confused.

She turned to Snapper, "What do you get out of this? Seriously? You don't know me. You heard me sing covers and now, out of the blue, you want to hook me up with Mr. Garnet and sponsor my career. You do see how that sounds sketchy, right?"

Snapper hadn't thought of it that way. Most of the time when he offer to help someone they jumped at the chance without any questions. He had underestimated Jensen.

"I apologize, Ms. Jensen, that was not my intention. How about we start over with a different position. What if you allow me to pay you for your services at the party. There will be an invoice and receipt so that there is no tie to me if you decide to take Axel up on his offer of studio time. You would have the money to pay for it yourself. Would that work?"

"Interesting, but studio time isn't cheap and I don't think that five hundred bucks is going to get us much. I do appreciate the offer, though," she replied.

"Customarily your performance would bill for two-hundred and fifty for each member of the band times the number of hours. You performed for approximately six hours, so the payment would be seven thousand five hundred dollars. Does that sound fair?"

Jensen's head was about to explode. The most they had ever made was five hundred dollars – a hundred bucks a piece. She couldn't help but think he was conning her or at the very least elevating the cost.

"Mr. Blossom, that sounds not only fair, but it also sounds excessive. "

"I promise you this is the same amount that has been paid for the string quartets that have played at House of Blossom functions. Trust me they weren't as good as you. You and your band have truly earned it." Snapper paused, "Just so you know, those clients I handed you will all pay the same rate that I am quoting. If you'd like to call one of them and just ask in general terms and see what they quote. If it's lower, we can go down to a number that makes you comfortable."

She took him up on his offer. She called Mrs. Martha Pennington. She wanted the band for her daughter's sweet sixteen party in March. Without hesitation, Mrs. Pennington offered ten thousand dollars. To which Jensen promptly accepted and said they would be in touch to hammer out the details.

"Okay, you're not trying to play me. She offered ten grand and asked if that was too low. Do you rich people just throw money around?"

Snapper felt the proverbial slap in the face and it stung. "I'm actually rather frugal, especially compared to Mrs. Pennington. She has money from three dead husband's and she loves to spoil her daughter."

Although she was still hesitant to get involved with a Blossom, she knew that a demo would help to catapult her band to the next level. She could live off rich white people, she'd done it once before.

Chapter 34

By the end of February, things at Freedom Flowers Estate was going well for the siblings. Dio and Sam were officially dating, Nia was having some fun with one of her hacker friends, Mari was riding the high of the successful fall collection from Isabelle, Snapper had cemented his reputation as an excellent CEO for House of Blossom, and Oni was excited for graduation. The bond between the siblings was as solid as it had ever been and oddly Magnolia had not tried to interfere in their lives to mess it all up.

All of the siblings were going to graduate from Georgia Tech in May and Oni was already planning a bash for the occasion. Ever since her eighteenth birthday party, she wanted to celebrate everything. With all of them graduating together, she couldn't see a reason not to throw a party for the entire graduating class.

They had all sailed through their courses and even with the demands and pressures from work and the investigation, they made time to study together and to help each other with assignments. The rivalry that had existed between all of them was all but gone. It helped that they would each graduate summa cum laude. Although, Oni had the highest GPA of the seventy nine graduates from the MBA program. No one was surprised.

She was working with one of the top caterers in the area and had hired a decorator to make the gardens into a grand showcase for the graduates. She'd gotten all of their pictures and told the decorator to make sure that everyone was prominently represented at the party. She'd had arranged with the gardeners to bring in four potted topiaries to carve the numbers 2023 and she had the housekeepers completely refresh all of the guest houses. Her siblings thought she was going overboard, but she had a binder with all of the plans and ideas and she'd told them to leave everything to her. They gladly did just that.

With classes over, the next investigation meeting was scheduled for March fourth. Rudy had texted that he thought he was on the trail of something and hoped to have more to report at their meeting.

Thanks to the work of the hackers, Rudy was able to find out more about the activity that had been in one of the accounts for the Ailongam company.

"It wasn't activated until six months before it was depleted. I can only find the two accounts we know about under the company name. The one we think is tied to Conti and one that was depleted. Here's where it gets interesting. I don't think that second account was planned because I was able to associate a name besides Magnolia's to it – Rose. Does that mean anything to any of you?" he asked the siblings.

They all looked at each other but there was no recognition of the name for any of them. Snapper commented, "Mother loved roses. Father would buy her one dozen for each year they had been married. At some point they switched to one rose for each year. Maybe it was a code like RBJ. Has anyone figured that one out yet?"

"That one is still a mystery," stated Mari. Every employee record has been checked for any that have those initials but the three that matched were either dead or retired."

"Is it possible that the R is for Rose?" asked Oni.

"That's excellent," commented Dio.

"Maybe it's one of Mother's relatives. Someone could have blackmailed her for money or something. Mother does have a lot of secrets."

"But why deplete it?" Nia asked.

"Possibly the final payment was made and the person pulled all of the money out," Sam said with a question in his voice.

"We could speculate and create conjecture all day. The fact is that we don't know. We will just keep digging," stated Snapper.

The meeting continued with an update on Darrian from Sam. Detective Stone had been informed the day before that Conti's trial date had been set for Wednesday, July nineteenth, but unfortunately his lawyer had won his argument that Conti should be released on bail. A two million dollar bond was posted and Darrian surrendered his passport. Other than that, he was free to travel the United States as of that day. He was to be released at noon. Two hours. Flight records showed that his lawyer had already booked him a flight to Atlanta.

"We need to inform security at House of Blossom," Nia suggested.

"Rock, paper, scissors for who is going to tell Mother," Mari joked.

With a sigh, Snapper took one for the team and called her.

Lydia was in a panic when she called Snapper. "He's here. He's at the gate. He keeps buzzing wanting to be let in. After you called your mother all of the codes were changed and she had a locksmith come out and change all of the locks. What should I do? Your mother isn't answering her phone."

It's okay, calm down, Lydia, I'll take care of it." He walked out to Venus's desk, put his cell phone on mute, and snapped his fingers to get her attention. He instructed her to call the police and get them to Flora Fields immediately.

Unmuting he told Lydia, "The police are on their way to tell him to vacate the premises. You don't have to do anything. You were right to call me. Mother is in a meeting and will be there for at least another hour. Did you leave her any messages?"

"Yes. I left two voicemails and I texted once."

"Okay, I will get a message to her to ignore them. As soon as the police are there –"

She interrupted him, "I hear the sirens," she paused, "he heard them too. He just peeled out and he's leaving."

"Which way did he go, Lydia?"

"He went out to the left."

"Excellent. I'll relay that information to the police. Did you see the car?"

"It looked to be a white Ford, but I can't be sure."

"It's probably a rental so he can look inconspicuous."

"The police cars just flew by, they must be pursuing him," she relayed to Snapper.

"Where is the security team that Mother hired?"

"They don't start until tomorrow."

"I'll take care of that too. I won't have you there unprotected. He's up to something and it is telling that his plane landed just an hour ago and the first place he goes is there. He knows he's not allowed on any House of Blossom property. I'll call Detective Stone and see about a restraining order. If you have any other issues, just call me or one of my sisters. You know how Mother hates a cell phone."

Snapper called Stone and requested a restraining order for all of his family members, including his mother and Lydia. He knew as long as Darrian was in town he would try to get to one of them. If he gets arrested for ignoring any of the orders his bail would be revoked, which would suit Snapper just fine.

While he had him on the phone, Stone informed him that Isabelle was refusing to testify against Conti. Without her testimony there wasn't a case for kidnapping.

Snapper said that he would speak with her, but he wasn't going to push. He knew that the case of trespassing was solid and if convicted he was looking at up to seven years.

Nothing else was heard from Darrian the rest of the day, but Snapper wasn't taking any chances. Not that he was a hardened criminal, but he blamed the Blossom's for his arrest, the ruination of his reputation, having to sit in jail for months, and facing years in jail for something as simple as trespassing.

Stone was having a hard time finding him. He wasn't registered at any of the local hotels and no rental company had record of him renting a car. It was like his plane landed and then he just appeared at Flora Fields. Even though the police arrived there within seconds of him leaving the gate, he disappeared. With no family in the area and him not being at his previous residence, Stone didn't have anything to go on in order to find him until about an hour later when Venus called him.

"He's walking up the stairs right now. I don't think he spotted me. I'm just running across the street for a bite to eat. He's approaching the front doors now." Venus was giving Stone a minute-by-minute report of his movements as Stone raced to the scene.

When he finally got there, Darrian was arguing with the security guard that he had to see Magnolia. All of security was on high alert for his arrival. By the time Stone entered the building, Conti was surrounded by three burly security guards who were blocking his path to the bank of elevators.

Stone grabbed him by the arm and drug him outside. Conti tried to resist, but he thought better of it. They went to Stone's car and instead of putting Darrian in the back, he asked him to take a seat in the passenger's side of the car.

"Look Conti, the Blossoms are heavily guarded, as you can see. You're not getting to any of them. To make that point clear, each of them have taken out restraining orders against you."

Stone reached in his backseat and pulled up his briefcase. With two clicks of the locks, it popped open. He pulled out a handful of papers and handed them to Darrian. "Mr. Conti, you have been served. You are not allowed within one thousand feet of any of the Blossom's. Do you understand?"

The wheels in Darrian's head were spinning. He would try to figure out a way to get around the orders, but for now, he would obey. He nodded in confirmation. "Can I go now?"

"One more thing. Write down where you are staying and the make and model of the car you are driving. Is that your car?"

"Oh, God no," he said with disgust. "I borrowed it from a friend. I do still have a few of those in this town."

After Stone verified it was a real address, he allowed Conti to leave with a warning that any infraction would land him right back in jail. He hoped that would be enough of a threat to keep Darrian on the straight and narrow while he was in town, but he doubted it.

There was something in his eyes that Stone didn't like and he texted Snapper to continue being on alert. Just because Darrian had the paperwork didn't mean that he would follow it. There were too many variables with him and he was determined to get to Magnolia.

Chapter 35

A text woke Snapper at three o'clock in the morning. It was from Sam. "The meet is on. Need the crypto transferred." The next text was a QR code.

Snapper jumped out of bed and went to his computer. The crypto he'd parked was ready to be transferred. He scanned the QR code and within seconds the confirmation popped up on the screen. He didn't know who he had just sent a million dollars' worth of digital money to, but oddly he hoped it was the guy who was hired to kill his father.

Another text. "Received. Will text details when I get them."

Now wide awake and feeling anxious, Snapper decided there wasn't any reason to go back to bed. He went downstairs to get some water and start the coffee maker that wasn't set to go off until five.

After pouring his coffee, he decided to go sit out by the pool. The air was warm, but there was a gentle breeze that felt good against his sleepy face. Just as he had taken his first sip and placed the cup on the table he heard someone moving around in the kitchen. His first thought – the Italian.

He approached the door cautiously and looked around the corner. He found Mari making herself a cup of coffee.

"Good morning," she said in a cheery voice.

"What are you doing up?"

"I heard you jog down the stairs. You know you have heavy steps?"

"I'm so sorry, Goldie."

"No worries. Come on let's go outside."

Sam texted. "I sent the funds to the guy."

"Well, that's done," Snapper announced.

"What's done?" Mari asked.

Snapper explained why he was awake and that he had just gotten confirmation from Sam that there was no turning back on the transaction or their mission.

"Are you sure this is a good idea?"

"I know it's an idea and it's a step in a direction. It's been a year and a half since Father's murder and this is the first solid lead we've had. It's like we all agreed, it's worth the risk."

They continued talking about more innocuous subjects like Dio and Sam, sales projections, the success of the summer collection, how Isabelle was doing after her frightening ordeal with the Italian, and that brought up the subject of their mother.

Mari had spent more time with her as Magnolia was in the design studio quite a bit helping Isabelle. She had seen a softer side to her mother, one that had never been shown to her, but she would catch moments when Magnolia would look up at her and smile. Not her devious, I have a plan for you smile, but a genuine almost heartfelt smile.

She wanted to know if Snapper had noticed any difference in their mother since their father died because Mari had concluded that was when things started to slowly change.

Snapper did not agree with the timing, but he did agree that she did seem less harsh. He surmised that the change took place when the Italian left the picture. He'd been in her life for over ten years. He may have been an anchor around her neck that she didn't know how to or didn't want to rid herself from until the option was presented.

"I had a thought that maybe we should invite Mother to graduation or at least the party," said Mari with a little trepidation.

"I can tell you now that she would never come to graduation. Too many common people in one space for her. But she may come to the party. It would have to be a unanimous decision. If even one of us doesn't want her there, then we don't invite her. I'm okay with it. She'll be on her best behavior in a public setting like the party."

They continued to talk until the dark melted into day with the first rays of the sun. It was predicted to be a beautiful Sunday, so they decided to go back into the kitchen and cook breakfast for everyone to the delight of their chef who had been in the kitchen only five minutes before they gave him the day off.

The smell of pancakes and bacon drew each of the siblings one by one down to breakfast. When the last one shuffled down the stairs, Oni, they all sat down and shared a meal together.

Snapper gave them an update on the meet and the transfer and Mari broached the subject of their mother coming to graduation or the party. No one was exactly opposed to the idea, they just wanted to know why Mari had even thought about it.

She explained what she had seen from their mother in recent months and they all agreed that she had displayed a slight change since the Italian was out of her life.

Dio wondered if Magnolia had any idea that he had planned to propose to her and Nia replied that if she had, he would have been kicked to the curb long before he was arrested.

Dio updated the siblings about Carnell and how well he was doing at his gas station job. She had delivered the shoes and a large pack of Big Red to him the next day as promised. He was thrilled and from that moment on, they couldn't get him to stop talking. It was like he had been bottled up for so long that it all just poured out of him.

She had a barber come to Salvation House and give all of the men haircuts and she helped Carnell apply for a job. He only had an elementary education, so some of the questions and sections were difficult for him. But with a little effort he turned it in to the owner of the gas station that was four blocks from Salvation House and he was hired to start the next day. He used the money he earned to help the other men at his new home.

There was no talk of the murder, the investigation, or any additional mention of their mother. It was just a simple morning as they shared their lives before they went off to work.

"How is that possible?" Mari yelled into the phone. "I don't care, that is a *you* problem. I'll expect those fabrics first thing in the morning. You can do an overnight delivery or you can fly them over yourself. Either way, they had better be on my cutting boards before noon tomorrow." She hung up the phone and turned to Isabelle.

"Someone cancelled the order according to them. My first question was why was that not confirmed through me as is procedure – he couldn't give me an answer. He had no answers. I think it's time to find a new vendor."

Isabelle just stood in awe of how confident and self-assured Mari was in her job. Isabelle was still trying to learn those skills.

"I know a vendor," Isabelle said meekly.

Mari waited for more information.

"Um, I used Silk Factory when I was in the Philippines. It's in Cambodia and their silks are luscious and vibrant. It's a fraction of the cost we have with our current vendor and I vetted them before I started working with them. They do not employ children and the people who work there work a ten hour shift then they have the next day off. The factory is in production twenty-four hours a day."

"They sound fantastic. I don't know why I haven't heard of them before. I'll find their contact information and set something up. Would you be up for a trip to Cambodia to help me assess their products?"

Isabelle was thrilled that Mari had that much respect for her. She couldn't get "Yes" out of her mouth fast enough.

Just then, Magnolia entered the studio.

"Good morning, Mother," Mari greeted her.

"Good morning, Marigold." she replied. "Good morning, Isabelle." She looked around. Where are the silks?"

Mari explained the situation and told her mother about Isabelle's suggestion of using the Cambodian based company. Magnolia agreed that an inspection of the facility would be worthwhile, especially if they were less expensive. As the conversation between the three flowed, Mari asked her mother if she could talk to her in private.

Curious, Magnolia excused them from Isabelle and walked with Mari to the other end of the studio. Mari was a little nervous as she hadn't been alone with her mother in months.

"Mother, I don't know if you are aware, but the five of us are graduating from Georgia Tech next month."

"Yes, I'm aware."

"We are having a party at Freedom Flowers Estate for all of the graduates and all of us would appreciate it if you would join us." Before Magnolia could reply, Mari added, "of course, you don't have to stay for the entire party, but maybe you could come for a little while." Her words were quickened and exposed her anxiety.

Magnolia thought for a moment. She wasn't sure if this was some type of manipulation or if her daughter was being genuine. She read Mari's face, but it could have gone either way. Magnolia had to make a decision. It was getting awkward standing there in silence.

"I appreciate the invitation," she paused.

Mari braced herself for a rejection and words of disapproval.

Magnolia continued, "I would like to celebrate the accomplishments of my children."

Mari was confused. *Was that a yes or a statement?* "So, I can put you on the guest list?"

"Yes, please do."

Mari almost fainted. She couldn't remember a single time in her life that Magnolia had said the word 'please' in her direction.

"Is that all?" Magnolia asked.

"Yes, Mother. Thank you."

Magnolia nodded, gracefully turned, and headed back to her office.

For a few minutes, Mari stood in the same spot. Stunned, shocked, amazed. When she gained her composure, she texted her siblings that their mother had actually agreed to come to the party.

Oni replied, "Great! Now the place has to be perfect!"

Snapper and Dio just gave a thumbs up while Nia replied, "Oni, she probably won't even show."

Mari commented, "Trust me, she's coming. I think she actually appreciated the invitation. She was oddly nice to me. She said 'please.' What do I do with that?"

Oni sent a shrug emoji. None of the others replied because Oni's said it all.

After a few more texts, Mari got back to work with Isabelle who was sketching some new swimsuits she wanted to add to her collection. She was into black spandex with accents of light colors.

"Waves," she said as Mari approached. "I see waves. How about midnight waves. Using the colors of the beach at midnight. No, that's stupid, or is it?"

"You're spiraling. Let me see what you have so far." She looked over the sketches. "Have you thought about using the colors of sunset. They are darker like you have here, but more contemporary. I don't see you with a collection with a base of black. It would be off brand for your aesthetic.

Mari's phone buzzed. It was an unknown caller.

"Mari don't hang up, it's Darrian."

Chapter 36

Mari tried to hold her composure and held up a finger to Isabelle with a smile on her face before she turned and walked away. Rushing to her office, she mouthed to her assistant, "no interruptions," and closed the door.

"What in the actual fuck do you want?" Mari spat every word into the phone.

"Mari, thank you. I'm so sorry to call you, but I can't get anyone to talk to me. Your mother has completely shut me out and I'm honestly scared to talk to Snapper. You're the only one at that company I trust."

"Well, I don't trust you."

"I understand. That's fair. But please hear me out. I'm not the one you should be worried about. There is someone else I think may be after your family."

"You are crazy! Look, I'm not doing this with you. Call me again and I will take out a no contact order to go along with the restraining order. If for no other reason to hate you, oh, but trust me, I have plenty, the fact that you terrified Isabelle in New York makes you number one on my hit list."

"I understand. I was being petty. I just want to talk to your mother and explain. Can you please help me get her to talk to me?"

"Absolutely not. Goodbye Darrian and don't call again." She hung up the phone.

She left her office and headed straight for Snapper, but Venus had to stop her. Snapper was in a closed door meeting. Mari didn't care. It was too important for him not to know immediately. She gave Venus a 'I dare you to stop me' look as she picked up the desk phone and paged into Snapper's office.

His voice was annoyed but calm when he answered, "Yes, Venus."

"Dragon, it's me. The Italian just called me."

He didn't need to hear any more. Within seconds he was out of his office. "Venus, offer the gentleman a beverage or take their lunch order. I'll be right back. "Your office," he directed Mari."

They walked down the hallway and around the corner to Mari's office.

"What do you mean he called you?" he inquired as he seethed, his voice dripping with anger.

She explained everything. His begging, his cryptic statement about someone else to worry about, pleading to talk to their mother, and of course, hanging up on him.

"No, he didn't threaten me. It was actually the other way around. I told him I would get a no contact order."

"That is going to happen right now. I would have thought that the restraining order would have been enough." He pulled out his phone and texted Stone about what had happened and requested no contact orders.

"Goldie, are you okay?"

"Yes, of course. She stood with her shoulders squared. That asshole can't do anything to me and his call was just an inconvenience. I'm actually worried about Mother. He is determined to contact her."

"Mother is fine, She has a bodyguard and a complete security detail both here and at the house. I might not be her biggest fan, or a fan really, but she is our mother and I will not let anything happen to her."

"If you're good, I have to get back to my meeting."

"Yes, go, go." She shooed him out of her office.

As he returned, Venus let him know that the men in his office had ordered lunch and that it would be there in thirty minutes. With that he re-entered the negotiations.

Still angry by the time he was done with his day, Snapper texted to meet with Stone at a local bar. Snapper needed a drink. It had been a long day and while it ended well with the negotiations for House of Blossom to acquire a small ready-to-wear company that was on the rise through it social media presence, Oni had thought that the House could add to their resources while it increased profits.

She'd turned out to be correct. With seventy-eight percent ownership, House of Blossom was positioned to increase revenue for the company by twenty five percent within the next quarter. Unfortunately, it was all tainted by the Italian and his ridiculous call to Mari.

"Conti can fuck with just about anyone else, besides Oni, but Mari is completely off limits. I will personally beat the shit out of him if he contacts her again," Snapper told Stone.

"There's no need for violence. I have put in the request for no contact orders and I'll find him as soon as they are issued. Just tell your family to not answer any calls from unknown caller or unknown numbers. If it's important they will leave a message," Stone suggested.

Snapper rubbed his temples. "I don't know how much more I can take. This guy is a drain on my family. Look at how many resources we have had to deploy for just one man. One man. A fucking idiot at that. He knows none of us are going to help him and you'd think after over ten years around my mother he'd know that when she is done, she is done."

"He's a desperate man who is in love with your mother. I've seen this movie a hundred times in my career. I do think he's harmless, but desperation makes a person do very foolish things, so I wouldn't let down your guard just yet."

"Trust me, that's not happening. I have to protect the girls…" he took a breath and let it out as he continued, "and Mother."

"I got Oni's request for a police presence at your graduation party. I've asked around and so far I have three officers who are willing to sign on to moonlight for y'all. Everyone knows the pay would be worth the lost hours, but we are stretched really thin these days," Stone said in an exhausted tone.

"Three should be plenty. We really appreciate everything you've done for our family. I don't know why, but I have a feeling this is the year we catch the killer." Snapper raised his glass.

"Here's hoping," Stone replied as they clinked their drinks together.

Darrian was completely at his wits end trying to get someone in the Blossom family to talk to him. Mari was his last hope of getting to Magnolia. He was smart enough to know that she was done with him but he thought that all of their years together would have at least meant something.

He just knew that if he could explain everyone would know that he was sorry and that they would drop the charges. He couldn't stand the thought of being in jail any more than he already had been, it was horrible. Jail was so below his standards of living.

He'd finally gone back to his home and was driving his Mercedes. His friend's old Ford Taurus was transportation, but it was so not the luxury he was used to, which was unacceptable.

Darrian wasn't the grateful kind of man. His friend, if that was what she could be called as she was one of the seamstresses from the House. He'd just shown up on her doorstep when he had gotten back into town. Still being enamored by him, she offered her home and car to him. He swore her to secrecy.

He left five hundred dollars on the entry way table a few mornings earlier with a note that said, "Thanks. D." He treated her hospitality more like a hotel than a friend. Which was completely on par with who Darrian was and how he treated people.

He tried to think, as he drove around Atlanta, of how he could possibly talk to the Blossom's. He was sure that after his disastrous phone call with Mari that no contact orders would in fact follow, but until then he would continue to try.

As if luck was on his side, he spotted Snapper's car outside of a local bar. He circled the block to make sure. As soon as he saw the BLOSSOM 3 license tag, he knew it would be his last chance to set the record straight.

His problem – the restraining order. He shouldn't actually even be in the parking lot.

He took out a notepad from his attaché case. His only recourse was to leave a message on the car.

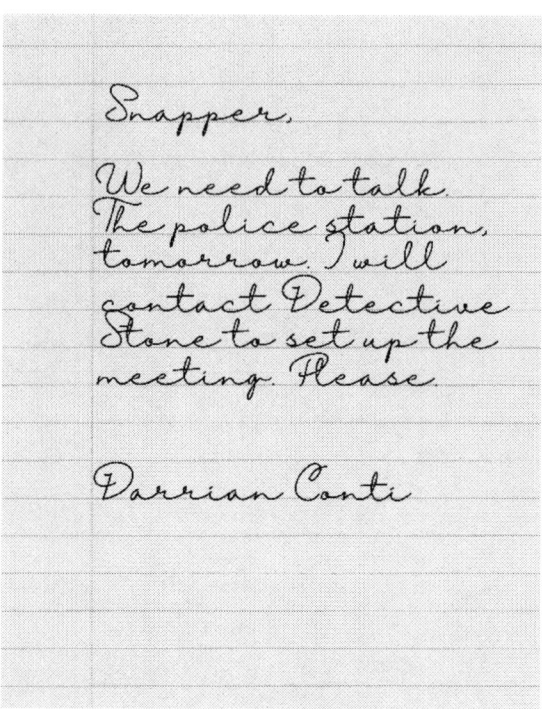

Snapper,

We need to talk. The police station, tomorrow. I will contact Detective Stone to set up the meeting. Please.

Darrian Conti

When Snapper and Stone found the note, Snapper only had one thing to say, "We need those no contact orders now."

Stone was a little more collected. "When he calls, I will explain to him that you will not be meeting with him." He paused. "You've got to give it to him, he is tenacious." He chuckled.

"I'm not sure where the humor is in this situation, Detective."

"You know, it wouldn't hurt for you to meet with him. I'd be right there."

"You can't be serious?" Snapper was appalled at the thought.

"You can hear him out. That would put an end to the harassment. It could be a win-win."

"Fine. When he calls, set it up."

Chapter 37

The meeting with Darrian had to be postponed because Sam had texted that the meet with the ex-military guy was a go. It was set up at the last minute with no warning. This didn't surprise Sam, but the siblings were caught completely off guard.

All of the them were glued to their phones that morning. The meet was set for ten, but like everything else that had happened with the investigation, they couldn't be certain.

Dio was a nervous wreck so she had her assistant shift her schedule to lighter work that she could do on auto pilot. She wanted to be able to drop whatever she was doing with a seconds notice.

She and Sam had gotten serious in a short amount of time. He'd promised to take her away for a weekend if everything worked out with the meeting. She countered with she would take him in the jet anywhere in the world. They were good either way, as long as they were together with no interruptions for the entire weekend.

As ten approached the siblings gathered in Snapper's office. Nia was sitting on the light green sofa nervously kicking her leg with Oni sitting beside her just staring at the wall. Mari was sitting at the table by the window looking out over the city. Dio was pacing as Snapper sat at his desk with his cell phone placed squarely in front of him.

They all knew the risk and danger that Sam had placed himself in for them. Even though it started out as a job to find their father's killer, it had turned into so much more. Sam was a friend and they all worried for his safety. Not a word was spoken as they waited.

Ten came and went, which they expected, but when eleven rolled around Dio was frantic. There had been no disclosure of information other than the meet was happening. There was no location, no names, no anything.

It was hard for Sam to let go of Dio that morning as they woke up in each other's arms. She had begged him for at least a location, but he knew better. If she thought for one second that he was in trouble she would call out the National Guard to extract him.

No, he had to stick to the plan and follow the strict instructions that had been forwarded to him.

- If your vehicle has any tracking devices, find one that doesn't. Nothing newer than 1999.
- Leave cell phone behind. Only carry the encrypted burner phone provided. I will contact you with information. You do not reply.
- Avoid main roads as much as possible. Take routes that do not have CCTV.
- When you arrive at the provided location, do a visual sweep for any cars, civilians, or surveillance. If any are present, leave.
- A new location will be texted.
- Once a suitable location is established you will stay in your vehicle.

- Communication will be done by phone. Use the voice modulator when speaking on the phone.
- You will ask no questions.
- Information will be provided and questions will be asked of you.
- If any of these instructions are ignored or corrupted, the meet will be canceled and you forfeit the fee. No services will be rendered.
- Tell NO ONE!

Sam followed the instructions to the letter. He had paid cash for a 1998 Ford F150 and hidden it in a storage unit. At nine he switched vehicles and parked as he waited. Five minutes later a text was received.

"Head North to Holly Springs. Further instructions in 45 minutes."

Just before Sam entered the town limits, another text.

"Continue to South Canton."

Fifteen minutes later, "Oakdale Rd to W Hayes Rd"

By this time, it was ten-thirty. Another text, "Turn right onto the dirt service road. Toward Etowah River. Stop at end."

Sam carefully made his way looking for the service road. He was not familiar with the area. He'd never heard of Etowah River. He was going on instinct and sheer determination.

When he got to the end of the road, he stopped the truck and looked around for any possible reason that the location was not secure. He found none. He stayed in the truck, as instructed.

Five minutes later, the phone rang. He attached the voice modulator.

"What is your purpose?" the garbled voice on the other end asked.

"I am investigating the Heliotrope Blossom murder. I was told you had information."

"I do. It was a clean hit. Anything else?"

Sam had to stop himself from asking questions. "Yes."

"Is your inquiry about who did the hit or who hired it to be done?"

Sam knew that he could select only one or the other. "Who hired the hit." He thought if he knew that information that he might be able to find out the latter at a different time.

"A woman. Only a first name – Rose."

Sam remembered back to the account associated with Ailongam · that had been opened and depleted.

"You have followed the rules. You get one question."

Sam hadn't thought of any questions, but there was just one that the siblings wanted to know, "Why?"

"Retribution."

The phone went dead.

Sam sat there for a minute. He rolled down the window and looked around to see if he could hear a car or see anything move. He saw nothing.

The information didn't make any sense based on the year and a half of investigation they had done. It was just more cryptic clues. He started the truck and drove back out of the service road. He couldn't let anyone know that he was okay. He wiped his fingerprints off the phone with his shirt tail, broke it in half, tossed it out into the road, and ran over it.

He got back to the storage unit as quickly as he could to trade vehicles again. Then he went straight to House of Blossom. It was against his own rules to meet clients at work, but as Dio's boyfriend he decided he could use that cover and risk it.

Dio's assistant buzzed Venus to let her know that a gentleman was present to see Dio. Venus called into Snapper's office. All of the siblings jumped and turned toward the phone. They examined

Snapper's face hoping for some sign that it was information about Sam.

"Sam is here to see Dio," she told him.

Snapper took a breath and said with a smile, "Dio, you might want to open the door."

She quickly opened it to find Sam standing there. She was so relieved that she didn't care she was in public, she kissed him hard and wrapped her arms around him.

After the passionate kiss ended, she didn't let go of his hand and they walked back into Snapper's office.

Sam told them everything that had transpired with the elusive hit man. It was more than confirmed in their minds that the voice on the other end of the phone was the man who had shot their father, but Sam had made the correct decision in asking 'why' as far as the siblings were concerned.

They didn't know anyone named Rose and absolutely no one who needed to exact some type of vengeance against their father.

"With a floral name, it has to be someone in the family, but the last Rose I know of is a cousin who is in her fifties. She has no dealings with the company and I can't imagine Father doing anything that warranted being murdered by her," Nia reasoned.

"Oni call Rudy. He needs to know all of this. Ask him to look harder into that Rose account with the code RBJ. There's something there that we need to decipher." Sam requested.

"Well," Mari started, "we know the who, what, when, where, why, and how, we just need to connect them all to the mysterious Rose.

Chapter 38

Oni couldn't sleep. She was too excited. It was graduation day. May fifth had finally arrived. All of the Blossom siblings were graduating with an MBA. She had already decided to take at least a gap year before she decided if she was going to go back to college to get a doctorate in something. She was thinking Digital Media. For now, she was just thrilled to be done with college.

It was five in the morning and she hopped out of bed and went downstairs where the coffee pot had started brewing. The smell only added to her invigorated energy. She popped a couple of grapes in her mouth from the bowl on the counter while she waited.

She plucked her favorite mug from the cabinet. Her father had given it to her for Christmas when she was five. He told her that everyone should have a favorite mug. He would make her homemade hot chocolate and pour it straight into her mug during the winter months each year.

The mug had a multi-colored happy bunny rabbit on it. When she was five, she had a rabbit names Scarlett O'Hare. Her room was decorated in everything rabbits. For her sixth birthday Helio purchased fifty rabbits to roam free on Flora Fields. Their descendants still lived there.

As she sipped her coffee she thought of how proud her father would have been to see her graduate. He was always proud of her, but he was especially so when it came to her academic and business accomplishments. It was his encouragement that took her to Georgia Tech. He had supported their business program for many years and just like at Parsons he had a scholarship for students who attended for their bachelors in the business field. He believed in post-secondary education and was a proponent of its merits. While she loved being a student, she knew it wasn't for everyone.

She had been talking to some of Nia's hacker friends who learned everything from doing. Only a handful of them had a college degree, but all of them were the guys who could get just about any information if it was connected to a computer - degree, or no degree.

She was good with computers when it came to social media. She knew the ins and outs of Instagram, Tik Tok, Facebook, Snapchat, YouTube, and a few others that most people didn't use much or even knew about, but when a new app came out, she was on it.

With her mind racing, she had to calm herself. She went back upstairs and changed into one of Isabelle's custom bathing suits and went back down to take a swim.

She'd been a champion swimmer in high school, but even with a pool in the backyard, she didn't have as much time to get into it as she would have liked. She focused on her breathing and her strokes until her mind eventually unwound and it was just her and the water.

Simultaneously all of the alarms in the bedrooms went off at six. They had all taken the day off to relax and enjoy their graduation. It wasn't every day that five siblings graduated together.

Snapper could hear the stage being built out on the grounds. He'd hired Jensen to perform at the party.

The band had been busy over the past five months. As Snapper had predicted they were making good money working the Atlanta circuit of events. They had finished their demo and Axel agreed to produce it instead of giving it to one of the junior producers. He knew his name being on it would bolster their prospects of actually being heard by a record label.

Snapper had spoken to Jensen a few times since their meeting after the New Year's Eve party. She was happy and had even apologized for being so suspicious and abrasive when he'd first introduced her to Axel. He was excited to see her. He wanted to hear all about the gigs she'd done and he didn't know what it was, but there was something familiar about her. He wanted to know more about her.

Dio immediately called Sam when she woke up. She had wanted him to stay over, but he had another case that involved the murder of a young woman that he needed to prepare before he met her parents that morning. He promised to be back before they left for the stadium where the graduation was being held.

Her next call was to Carnell. She had invited him to the graduation and wanted to make sure he didn't need anything before she started her day. She'd even arranged for a car to pick him up so he wasn't late. He had been doing very well. He was promoted at work and had saved enough money to get himself an apartment that was only a few blocks from work and Salvation House.

She didn't take on Salvation House as a charity, she considered it a salvation for her own soul. She helped with her time and simple resources. She always cleared everything through Jerry and he was the balance between a handout and a hand up. She'd always just given money, but never got personally involved, but now she was a vital participant in the progress of the program. She was learning that it was worth listening to everyone's story.

She was most excited about her relationship with Sam. He'd dropped the "L" word on their weekend together in Paris after the meet with the ex-military guy. She didn't reciprocate at the time. She did love him, but she was scared of what it meant. He told her that there was no pressure, he just wanted her to know how he felt. He was a patient man. She was planning to tell him at the party that night.

Nia's friends with benefits had turned into a more frequent and somewhat serious relationship. She texted Jack when she got out of the shower. He was a brilliant hacker and one of those guys that Oni had been thinking about earlier who didn't have a degree. Magnolia would not approve.

She was excited for the weekend. Jack was going with her to all of her animal shelters. It was going to be a whirlwind weekend of puppies and kitties. She couldn't wait. She was in negotiations to acquire some land in Oklahoma.

She wanted to start an equestrian shelter complete with all of the care needed to nurse even the sickest of horses back to health or give space for older horses to live in luxury. She wanted to start a program to donate horses to police stations and she had even bigger plans for an equestrian therapy center.

Mari was usually the last one to get out of bed. She didn't have the duty of a boyfriend to call like her sisters, so she lazily stretched as she pressed the snooze button on her phone. She propped up her pillows and grabbed a book from her nightstand. Reading in the morning was one of her favorite things. It was a little escape from reality. That day's escape was into the world of Elizabeth Zott in *Lessons in Chemistry* by Bonnie Garmus.

After a few chapters, she lumbered out of bed and looked out her bedroom window that overlooked the back of the property. It was a beautiful day for a graduation.

Then she noticed that Oni was swimming and thought that would be a great way to wake up. Quickly, she put on her favorite bikini that Isabelle had made for her and went down to join her. No one else was downstairs yet, so the coffee pot was still almost full. Being the last one up, usually meant that all of the coffee was gone and she had to make a fresh pot because her siblings thought it was funny.

Chapter 39

Sam, Carnell, Jack, Detective Stone, and Rudy all stood and cheered when each of the siblings names were called at the graduation. The Blossom children had been surrounded their whole lives by people who were friends with their money more than them, but on that day, the five people they looked to find in the stands were their friends because of who they were as people.

The tragedy of their father's death had brought all of these people into their lives in some way or another. Snapper had promised, at the unveiling of his statue, the siblings were doing what it took to carry on Helio's legacy. They wanted to make sure they did that in a way in which he would have been proud.

Once the excitement of the graduation ceremony had commenced, it was time to party. All of them piled into a stretch limousine to head back to Freedom Flowers Estate. The graduation ended shortly after six that evening and guests were invited to arrive at the party starting at eight, so that gave all of them just a little time to get changed and be ready to receive their fellow graduates.

Unlike the New Year's Eve party where hundreds attended, this was to be more intimate and held in the garden. The sophistication level was heightened but Oni had put together a party that would be epic.

At seven forty five the siblings met at the outdoor bar under the pergola to toast their success. Oni was the only one who was thinking about returning to college in the future. The rest of the siblings had all sworn off ever stepping foot in a classroom again. While they were toasting, the band was doing a last minute sound check.

Due to the smaller setting, they had lowered the levels and were going to play a set that was more family friendly since some of the graduates were bringing their children.

Oni had hired a local farmer to bring some of his animals for the children to pet and interact with as well as a small assortment of carnival games and rides. She had also employed, for the evening, eight top tier nannies from the Atlanta area. The family chef had even volunteered his services to grill hamburgers and hot dogs for the little ones.

Security radioed that the first guest had arrived and the message was relayed to the siblings. They positioned themselves on the front steps of their home to greet each person as they exited the valet area. Georgia Tech gold runner carpets had been strategically placed throughout the space to lead the party goers to all of the festive areas of the garden.

Oni had arranged with Jensen to take the stage promptly at nine thirty to make an announcement. "Welcome everyone and thank you for coming to celebrate the 2023 graduates." Rousing applause and cheers came from the crowd that had made their way to the stage. "My siblings and I just want to let you all know how much we appreciate and celebrate you and all of the hard work we all put into the MBA program. It has been a true pleasure studying aside each of you, but I hope we don't do it again anytime soon." Laughter erupted. "Now for your visual entertainment, a sky extravaganza of fireworks."

Ohs and awes cascaded as the first creation was a Georgia Tech G in gold. That was followed by a graduation cap and an assortment of glorious streams of colors that looked like they were being placed among the stars. The spectacular ended with the word "Congratulations" written in cursive that fell to the Earth in ever changing colors.

When the last flicker had fallen from the sky, Dio turned to Sam and in a sweet and soft voice, she looked him in the eyes and said, "Sam, I love you."

He scooped her up in his arms and kissed her.

As their kiss ended, Dio saw Magnolia enter the garden. The siblings had taken bets if she would actually show. Snapper, Nia, and Dio owed Mari and Oni a thousand bucks each.

The Blossom's gravitated together to greet her. "Mother," they said in unison.

"Children. Congratulations."

"Thank you, Mother. It is gracious of you to come and join us. May I show you around the garden?" Snapper asked. He knew the others were nervous and feeling awkward, so he stepped right back into the favorite child role. The others were relieved and thankful. They all went to the far side of the garden while Snapper escorted their mother toward the bar.

"In anticipation of your visit, I have your favorite, Mother." He turned to the bartender, "Mccallan 18, please sir."

"That is very generous of you, Snapdragon."

"I will admit that I had my reservations about coming, but now that I'm here I am impressed. Did you use Darlene for the décor?"

"Yes, we did. You have an excellent eye, Mother." Snapper was showering his mother with platitudes.

He introduced her to most of the guest and he showed her the beautiful topiaries that had been trimmed for the occasion. They were lit from within to add a glow to the designs.

"Your home is lovely, Snapdragon. If you can't be at Flora Fields, I think you and your sisters have done well here."

"Mother, the compliments are lovely and excuse my candor, but a bit unexpected."

"I understand. I have not been very gracious to you or your sisters. I will admit, the house is rather empty without your presence. But as always, we persevere." She paused and the moment of vulnerability passed. "I believe I have seen enough for one night. Would you escort me back to the valet? I told him to park it close."

"Yes, Mother, of course." He linked her arm in his and he led the way toward the front of the home. To get her there in the most expedient manner, they cut through in front of the stage.

"Oh, Snapdragon, is it necessary to go this w…" she abruptly stopped speaking when she glanced up and saw the band.

Snapper wasn't sure, but he thought he saw a glare of recognition and animosity fly through the air between them. He was almost sure about it when his mother quickened her steps. But he excused it that she didn't like the music and being right by the speakers.

He kissed his mother on the cheek and thanked her for coming when the valet brought her car around. He attempted to end the encounter with a pleasantry. "Perhaps you will visit again and I can take you on a tour of our home."

"That won't be necessary, but the offer is appreciated," she replied as she closed the door and drove off.

With that, Snapper went to find his siblings.

The revelry continued until around midnight, although most had left by eleven, especially those with children and after the petting arena was packed up so the animals could get a rest.

The party had been received well by everyone and Jensen was offered three more events during their break.

While they were packing up, Snapper walked over to congratulate them on another fabulous performance. He was really enamored with Jensen.

He tried some small talk with her, "Are you from Atlanta?" he asked.

"Born and raised, she said proudly," she replied as she packed up her guitar.

For a person with excellent people skills, he was stymied as to what to say next. "That's interesting," was the best he had.

"Oh, yeah," she looked up from her case over her shoulder, "what's interesting about it?"

"Well," he started, "interesting in that most people here are transplants. They move here for jobs more than being an original."

"Guess you're right," she agreed as she continued to gather equipment and cords."

"How's it been working with Axel? I've been in the studio a few times when he's been working. I am amazed at how he knows exactly what needs to be done to push a vocal or instrument forward or backward."

"He's a genius. We sound better in the studio than we could ever sound in person. He's patient too. I messed up countless times and he just rolled with it. Thanks again for the introduction."

"My pleasure." He stopped talking. He thought it was going well and he didn't want to say too much.

"I think that's it," she announced. "Gotta' hit the road. We have another gig tomorrow night in Decatur."

"Sure," he replied. "Hey, one more question. What was that with you and my mother?"

"You'll have to ask her," she replied before jumping into the passenger seat of the band's van.

Chapter 40

Putting his distaste for the Italian aside, Snapper had agreed to a meeting with him. Stone had set it up for the Monday after the graduation since the first time was postponed. Darrian had assured Stone that the information he had was going to be helpful and it may persuade Snapper to drop the charges.

Stone told him not to hold his breath, although, he wasn't privy to what he had to say. Darrian refused to talk until Snapper was present. His one other request was that none of his sisters be there and absolutely not their mother.

Despite his feelings for her, time had healed Darrian's heart and now he was going to do the one thing he could do to get her attention – exact vengeance. He had been holding onto a piece of information that was going to blow up the Blossom family, which was exactly what he wanted to do. It was only fair, he reasoned. His career was over, his reputation was ruined, and he was facing jail time.

He was practically salivating at the thought of how Snapper would react. He was honestly hoping that he would attack him and call him a liar. Darrian wouldn't waste a second accusing him of assault. He thought that a pretty boy like Snapdragon Blossom wouldn't last a month in jail.

Begrudgingly, Snapper arrived at the police station at ten fifteen for their ten thirty meeting. Stone was waiting for him in the lobby.

"Conti is in the soft room. You ready?" Stone asked.

"Let's just get this over with. I have more important things to do than waste my time with the Italian."

Stone placed his hand on Snapper shoulder and directed him to the room where Darrian was waiting.

When the door cracked open, Darrian stood. "Snapper," he said in a timid voice. Having him in front of him shook his resolve.

"Everyone sit, please," directed Stone.

The three of them unconsciously formed a triangle, leaving as much space as possible between them.

"Okay, Darrian, you've got my attention. You have five minutes to fill me in with this bombshell that I just have to know."

Darrian cleared his throat. He could hear the hostility in Snapper's voice. He decided to match his energy. "I'm just going to come out and say it. Did you know that your father had a child long before any of you privileged brats were born?"

Snapper's face turned red. "You fucking idiot!" he screamed, "Are you seriously trying to ruin my father's good name with an illegitimate child." Snapper stood up and got in Darrian's face. "Just because you ruined your reputation does not mean that I am going to let you take my father down with you. He was always good to you. Can you say the same of yourself toward him? I'll answer that for you. Fucking hell, no considering you were screwing his wife for ten years." He turned to Stone. "I'm done with this trash. Please keep him away from me and my family."

As Snapper stomped forcefully toward the door, Darrian said a name, "Rose."

Snapper stopped in his tracks. "What did you say?," he turn back toward him slowly with fierceness on his face that truly scared Darrian.

He almost decided to stay silent, but he doubled down instead. "I said, Rose. Her name is Rose and your mother knows about her, has for years."

Snapper was deeply confused. His head spun with how many times the name Rose had come up in the investigation into his father's murder, but there was no connection to anyone he knew. He dismissed the thought. It was a ploy. Darrian was rich, he may have done research and found the name just like they had. He concluded that Darrian was antagonizing him.

"I don't know what game you're playing or where you got that name, but I mean it if you come near or contact my family ever again, I promise you I will find a way to put you under the jail."

With that, he walked out of the room and with quick steps made his way back to his car. He sat behind the steering wheel with white knuckles. The possibility of Darrian finding that name was slim to none in reality. But how…how would he know that name and that she is connected somehow to his father's murder. Mother, that's how.

He thought about going back to the office and confronting her, but he knew that would be a disaster. Instead, he opted to text his siblings, Sam, and Rudy. In their group chat he sent, "Emergency meeting in the war room tonight. IT IS URGENT!"

Within seconds they all replied with a thumbs up. Snapper used to hate that emoji. It was the only thing that their mother would accept in a text. It represented disdain and made him feel worthless. Now when he saw it from his sisters and friends he knew it meant that they supported him and would be wherever he needed them.

He didn't go back to the office. He needed to go to the war room and prepare. Plus, he didn't want to run into his mother. He didn't have any meeting that day that couldn't be pushed, so he called Venus and told her to do whatever she needed to do. If something had to be handled, he would work from home.

He went back through the files and accounts that had to do with Rose. He looked up if there was another Rose in the family that they didn't know about, but the family Bible didn't have the name other than his father's cousin and Ancestry.com showed a Rose who died in 1958.

He wanted to get the hackers on looking up birth records, but he didn't have a year. He called Jack but hung up as soon as it rang once. He texted quickly, "Sorry, accident." He couldn't involve Jack. He would call Nia. No, as frustrated as he was, he would have to wait until everyone got home.

When everyone was present in the war room, Snapper shared his encounter with the Italian.

"Are you saying that somewhere out there we have *another* sister and Mother knows her?" Dio said with doubt in her voice.

"There is no way that Father cheated on Mother," Oni declared.

"This is the most absurd thing I have ever heard," agreed Nia.

"I agree, but the name, Rose, how would he know *that* name?" Mari asked with trepidation that she wasn't staunchly on board with the information being bogus.

"Mari, you have got to be kidding," Dio ranted. "It's the most common flower out there, that's why the name isn't used. It's cliché. Darrian wouldn't know that, it's a family thing. He probably just pulled it out of his ass to stir up shit."

Now that everyone knew, Snapper asked, "How about we take a week and try to disprove it. If we don't we'll always have a hint of doubt. Nia, can Jack go through birth records? I guess start with Father's name to see if he did have a child with someone else. If that doesn't yield any results, we can try to find out if there were babies born during their marriage named Rose. Damn that fucking Italian."

"Rudy and I will concentrate on the accounts and try to get more on the code. I'm more convinced than ever that the R in RBJ is for Rose. We also need to find out where and how the money was taken out of the account. There has to be some CCTV at a bank," Sam said.

"Okay," Snapper sighed, "We will either find something or we will prove that this is a wild goose chase. Either way, we might be able to identify Rose and track her down. She has to have some connection to Mother."

"Speaking of, I say we all steer clear of her as much as possible this week until we have some reason to speak to her," suggested Dio.

That they could all agree on.

When they disbursed, Mari hung back to talk to Snapper. "Dragon, you know that there is something to this. I don't care what Dio said about the family tradition of not using the name Rose, I just have a bad feeling that this is going to be the lead that gets us to the person who ordered the hit on Father."

"Goldie, I couldn't say it in front of the others, but I have a gut feeling that we are not the only Blossom children. I don't see Father cheating on Mother, but anything is possible."

Chapter 41

Jack couldn't find any birth records with Helio's name except for the five Blossom siblings. It was another dead end. By Thursday evening everyone was ready to give up on the search for the elusive Rose. They had no leads, no additional information, and no other avenues to pursue. They had given themselves a week, but it was looking like they didn't even need that much time.

Rudy and Sam had exhausted all of their tracking into the Rose account and other than speculation that the first letter of the RBJ code stood for Rose, they weren't able to access any more information. Something as simple as three letters had them all stymied and frustrated.

For all of the brilliance that flowed through the veins of the Blossom children, none of them knew where to go or what to do. They felt like they were losing their father all over again. For all of their work and dedication, their investigation had yielded little.

"Maybe I should go back and talk to Darrian," Snapper said to Mari in a defeated tone.

"No, absolutely note," she replied. "Even if he knows something I seriously doubt at this point he would tell you anything."

"I don't know, it might be worth it, we can't lose anything," Dio commented.

As the siblings sat around the dining table that morning they rehashed all that they had uncovered and avoided the one thing they all knew that needed to be done to get more answers.

Nia was the only one brave enough to say it out loud. "We all know what we have to do. Talk to Mother."

"Who is going to take that bullet," Oni asked.

"Dragon, you know it has to be you. We won't listen to any of us," Mari said.

With a sigh, Snapper knew she was right. From all they knew, the answers were with their mother. They had avoid talking to her or even giving a hint of what they were doing to her. They had all come to the realization that she was the key to everything. She was either the one who had him killed or she knew who did. Neither option sat well with the them.

"How would even bring it up? Hey. Mother, did Father have another kid?" Snapper scoffed. It was a genuine question. The last time he crossed her – rolled his eyes – she slapped him. Not that he was afraid she'd ever do that again after he threatened her, but he knew that if something, even ever so slightly made her angry, it was going to unleash her inner Fury.

They discussed, briefly, the possibility of showing a united front and all of them confronting her, but that was quickly scratched from the list. The siblings were in an impossible situation.

While still mulling over what to do, Snapper had a flash. "Wait!" he exclaimed.

All of his sisters stared at him blankly. He hadn't continued and they weren't sure if they should ask why they should wait or let him collect his thoughts.

Sure enough, a moment later he continued. "When I met with Darrian he said something that I had completely glossed over. I dismissed almost everything he said, but I missed something in his words."

The girls were perplexed and intrigued.

"He said that Father had a child *before* any of us were born. If that's true, then we have been looking in the wrong place. We need to go back to before the twins were born."

"You think that there is an older sister out there somewhere?" Dio asked with a hint of 'there'd better not be." She liked being the oldest and to think that someone else held that position was preposterous to her.

"Is it possible that Mother and Father had a child before they got married and gave it up for adoption? You said that Mother knows," asked Mari.

"That's a possibility. But if that happened, why didn't they just get married before it was born? Why put it up for adoption if they were going to get married anyway?" Nia pondered.

"That would explain why Father's name isn't on any other birth records. When a child is adopted, those names are put on the birth certificate, not the biological parents. So, it wouldn't do any good to search for Mother's name either." Oni added.

Snapper looked at her with his head tilted slightly to the right. "How do you know that?"

"I have a friend who was adopted as a baby. She doesn't know who her biological parents are because her birth certificate is in your adoptive parents' names. She tried to get information from social services, but everything was redacted that had anything to do with her biology. Her's was a closed adoption, so no one knows anything other than where she was born and when."

"Fascinating," Snapper replied. " Swear you get smarter by the minute. I know nothing about that process. I don't even think I know anyone who is adopted. Then again, how would I know if they didn't tell me?"

"Exactly. I didn't know until we had a random conversation about who in our family we looked like the most. She doesn't look like either of her parents. They both have dark hair and brown eyes with olive skin. She is a blonde haired blue-eyed fair-skinned kid. No connection there in the DNA."

"That gives me an idea," said Nia. "What if we did one of those DNA tests? Only one of us would need to submit it. We might get a match."

It was the first solid and good idea anyone had in a while, so Snapper volunteered to be the Guinea pig. They decided to order the kit right then and have it delivered overnight. It was too late to call Stone, but Dio thought that it might be prudent to run the DNA through the crime lab, if that was allowed.

"You know Stone isn't going to go for that," Snapper scoffed.

"He might if we remind him that it could help to solve a murder," Dio reasoned. "For all we know this Rose person is a hardened criminal. Maybe that's why we don't know that she exists. Maybe that's what Mother knows but she can't bear to send her child to prison for murdering Father."

They all busted out laughing. They knew that Magnolia would have marched the police to their doorstep if she thought any of them had something to do with Helio's murder, much less an errant child.

When the box with the DNA kit arrived first thing Saturday morning, the siblings were anxious to see how it worked. From what they knew from movies it was a simple buccal swab, but they figured that it was probably more complicated than that.

Carefully, they opened it and found the instructions. "I'll read them," Oni stated as she grab them out of Nia's hand. "You'll probably mess it up," she teased. "Snapper get down here. Remember, you volunteered for this torture." She yelled to him up the stairs with a giggled.

Snapper was in his bathroom brushing his teeth. He didn't want the DNA people to think he had bad dental hygiene.

He bound down the stairs a few minutes later. "Okay, I'm ready." He made a big grin to show off his pearly white, perfectly straight teeth. "All clean."

Oni smacked him with the instruction booklet. "You dumbass. It says right here in the Do's and Don'ts section, "Don't brush your teeth within thirty minutes of performing the DNA swab."

"Oops," he shrugged. "Since we have to wait, who wants to go for a swim?"

They all went and put on their bathing suits to kill time in the pool. At Flora Fields they were not allowed to use the pool for anything other than practice. They each took swimming lessons as children and all of them had been on the swim team in high school.

When they were much younger, Helio would play with them and toss them around, to Magnolia's dismay. She wanted to sunbathe, not hear giggly, screeching children when she was by the pool. It was one of the few times in their marriage that Helio did not abide by her rules.

He loved the pool and seeing the children happy made his heart sing. Especially since most of the time they were so shy and quiet. He had made a compromise with Magnolia that he wouldn't have the children out there while she was soaking up the sun and he had the pool heated so he and the children could enjoy the pool in the winter months. Magnolia never went out there after September.

The girls decided to play chicken and Snapper was the referee. Oni was on Nia's shoulders and Mari was on Dio's. It was an equal battle, but Oni got the perfect angle under Mari's shoulder and pushed her right off. Snapper tried to call it an illegal hit, but Oni was having none of it.

Mari came back up from under the water laughing, so Snapper had to concede. Their laughter echoed through the grounds as they had a fun time like they had once done with their father.

"Okay you," Mari addressed Snapper, "let's get you in there and see what you are made of," she teased.

Chapter 42

"No, Snapper, I cannot put your DNA into the database and see if you've got a match. That's not how it works," Stone replied to Snapper's request. "You're just going to have to wait for your results to come back from the ancestry kit. Besides, we have something pressing we need to talk about."

"I know. His trial date is in two days. I'm meeting with my lawyer this afternoon to prep."

"I still don't know why you insisted on being put on the witness list. Any of the managers from the New York office could have testified about the protocols. They even have the security guard who was on duty that night ready to take the stand… Apparently, he's never liked Conti."

"I think that it will carry more weight with the judge if the CEO testifies. I'm telling you; he needs to get jail time. I'm not saying seven years, but something since Isabelle just can't bring herself to testify. She doesn't want to be in the same room with him. She was shaking when I asked her about it one last time last week," replied Snapper. "What baffles me is that Conti opted to have a bench trial instead of a jury trial. I would have thought that he would use his status to influence a jury." He continued.

"From what I've heard, his lawyer advised against a jury trial. He's thinking that the judge won't find him guilty, so the less media coverage the more likely he is to be embraced back into the fashion world. It's logical, but I'm not saying it's sound logic," Stone postured.

Changing the subject, Snapper asked, "I know the answer, but is there anything new on my father's case? I can't believe it's almost been two years."

"I'm afraid not. I am still working it in between my other cases. Summer in Atlanta makes people do stupid things, like kill each other. Summer and the holidays are stacked around here. I wish I had something to tell you," Stone replied with a sigh.

"Sam and Rudy are working with Jack to crack the RBJ code, but they've hit a new roadblock. The account was closed three days ago. We don't know what it means, but they think it means they are getting close and that someone got nervous."

"That's possible. Criminals are dumb by nature. They think they are smarter than everyone else so when they get away with their crime they get complacent and lose focus. Not every criminal makes a sidestep, but most of them do eventually."

That was the encouraging word that Snapper needed to hear – eventually. He could hold on to hope with that as his faith in ever finding his father's killer had been waning.

The honorable Judge Atkins was assigned to the case of the People versus Darrian Issac Conti. As soon as Snapper heard his full name read aloud he knew who owned DIC Unlimited, but he had to file that away for later.

"Yes, your honor, we'd like to call Snapdragon Blossom to the stand," the prosecuting attorney stated.

Snapper didn't even acknowledge Darrian. He looked directly at the attorney the entire time. He hadn't realized how much he still hated Darrian until he was in the same room with him.

"Mr. Blossom as CEO of House of Blossom is it part of your job to ensure that all of your employees are safe?" the prosecutor asked.

"Yes, that is correct."

"In doing so, does your company have strict protocols that state how and when your buildings can be entered and by whom?"

"Yes. Each building, depending on where it is located, abides by not only the local and state laws, but we have state-of-the-art security systems, patrol and lobby guards during the day, and shift guards in the lobby overnight. All of these employees are former police or military and are retrained each year on the House of Blossom entry protocols."

"Mr. Blossom would you please walk us through a typical entry into your building between the hours of nine in the evening to three in the morning?"

"There are two shift guards in the lobby until eleven, then there is one until three. In order to enter the building a person would have to go to the front doors of the building, scan their work badge to acquire entry and present themselves to the shift guard, who has the final say if the person can continue to the elevators after signing in again with their picture identification badge. Depending on the time of year, we do have employees coming and going around the clock. If by chance, which this has never happened, someone does get by the shift guard, then the police are called immediately."

"One last question, if someone does not follow the protocols and enters the building in a different manner, what is House of Blossom's procedure?"

"The person is considered to be trespassing and the local law enforcement is called to handle the situation. "With that, Snapper stepped down and the shift guard was called to corroborate and give his testimony.

Once the prosecution rested, the defense called Darrian to take the stand. He had pled not guilty and stated that he was not aware of such protocols. He had entered House of Blossom properties through many side doors in the past and he did not realize that entering through the loading dock was a crime."

Snapper did all he could not to roll his eyes. Unlike Snapper, Darrian looked directly at him the entire time. He was trying to plead his case to him more than he was to the court. Darrian really did not want to go back to jail and he still thought there might be a chance that Snapper would speak on his behalf during sentencing.

"Call your next witness," the judge instructed the defense council.

"Yes, your Honor. We would like to call a character witness, Mrs. Magnolia Blossom."

Snapper and Darrian both whipped their heads around to see Magnolia being escorted in from the lobby of the courtroom. Snapper glared while Darrian beamed. No one other than the attorney knew she was being called.

The prosecution objected, as she was not on the witness list, but the defense stated that she had just called that morning and asked to speak to Mr. Conti's character. The judge overruled the objection and allowed Magnolia to take the stand.

The click of her heels echoed through the courtroom as her delicate steps made her look like she was gliding across the hardwood floor. Her hair was tightly pulled back into a luxurious ponytail that sat just below the crown of her head. She wear diamond earrings that created a slight hue to the edges of her face from the radiant rays of sunshine that lit the space.

She was, of course, impeccably outfitted in a House of Blossom dress. The white color made her skin look like she had just returned from the tropics and the knee length accentuated her long legs.

"Mrs. Blossom is it your desire in court today to speak on behalf of Mr. Darrian Conti's character?" the defense asked.

"Yes, I have known Mr. Conti for over ten years as he has worked for my company," she gave a pointed look at Snapper, "as a designer and has recently been promoted to Head Designer in our Milan headquarters."

"Would you say that Mr. Conti has any ill-will against your company?"

"I can't state that I know of any cause for him to have any malice toward House of Blossom." She chose her words carefully.

"Do you know it to be true that Mr. Conti has had privileges, such as entering buildings without signing in during his tenure with your company?"

"Yes. During Fashion Week, as that is when this took place, designers are not held to the strict protocols of entry as they may need to visit the design studio for various reasons with only moments to spare. While I encourage all employees, including designers, to follow the protocols, when I am not there to supervise, I cannot monitor that activity."

Snapper was dumbfounded at how all of his months of work to put Darrian away had just been unraveled by his mother. While he kept a calm, blank face in the court, he was screaming at her in his head. He also couldn't help but to notice in his peripheral vision that Conti was smiling from ear to ear which made him even madder.

With her testimony concluded, the judge proceeded to closing arguments. The prosecutor argued that despite Mrs. Blossom's testimony that the rules are sometimes bent, the law was clear when it came to trespassing. Conti did not have permission or a reason to be in the New York building on the night in question yet the CCTV footage clearly showed, in color and HD, that the person who had entered the building through the loading dock was Darrian Conti.

The defense put more credence on Magnolia's testimony by stating that it was an unwritten rule that during Fashion Week the designers would enter the building without going through the lobby and checking in with the shift guard. He contended that Conti did not have any malice and he did not cause any harm during his time in the building.

After hearing both sides, the judge recessed for lunch and stated that he would render his verdict at two that afternoon.

Snapper quickly made his way to the lobby, but his mother was long gone by that point. She'd inflicted the damage to the case she had planned and he knew she had just thrown down the gauntlet toward him. He thought, "Game on, Mother."

When Judge Atkins returned to the bench he was quick with his verdict. He laid out his thought process as to how he came to his decision. He addressed Conti directly and told him that he had no doubt that his intentions the night he went into the building were nefarious; however, the prosecutor had failed to prove any malice. He added that since it was a regular practice for designers to move about the House of Blossom properties during Fashion Week without following protocols, he could not conclude that Mr. Conti entered the property by deliberately disregarding the company's processes and procedures even though he was aware that they existed. With that conclusion he rendered a verdict of not guilty.

"Mr. Conti, you are free to go," the judge stated.

Snapper was furious and walked out of the courtroom in a blinding rage toward his mother. She had ruined everything, but for what reason? She had cut Conti off, dismissed him like a dog, and refused to talk to him. Why at the last minute would she come in knowing that her words would put him right back into her life?

Chapter 43

With the disastrous results of the not guilty verdict racing through his head, Snapper flew back to Atlanta to inform his sisters that Conti was free. The decision meant that he still worked for House of Blossom and with Magnolia circumventing Snapper's authority to bring him back to the Atlanta House, all of the Blossom children would once again have to work with him every day. Snapper worried mostly for Mari and Isabelle.

He called them both into his office to discuss the situation. He wanted to tell Isabelle in person and have Mari there for moral support as he knew that Isabelle was still traumatized by the incident from Fashion Week in New York.

Magnolia may have lost a few battles along the way in the war with her children, but through cunning precision and patience she had undermined all they had done to find their father's killer.

From the time she found the notepad in Oni's office, she knew they were doing more than talking to Detective Stone. She had loyal police officers who informed her of every move that was being made and it was no coincidence that she called the defense the morning of the trial and had the corporate jet fueled and ready to take her to New York.

She had sat back and let the children play out their theories, but when she was given the information that Darrian was running his mouth about Rose, she knew she had to put a stop to all of it. Her plan was simple and elegant. Stop Conti from being found guilty and bring him back into the fold of Atlanta so that she could control him. He was a wild card that needed to be tamed.

The one thing she didn't know was that Sam and Rudy were involved. They had kept low profiles and with Sam and Dio dating, there was no reason to suspect that he had any involvement. Rudy's presence could be explained as well. He had a small construction company that he often used as cover for his jobs. With the children remodeling most of the guest houses on the property, his frequent visits to Freedom Flowers Estate went virtually unnoticed.

"Isabelle, I'm so sorry that I did not see this coming. I should have known that she would pull a stunt like this," Snapper apologized.

With tears in her eyes, Isabelle replied, "It's my fault. I should have testified. I should have held him accountable. I was just scared because I couldn't identify him. I knew they would ask me if I had seen him, but I didn't. I thought I would hurt the case. What I feared would happen with me, happened because of me." She began to openly weep as she covered her face.

Mari walked over to her and put her arm around her in an attempt to comfort the young designer.

"Isabelle, there was nothing you could have done to change the outcome. Our mother is to blame, not you," Snapper reassured her. He called his sister to his desk and spoke softly, "Goldie, take Isabelle to one of the comfort pods. Ask Emma to stay with her until she is feeling better. Then come back to my office. I'm going to text Nia, Oni, and Dio to join us."

Mari went back to Isabelle and gently coaxed her to stand and walk with her. On the eighth floor were four rooms that had been designated as safe spaces called comfort pods. They were designed to be a private space for employees where they could go to calm themselves or take a quiet break when needed.

They had been designed by Magnolia after she read that Google had nap rooms. While she wasn't a proponent of sleeping on the job, she did think that having a space to decompress was valuable.

The rooms were soundproof so a person who was crying or needed to let off stress with a good scream could do so without anyone hearing their distress. Each of them were painted in cool, neutral colors and provided luxurious and soft furniture. There was a stocked beverage cooler and freshly prepared snacks along with stuffed animals and fluffy pillows. In one corner there was a stress bat that was made of foam along with a punching bag. Many people used these to relieve stress, especially if they were having issues with a specific person. Ironically, Magnolia's face had been pictured on the bag many times.

One of the favorite parts of the room was the sound system. There were controls on the wall that allowed for a wide selection of music from therapeutic to heavy metal. Sometimes a person needed to rock out while others took advantage of the yoga mats and calming sounds to control their breathing.

Emma was the resident psychologist who maintained the pods. When someone asked, she would go into the room with them to either talk or comfort them. She loved her job and found that it was very rewarding in that she helped people deal with their emotions in a positive way.

Mari held Isabelle close to her as they approached the pod area. Emma heard her cries and immediately went to meet them. With Isabelle in good hands, Mari returned to Snapper's office.

When Mari returned, her sisters were being updated by Snapper about Isabelle. They all liked the new designer and were unsure how she and Darrian would be able to work together after what had happened. Mari was additionally angry with her mother because Isabelle looked up to Magnolia.

"To Mother, she is collateral damage," Snapper said bluntly.

Before anyone could comment, Magnolia walked into Snapper's office. She did not acknowledge any of the girls. She walked straight to Snapper's desk and said, "I hope you understand now that you cannot outsmart me, you cannot match wits with me, and you absolutely cannot beat me."

As he forcefully stood up, his chair slammed against the wall. "Beat you? Beat you at what? Destroying this family? You're right, I could never do as brilliant of a job on that one. You have singlehandedly crushed each of us under your five thousand dollar Louboutin's, but here is where you are wrong. You're wrong in underestimating us. All of your tricks and punishments just because we were unfortunate to be birthed by you, they don't defeat us, they make us stronger and we know that you hate that. You can't stand to see the five of us thrive and succeed. Especially where you failed."

Magnolia didn't flinch. She gracefully sat down in a chair placed in front of his desk and asked, "Are you through?"

"With you? Yes," he sat back down, "Yes, I'm through."

She chuckled in a maniacal tone. "Snapdragon, poor deluded, Snapdragon. How is it that I gave you everything, taught you everything, but you still have no clue who you are dealing with? I know *everything*. I know about your little *investigation* and your incredibly naïve notion that the five of you can possibly find out who killed your father."

The girls filed over to stand behind Snapper. They wanted to demonstrate that their mother needed to understand that they were united against her.

"Mother," Dio started, "You can pull all of the underhanded and despicable schemes you can dream up, but I can promise you that the Blossoms are not going to break because of you. Remember, we are Blossoms by blood, you just married into the family."

Magnolia was appalled and for a brief second her face showed her anger as she replied, "Gladiolus, it's nice to see that you have finally grown a backbone though I believe it is directed at the wrong person. You see, your brother was foolish in his pursuit of Mr. Conti. If he had been convicted it would have splashed House of Blossom onto every headline along with disgraced, felon designer. Now how would that have looked? Being a 'Blossom by blood,' as you put it, doesn't mean shit if you are willing to ruin the name. I did what had to be done."

"Mother, I believe that this conversation is going in circles. Nothing will be accomplished by continuing. Please leave," Snapper said calmly while he gritted his teeth together.

Magnolia nodded and stood up. As she walked to the door, Snapper added one more comment, "Oh, and Mother, remember I am your boss and you can be fired. So, if I were you, I wouldn't make any more decisions without running them by me first. I would hate to let you go for insubordination. That would look bad on the company."

She didn't react and continued to calmly walk away.

When she was gone, Oni closed the office door and asked, "What are we going to do about her. She said she knows everything, but how? We've been so careful."

"Apparently not careful enough. Someone has been feeding her information about what we have been doing. Now what?" Nia asked.

"Now we find who killed our father," Snapper declared.

Chapter 44

As usual, and with more fire in their souls, the siblings met with Sam and Rudy that Saturday. Snapper knew that they were running out of time to find out once and for all who had hired a hit on their father. He also knew that his mother's story about saving the company name was bullshit. There was a more complicated and complex reason and he was willing to bet that Conti knew exactly what it was.

Snapper paced the war room while his sisters and the private investigators reviewed the information Jack had been able to get for them. He'd provided them with a list of just over two hundred names of girls born in the Atlanta area and who had been adopted.

The siblings had speculated that Magnolia and Helio had given a child up for adoption before they were married. They asked Jack to procure the adoption records for any girls born within two years before their marriage with the name Rose. They were sure she was on the list.

"I'm telling you, there is something more going on here. This isn't just about keeping the birth of a baby a secret," Snapper stated.

"What else could it possibly be?" Mari asked. "I seriously doubt that some love child killed our father, but I still believe that finding her will get us more answers."

"More than likely, it will get us more questions than answers," Oni said under her breath.

"So, what if Mother and Father had another child before us? Why does it matter? The Rose account was most likely a pay off or something to keep her from surfacing. I think we need to get back to Darrian and Mother as the killers." Announced Dio.

"It's a fair point," Mari agreed. "Why else would Mother have gotten him set free?"

"But that doesn't make sense. She had completely frozen him out before the trespassing thing came up. Why save him?" Oni asked.

"He wasn't a liability before the trespassing charge. He was still a designer for House of Blossom. She probably thought he would beat the charge. When it went to trial, she had to act to protect her secrets," Sam reasoned.

Snapper sat down and took part of the list. Each person methodically researched all of the names to see if they could find any additional information. One-by-one the names were crossed off the list. As it got shorter and shorter they began to think the search was going to be fruitless.

Oni had floated the idea that Rose could be a middle name and that they were wrong about the R in RBJ standing for Rose. That would mean another job for Jack and more names to go through, which none of them felt particularly good about having to do.

Snapper was feeling the pressure. He felt like he needed to solve the case for his sisters. Where there had once been rivalry, he now felt protective of them. He wanted to find an ending to the investigation. He began to pace again, feeling like he had missed something in the nineteen months of studying every aspect and researching every avenue of the investigation.

"I know that I have said this before, but I'm telling you, Darrian knows something. I think that is why Mother testified. Keeping him out of jail had nothing to do with the company. She's up to something and I think she did that to keep him quiet. I need to talk to Darrian."

All of his sisters, like before, were against the idea, but Rudy suggested that they at least figure out a way to talk to him without it being confrontational. He reminded them that there was such a thing as a casual conversation.

"I'm going to be really straight with all of you, you're all too emotionally impacted by all of this, which is understandable, but it is clouding your judgement and making you all to wrapped up in this case. I think it is blinding you to the possibilities of looking outside of what your mother and Darrian have done. I realize that you are all angry because of how he disrespected your father and how he scared Isabelle, but when you take those out of the equation, he still has information that you need to know. Plus, he would be a lot easier to talk to than your mother."

While Rudy was talking, something click for Snapper, "He's right. Darrian does have more information and I have been way too damn emotional about all of it. When he tried to talk to me I couldn't stand to see his face. When I was in the courtroom with him, I couldn't look at him. All I could think was how awful he had been to Father. Maybe, I could ask him to have a civilized conversation with me."

The girls saw the merit in trying, although they weren't happy about the prospect of Snapper interacting with him again. He'd told them that if Stone had not been in the room that he would have absolutely beaten the shit out of Darrian. Snapper wasn't a violent person, so for him to feel that much rage scared them.

"What if I talk to him?" Mari asked.

"NO!" Snapper shouted.

"It makes the most sense, Dragon. He and I have been close for many years, we've worked side by side together, and I was the one person in the family he trusted to call when he couldn't get to Mother. I think he would talk to me."

Snapper walked over to Mari. "Goldie, you don't have to do this."

"Yes, I do. I can stay calm and he's not particularly intimidated by me like he is with you. Call Stone and have him drop the restraining orders and the no contact orders. It will be a show of good faith. Also, ask Stone if he will set up another meet with Darrian, but this time with me."

Snapper knew that when Mari had made up her mind to do something, it was always best for him to support her instead of trying to talk her out of it. She could be headstrong when she needed to be and he knew she would be in this situation.

"Okay," he relented," I'll make the call.

Reluctantly, Darrian agreed to meet with Mari. When Stone had first called him he was completely opposed to the idea. He wanted nothing to do with the Blossom children, but when Stone informed him that they had all dropped their restraining and no contact orders, hc did see it as Mari had thought – a gesture of good faith.

He and Mari had always gotten along. She was an excellent boss and he truly respected her. It wasn't until she wouldn't talk to him on the phone that he had developed less than honorable feelings toward her. He was willing to put that aside to see what she had to say.

They met the next morning at the police station. Snapper had insisted on driving her and he sat out in the car while she went inside. It was one thing for him to agree to the arrangement, it was another to allow her to be there alone.

Stone had assured him that he would be in the room the entire time and that he would guarantee that Conti would not be allowed to be any closer than across the table from her. But Snapper wasn't taking any chances. He asked Mari to call him before she got out of the car and to put it on speaker. He wanted to hear everything that was said in case Conti got out of line. She agreed and appreciated his protective nature.

Stone met her at the front door and escorted her back to the room where Darrian was waiting. He stood up as soon as the door opened, but unlike the aggressive stance he'd taken when Snapper had come to talk to him, he was relaxed and smiled as soon as he saw her.

She was lovely in a soft green House of Blossom dress with a lace collar and shoulder cuffs. It was one of Darrian's pieces from his 1986 summer collection. She pulled it from the vault especially for the meeting. It went beautifully with her green eyes, fair skin, and strawberry blond hair that was curled and ever so slightly bounced when she walked.

"My darling, Marigold," Darrian said as she entered the room. "You are a vision."

She appreciated the compliment and asked him if they could sit and chat for a bit. Stone sat in a chair that was positioned in the opposite corner of the room. She had asked him as they walked to the room if he could give some space for her to speak to Darrian in a more casual manner. She'd placed her phone on mute for a moment so Snapper could not hear the request.

After exchanging pleasantries, Mari got down to the business at hand. "Darrian, I want to talk to you about Rose. You'd mentioned her to Snapper, but he was not in a place to hear you. I can. I want to know if I have another sister."

"I know very little, just what your mother has mentioned. I would have thought she'd have told all of you by now. If for no other reason than out of pure spite."

"You know Mother likes to hold things close to the vest and keep secrets. She's most likely holding on to that card for a rainy day," she replied in a sweet, calm voice.

"Yes, you're probably right. Besides, she doesn't want the girl coming in and messing up everything."

"What do you mean?"

"Mari, your mother saved me from going to jail, I'm not sure I should repay that kindness by telling her business. If she hasn't told you, then there is a reason.

"Perhaps," she started, "however, you were willing to tell Snapper before all of that happened."

"I was angry with her. I wanted to hurt her for abandoning me. But now," he paused, "now, I'm not so sure."

"How about I ask questions and if you feel comfortable you answer them. If not, I'll move on to the next."

He agreed.

"Rose is older than the twins, correct?"

"Yes."

"Excellent. Was she put up for adoption?"

"No."

That answer shocked Mari. They were sure that was the case and had spent the better part of a month exploring that theory.

"Oh, does she live with any of Mother's family?"

Before he stopped to think, he blurted out, "Why would she live with the Talbot's, she's a Blossom." He knew he'd said too much. He realized that Snapper must not have remembered when he shouted that their father had a child before the twins. Darrian thought back and concluded that Snapper must have been too angry to put that piece of the puzzle together. He tried to backtrack.

"She's your sister, she's older. She lives on her own. That's all I meant."

Mari didn't buy it. "One more question," she stated, "did my Father cheat on my Mother?"

Darrian felt a pang of guilt with that question. All of the years that Helio had been his friend; he'd been secretly having sex with his wife. He answered honestly, "No."

Snapper went around and opened the passenger side door for Mari as she left the police station. He'd heard everything and he was proud of how Mari had handled herself. He realized that she was completely correct in suggesting that she talk to Darrian.

"Are you okay?" he asked knowing that the new information was a complete shock to both of them.

"Yes, we know a lot more than we did an hour ago. I'll text everyone and ask them to meet. I know Nia and Oni were going to get their nails done and Dio was going to lunch with Sam. I hate to ruin such a beautiful Sunday, but they need to know this information.

Snapper agreed and headed for home. They didn't talk about Mari's conversation with Darrian on the drive. All that was revealed was still being processed. The thought of their father having another daughter before he was with their mother was shocking.

Neither of them knew how to broach the subject and neither of them wanted to believe it was true.

Chapter 45

With everyone gathered in the war room, Mari went through what she had experienced with Darrian. She explained that she had asked questions and that he was selective on the ones that he would answer. However, the ones that he did answer would take the search for their older sister on a different path.

"Rose does exist and since she is only a half-sister, that means that father must have been a teenager when Rose was born. If I remember correctly, he and Mother started dating when he was twenty."

"Here's what I don't understand, why isn't she part of the family? I get it, in the sixties and seventies it was a mortal sin to have premarital sex and for a woman to have a baby out of wedlock, but that doesn't explain where she went. Father wouldn't have just left his own child behind," reasoned Oni.

"Is it possible that grandfather took her? I can't see him letting an illegitimate child besmirch the Blossom name," Dio asked.

"That is possible. He may have given the baby away," agreed Nia.

"Hold on, we are forgetting about the mother. Who is Rose's mother?" Mari added. "Darrian did confirm that Mother knows who she is, so there has to be some connection."

"Could it have been a friend of Mother's? No, that doesn't make sense either. Plus, there's the account named 'Rose.' Why would Mother's fake company have an account in her name?" asked Nia.

"Ladies, I think we have lost focus as to who Rose is besides being a half-sister. She's also the person who hired a man to kill our father. Her father. I don't care if grandfather absconded with her in the middle of the night, I don't care who her mother is, all I care about is finding her and bringing her to justice for Father." Snapper said with too much anger pointed toward his sisters.

They all agreed he was right and agreed that they should put away the question of who she is on the back burner and focus more on where and how to find her. They still believe that the trail began with the account in her name, but they weren't about to ask their mother anything after her exasperating display in Snapper's office.

Sam had a thought. "There was two million in that account, correct?"

They all agreed.

"The account was opened six months before your father died and drained just a week before. Stay with me." He walked around the room as he thought. "We paid a million just to meet with the shooter, what if the hit also cost a million dollars. I didn't think to get that information. He confirmed that Rose hired him, so it would make sense that the money was used for the hit," Sam continued.

Now they were all thinking. Dio wondered if Rose and their Mother were in on it together, Nia thought that maybe Rose had somehow played their mother for money, Oni surmised that Rose had possibly blackmailed their mother, and Mari and Snapper talked about how it was odd that their father wasn't involved.

"How did Mother know Rose? Would it make more sense for Father to have given her money?" Mari asked.

"Maybe Father refused and like she does, Mother took care of it not knowing she'd just handed Rose the means to kill Father." Snapper replied.

"I can't see Father turning away his own child. For him, two million wouldn't have amounted to much if he helped his child, blackmail or not," Dio reasoned.

Just then, Nia's phone rang. It was Jack with a report on his search for girls named Rose born within two years before Magnolia and Helio had started dating. He'd found over four hundred names, but it was a fresh start for the group. He emailed over the information and all of them started pouring over the names and looking for social media connections as they had done before. But it was getting late. They had to suspend their search after only a few names had been marked off.

"Somewhere in that stack is the name we need. I feel it," Oni said as they left the war room.

When Snapper got to his office the next morning, the shit had already hit the fan. Isabelle was waiting for him and before he could even punch in his office key code she was threatening to quit.

Darrian was scheduled to come back to work that day and she didn't have the strength to be in the same room with him, much less work with him. Then there was the issue of hierarchy. Would she be expected to work for him if she stayed? Would he take over her collections? Was her work her intellectual property or did it belong to House of Blossom? She had realized that she hadn't read the contract she'd signed very thoroughly and she was freaking out about what was going to happen to her, her ideas, and her career.

Snapper tried to calm her down. He asked Venus to get her some tea and he called Emma up to his office. He wasn't ready for a complete meltdown again.

He started with a proposal. If she did not want to work in Atlanta anymore, she could have her pick of any of the other House of Blossom headquarters anywhere in the world. He started rattling off the names of fabulous cities and assured her that any one of them would be happy to have her, but he added that he would hate to see her go. He believed in her talent and that her style and vision was just what the American market needed.

When Venus returned with Isabelle's tea, she informed Snapper that he'd better turn on the television.

He turned on one of the national news channels and to his horror, there was his mother's face with Darrian sitting beside her. She was holding a press conference that he knew nothing about and it was live. Snapper was livid as he turned up the volume.

"…as you all know, Mr. Darrian Conti has been a legend at House of Blossom for many years. We are thrilled to have him back in the States after his brief trip to lend his expertise to our Milan headquarters. He has already made significant headway in designing our next collection…," Magnolia beamed as she addressed the press.

"What is this? Where is she at?" Snapper yelled.

"I heard she's at the Waldorf. She secretly arranged everything last night. This is bad, isn't it?" Venus asked.

"The only person this is bad for is my mother. I warned her what would happen if she challenged me," Snapper seethed while his mother's voice continued to chatter in the background.

They continued to listen in mystified astonishment.

"As the owner of House of Blossom, I can assure you that all of House of Blossom is thrilled to welcome Mr. Conti back to Atlanta today. Thank you for joining us." Magnolia and Darrian exited the platform without answering any of the questions being asked of them by the press.

Snapper knew that she had just manipulated everyone, including him, into not only welcoming Darrian back into the fold, but also making it impossible for Isabelle to leave and for him to fire his mother. She was always one step ahead of him and he didn't know how to stop her.

All of his sisters came rushing into Snapper's office. They were watching the live feed on their tablets.

"Have you seen this…" Dio began to ask before she saw the look on his face and heard the news anchor recounting the press conference.

"How did none of us know about this?" Snapper yelled and threw the remote at the television, smashing the screen. "How in the literal FUCK did we not get a single text or phone call from someone about this? We all have contacts in the media, someone should have let us know. FUCK! She has all but cut my balls off." He shouted with fierce anger. "Get me Dawn on the phone. I want to know how this happened!

He went to his desk and sat down while complete rage reddened his face. "How am I supposed to run this God forsaken company with her constantly going behind my back?" It was a rhetorical question. "Did you see Darrian's face? He was smiling like the Cheshire cat up there. Just soaking up all of Mother's praise and admiration. That fucking prick!" He turned to Mari, "Mari, do you remember anything from your conversation with him that gave you any reason to believe that he'd talked to Mother, that she had coached him, anything?"

"Nothing that I can remember, but he was so evasive with most of my questions. She could have gotten to him." She held out her tablet where the news was still talking about Magnolia. If she can create this in one night, anything is possible," she added.

Snapper looked at the tablet. "Turn the sound back on, what is he saying?" Snapper had seen a flash of the closed captions.

"...when she generously handed the reigns over to her son, Snapdragon Blossom, as CEO after her husband's death..."

They cut to a previous recording of Magnolia being interviewed in the lobby of the Waldorf Historia. "His father and I had always planned for Snapdragon to be CEO of the company. With his father's passing, I felt like it was time that I stepped back and let the younger generation of our family take it into the future."

Snapper stood up and went to the door. "Get out! Everyone out of my office, NOW!" he screamed and pointed toward the door. As he slammed the door behind them, everyone cringed. They had never seen him so enraged.

The next thing they heard was glass breaking as Snapper took a golf club from the corner and smashed his glass top desk with it.

Chapter 46

An hour after Snapper had thoroughly destroyed everything in his office that his mother had designed, he heard an argument outside of his door.

He forcefully opened the door. He stiffened. Venus was arguing with his mother that she didn't have an appointment.

He calmed himself, "It's alright, Venus. Thank you. Mother," He gestured for her to enter.

She chuckled as she crossed the threshold and surveyed the scene of broken glass, papers strewn everywhere, the feathers from the down cushions of the sofa still lingering in the air and in big piles on the floor, the smashed television, and the slashed leather of the chairs with a letter opener still protruding from one of the seats.

"I take it you saw my press conference," she said smugly with a twinge of a smile pulling up the right side of her lips. Her plan to get under Snapper's skin had obviously work beautifully.

"I did. I was surprised at all of the high praise you had for Darrian considering you pushed him out of your life at the first sign of trouble."

She walked to the floor to ceiling windows and looked out over the city. "Snapdragon, you foolish boy. I did what I had to do. I knew that you would try to find a way to send him back to Milan, or to Paris, or somewhere else in the world. But, unfortunately for you, and a bit for me, I need him here. While he might be a disaster waiting to happen, he is brilliant and once again I had to save the House of Blossom before you tried to fuck it up again." She said without looking at him.

"He's dead weight in this company. Have you not seen what Isabelle has done in her short time here? Besides," he said with curiosity, "I thought you liked her."

"I do. She makes me so much money. I can admit that I am impressed with her strengths as a designer, but she needs training. Why do you think I have been spending time with her?" she turned to see his puzzled face.

"Oh," she chuckled, "you thought I was helping her because I wanted to be helpful. That's hilarious. Have you not seen her work since she's been here? Think back to what she presented in your little contest." She paused, "Now think about what her designs looked like in the last collection. Ah, there it is," she read his face. "I knew you'd figure it out. Everything she does has my taste, my influence, my ideas sown into every stitch."

"Well played," he said, "Not only have you placed your hand in the designs you made it look like I was not elected CEO, which everyone in the business world knows is not true."

"Perhaps, but the business world isn't the only world that watches CNN, MSNBC, and Fox News, now are they?" she asked rhetorically with a smug smile. "Snapdragon, when are you going to learn that this is my company no matter who sits in that chair? Well, not *that* chair."

The only thing that had survived his rage was the chair that he had selected for his office.

"Oh, dear, those were on loan from The Met," she commented when she saw the works of art cut from their frames and lying like trash on the floor.

"Son, you really should learn how to control your temper," she mocked.

"Now that you have more than solidified your place and mine, have you thought about the drama you will be inflecting on Isabelle having to work with Darrian?"

"Trauma? You really are melodramatic. She needs to get a tougher skin if she is going to make it in this business. There is no room for the weakness in this House or in fashion. If she can't work with him, or should I say, under him, then she's not House of Blossom material after all."

"What do you mean, under him? She is our featured designer."

"That was all well and good when Darrian was in Milan, but *you* promoted him to head designer. You can't possibly think that he would come back here for anything less. Again, how would that look for the House. Honestly, Snapdragon, I don't know where your head is these days. What is with all of this emotion and hostility? You really need to see someone about it. I have the names of several good therapists."

"What is all of this, Mother? Are you trying to put me in my place? Are you getting back at me because we are looking into Father's death?"

"Petty nonsense. The answer to all of your questions is no. You really don't understand, do you? I'm the one who lost a husband, I'm the one who lost control of my company, I'm the one who lost my lover, I'm the one who lost my children, I'm the one who has lost everything while you ungrateful, miniscule children go around playing amateur detectives and try to unravel something that is none of your business."

Snapper had had enough. It was time to ask the one question that needed to be asked. "Mother, who is Rose?"

She turned from where she had been looking out the window. "Who?" she asked, feigning disinterest.

"Rose, Mother, who is she? I know that you know her and I know that you are in contact with her. What I don't know is why."

"You sure do seem to know a lot about, who did you say and why what?" she turned back toward the window. "Is this part of your sleuthing? You found a rather ordinary name and you think there is some big conspiracy? Really, Snapdragon, I'd hoped better than average for you, but it looks like my hopes are dashed." She shrugged. "I blame your father." She turned and began to walk toward the door.

"You know we are going to find her. It's just a matter of time."

"Look all you like for some fictitious person," she said as she continued to leave.

"She's not fictitious and you know it. You are avoiding all of my questions. I know that play. Besides, Darrian told me everything. I just wanted to hear it from you," he said.

She stopped and turned around.

She thought before she spoke. "So, this is something you heard from Darrian? Well, that explains everything." She turned toward him and walked over to where he sat in his chair. She leaned forward ever so slightly like she was talking to a child.

He didn't blink.

With a lowered voice, she continued, "I told him to keep you busy while I planned my press conference. He was more than happy to oblige. He must have done a really good job. I don't even think I would have thought to create a fake person for you to investigate. Rather clever of him, don't you think? She leaned a little further and placed her hands on the arms of the chair and pushed him backwards.

He caught himself before the chair hit the wall.

She stood back up straight. "I'll have to give him some praise for his efforts. You know, like I used to do for you. I do miss our talks and how you would always have nice things to say about me. What happened to that son?

"He grew up and saw you for who you are – a vindictive bitch."

She raised her hand to slap him.

He rose from his chair with complete calm, "That is not advisable, Mother. The son you had no longer exists. He died with his father. Now it's just you in your lonely mansion with no one to blame but yourself."

"Looks like you've been taking some backbone lessons from your big sister, Gladiolus. What fun, bonding. The five of you make me ill. Complete disappointments, the lot of you."

"You forget, Mother, we don't need your words of affirmation or your approval anymore."

"Says the boy who lives with his sisters. I am curious, why didn't you get a place of your own?"

"Because they are my family and unlike you, I protect my family."

"I should have slapped you. You are so stupid. All I do is protect this family. If it weren't for me there would be no family, no company, no money, nothing. So, don't you dare talk to me about family. I have sacrificed more than you will ever know," she said in a raised voice.

Instantly, she calmed herself. "Anyway, you really should have someone come and clean up this mess. Honestly, Snapdragon, this is no place for a CEO to conduct business. It looks like a child works here."

Chapter 47

Venus had already called a cleanup crew and the decorator by the time Magnolia left Snapper's office. When she looked in, she found him still sitting in his chair surrounded by everything that was broken.

He looked up and saw that her eyes were filled with worry and a bit of pity. An eerie calm came over him and he began to chuckle at the ridiculousness of his actions, the situation, and his mother.

"He gestured to all of the debris, "I think I need furniture that can stand up to a golf club." He picked up the club off the floor where he had dropped it right beside him and stood it upright in front of him only to let it fall again with a thud.

She walked in, stepping over the papers and broken glass, to stand next to him. She put her hand on his shoulder.

"Go home," Venus suggested. "You're not going to be any good here today and I can push your calendar until tomorrow. When you return in the morning this office will look like nothing happened, but more importantly, it will be your style and taste, not hers.

"I don't know why," he started, "but breaking everything in here that she thought was best for me, felt amazing."

"Sure, you do, "she replied, "this was the one last piece of her that was holding you down. You'd gotten rid of everything else, including her, but every day you walked into this office, it wasn't yours. Hell, it was practically a carbon copy of her office. Now that it's gone, you can let go of her completely."

"Thank you for that," he replied. "Oh, and if my sisters ask, just tell them I'm working from home today, but don't tell them about Mother. I need to do that in person when they get home tonight.

She nodded as she picked up his briefcase and handed it to him. "Good thing your laptop was in here," she patted the briefcase, "or IT would have to get you a new one of those too," Venus teased trying to make him smile.

He appreciated the effort, but he just needed to get out of there and clear his head. His mother's game of mindfuck had twisted it in all directions and he needed to figure out what was fact from fiction.

As he stood up to leave, she took his hand and said, "If you need me, just text. I can meet you."

He knew what she meant and on most occasions he would have taken her up on the offer, but he was too mentally and physically exhausted. He nodded and gave her a quick kiss on the cheek and squeezed her hand before he made his way through the minefield of broken glass and debris to exit his office.

Magnolia wasn't fairing all that well either after her deliberate run in with Snapper. She'd made her point with him but finding out that Darrian had run his mouth to the children again infuriated her. It made what she considered to be her victory less satisfying.

"Fucking Darrian," she said to herself as she entered her office and flung her bag and purse onto the loveseat. She was fuming and needed to know immediately what he'd told the children about Rose. She called him and demanded that he stop whatever he was doing and get to her office now. She was sick of dealing with her incessant children and having to constantly clean up Darrian's screw ups.

When she contacted him before the trespassing trial, he confessed to her that he had been so angry and upset with her, that the only way he thought he could get her attention was to drop a hint about Rose to Snapper. His plan, he told her, was that he would pique Snapper's interest, Snapper would confront Magnolia, and then she would have no choice but to contact him.

Unfortunately for Darrian, the plan backfired when he realized that Snapper already knew about Rose.

Magnolia thought she had made herself clear with him when she threatened to let him rot in jail if he ever said another word about Rose to the children.

Apparently, he didn't think that applied when she instructed him to distract them the night before the press conference, because she certainly did not mean with more information about Rose.

She thought to herself, "Fucking Saturday night pillow talk". It was one of the rare times she felt vulnerable and she had shared many secrets with Darrian over the years. She was seriously regretting that now.

Darrian came strolling through the doorway of her office happy as a lark. He bowed as if she were royalty, "I'm here at your request, madam."

"Cut the bullshit, Darrian, and close the door." After he closed the door she instructed him to sit in the chair facing her desk.

"I'm going to need to know everything you have said to my children about anything that you should not have been talking about to them."

He looked at her with understanding and confusion. He didn't want to confess to something but her convoluted statement had him in a twist.

"So, you want to know every conversation I have had with your children?" he questioned, trying to buy himself some time to think.

"Why must you be difficult? Let's narrow it down to the last few months. Is there a specific subject that has come up that isn't business related?"

He knew exactly what she was asking, but he also knew that she would be most unhappy with him. He figured she already knew or she wouldn't be asking the question.

"I'm not certain as to what you are referring to, but I may have mentioned a few things you told me in confidence about the person who's name shall not be mentioned."

She exhaled loudly, "Darrian, I swear I will throw you out of that window if you do not tell me now."

"Wait, those windows open..." he saw the look on her face and thought better than to continue the question. "Yes, I was angry at you for sending me off to be your errand boy once again, so when Mari asked about Rose, I answered most of her questions. Is that what you want to hear?" he paused, "besides like I told you before they already knew, they just wanted details. Which by the way, I did not give.

"What do they know?" she demanded.

"I don't know what they know outside of what I told them. I said she exists, she's Helio's daughter, and that she's older than all of them. Oh, and that he didn't cheat on you."

"That's it?" she said with relief.

"You want to know another secret? she asked, planting a seed to entice him. She knew if this information got back to the children there was only one source.

"They've already met Rose; they just don't know it."

Chapter 48

The siblings promptly went to the war room after Snapper detailed how their mother had reacted to him asking about Rose. They still had pages of names to go through and Snapper's resolve to find Rose had been fueled by his mother's insistence that she didn't exist. This, to him, was the battle that needed to be won to stop the war.

"No," Snapper whispered to himself as he looked at the name on the sheet, "it can't be. That's impossible." His stunned tone made everyone stop and look up at him.

"Snapper, what's wrong? What did you find?" Mari asked.

He didn't say a word, he just pointed at the name on the list – Rose Blossom Jensen. Mari gasped and put her hand over her mouth.

"No, that's just a coincidence," Mari reasoned. "I thought Jensen was her first name."

Snapper rubbed his forehead, "I don't know, I simply don't know. I never asked. I just assumed."

"What are the odds?" he asked.

"What is he talking about, Mari?" Dio asked. "Who's Jensen?"

"You know the singer from the band. She goes by Jensen, but Snapper just found the name Rose Blossom Jensen on his list."

Oni quickly started looking up the name on social media. A few minutes later she said, "The only thing I can find is a comment on a post from about ten years ago that says, 'Great job tonight, Rosie.' Other than that, I cannot find one reference to being Rose Blossom.

"Who posted the comment?" Nia asked.

"Someone named Gia Jensen."

Nia began searching the internet for Gia Jensen. "I think I found her," she said with a sad tone. "It's an obituary."

She transferred it to the screen on the wall. "She is survived by her daughter, Rose Blossom Jensen…" Nia trailed off.

"That's just six months before father was murdered," Mari stated.

"So, her mother dies and six months later she has Father killed? Why? And how does Mother end up giving her two million dollars?" Dio asked confused.

"It's her, I know it is," Snapper said softly. " I knew from the first time I saw her that there was something familiar, something that drew me to her. It was Father. She has some of his features. I can see it now."

"What do we do now?" asked Oni.

"I'm calling Stone," Snapper replied.

"She doesn't have a criminal history," Stone replied.

The siblings had raced over to the police station to have Stone evaluate everything they had found. They were anxious to see if she could be not only their sister, but the one who killed their father.

"Of course, it's possible she's your sister, but what evidence is there that she hired the hit?" Stone asked.

"It's just speculation," Dio admitted. "We found an account in Mother's records that was named Rose with a code of RBJ. We figured the R was for Rose, but this makes a direct link to Rose Blossom Jensen. There was two million dollars placed in that account six months before father died. From the obituary that was close to the same time her mother, Gia Jensen, died. Do you have anything on her?"

Stone checked the records for Gia Jensen. "She had some petty theft charges from the nighties, teenage stuff, but nothing since then."

"Does it say what she stole?" Oni asked.

"I'd have to pull her file for that," Stone replied. "Be right back."

"Why does that matter?" Nia asked.

"I don't know, but I have a hunch. People steal when their desperate, why would someone who associated with Father be in a desperate position?"

"You have to remember; Father wasn't always rich. Grandfather didn't give him money; he made him work for everything. I think that is why Father was so generous with all of us. He didn't want to be like his father," Mari replied.

"I still can't imagine that Father would just leave his pregnant girlfriend to fend for herself. He would have taken care of her and the baby," Snapper commented.

"Maybe. But who says he knew about it? His name isn't on any birth certificates but ours. I'll get Jack to pull Rose's birth certificate. That might give us some more information," Nia added.

When Stone returned he confirmed Oni's suspicion. "She was picked up twice. Once for stealing diapers in 1991 and once for stealing children's cold medicine in 1994. No other arrests after that."

"Jack's calling, hang on." Nia turned to Stone, "What's your email? Jack's sending over the birth certificate."

"I don't even want to know how he got that," Stone replied. He rattled over his email address and a few seconds later the document popped up on his screen.

It listed the father's name as unknown and had Gia at the age of eighteen.

"Why would she go all the way to Southside Medical to give birth?" Dio pondered.

"She might have been from that area?" Nia answered.

The siblings realized that they had even more questions than ever before and that only one person could answer them – their mother."

"We have to go talk to her," Snapper insisted.

"Hang on now." Stone said. "You can't just go barging in on your mother, ask her a bunch of questions, and then go all vigilante on this Rose person. All you have is speculation that she had something to do with your father's death. Let me handle this."

"We're going with you," they all said in unison.

Stone sighed knowing he wouldn't talk them out of it. "Fine," he relented, "But we go in my car and I will do all of the talking. Not that I expect your mother to give me any answers," he added.

The ride to their mother's was rather quiet. They hadn't been back to Flora Fields since they moved out. With the manipulation and backstabbing their mother had been doing, they knew that going to see her was a bad idea. Unfortunately, it was the only idea they had.

When they got to the gate, Stone buzzed the speaker. Lydia answered. The siblings were relieved. Anyone else most likely wouldn't have let them in. She opened the gate and met them at the front door.

"Your mother is in the sunroom. I informed her that you all are here. She's not happy, so I was surprised when she said to bring you to her."

As they entered the sunroom, Magnolia was sitting in an overstuffed light tan chair reading a book. She was casually dressed dark grey, silk, wide-legged pants, and a white pullover silk blouse but her makeup was impeccable and her hair was wrapped in a tight bun atop her head.

She stood and gracefully cross the expanse between her and Stone. "Detective Stone. Children. What brings you here at this hour? Please have a seat. I'm excited to hear what you have to say," she said with a hint of sarcasm through her Southern charm and hospitality.

"Mrs. Blossom," Stone started, "Thank you for seeing us. We apologize for the hour and for showing up uninvited. The truth of the matter is that I have received some information that I need to discuss with you."

"Shall I assume that the information came from my children, since they are all sitting there with pouts on their faces. Children, at least sit up straight. There is no need for bad posture."

"Yes ma'am. Your children have brought some information to me that I believe you can clarify."

"Please do not keep me in suspense, Detective Stone, how can I be of service?"

Stone ignored her condescension. He knew enough about her to read between the lines of anything she said. He decided to go straight for the gut punch.

"It has come to my attention that your late husband fathered a child in 1991. Were you aware?"

Magnolia was angry, but she kept her composure. "Detective, I don't know what my children have told you, but I explained to Snapper that this Rose person, I assume that's who you are speaking of, is merely a fictitious person that was made up by Darrian Conti to upset them while he was awaiting trial for the absurd trespassing charge that was leveled against him." She looked directly at Snapper and shot him an evil look.

"Ma'am, I can assure you that Rose is real and I believe you know who she is and have been in contact with her."

Magnolia resented the allegation and had a hard time keeping her face from giving her away.

"You think I am in contact with a child that Helio had before I ever met him? I'm not sure where you are going with this, but I believe our time together is up." She turned her head toward the door. "Lydia."

Lydia appeared quickly from around the corner.

"Could you please escort our guests —"

Stone interrupted her. "Mrs. Blossom, we are not finished. I'm going to give it to you straight. I have reason to believe that Rose Blossom Jensen was the person who hired the hit on your husband. Now is that reason enough for us to continue our conversation."

Magnolia gasped and waved Lydia away. She sat stoically for a moment. Trying to collect her thoughts and trying to comprehend what she had just heard. She knew that she had to tell the truth.

Chapter 49

Magnolia stood and instructed her guests to follow her to the library. As they walked, the siblings just looked at each other. Each suspicious and curious as to what their mother was about to reveal.

The library boasted twenty-five-foot tall ceilings and every wall was a bookshelf. It resembled an old library from the turn of the century with sliding ladders and intricate wood carvings. In the center of the room were three turn-of-the-century tufted leather sofas set in a U shape in front of a mahogany desk with a tufted leather chair that matched the sofa. At the far end of the room was a fireplace with a sitting space that matched the furniture in the center.

"Have a seat," Magnolia directed them to the sofas as she walked over to one of the bookshelves.

She pulled out a copy of the Voynich Manuscript that had belonged to her father. When it was removed, the bookcase popped open with a small click. She placed her hand in a groove that was carved into the side of the bookcase and pulled it open to reveal a safe that was hidden behind it.

The siblings were astonished. They had never known about the hidden compartment in all of the hours they had spent reading books or listening to their father read to them in the library.

She opened the safe and secured a stack of documents organized into various folders. As she closed the safe and locked the bookcase back into place, her shoulders were slightly curled forward and the expression of indignant righteousness had completely left her face. She was solemn and truly looked tired and worried.

She sat at the desk and began to sort out the folders neatly in front of her. She looked up at her children first. Not with a look of discontent or even anger, it was more thoughtful and concerned.

"Yes, I know Rose. She is a child that was produced from a one night stand your father had when he was nineteen," she began. "He never knew about her. I have found through my own research that they met at a party and as it was in the early nineties, they got drunk and apparently ended up in the back of his car." She shuttered at the thought.

She pulled out what looked to be financial records and reached out in the direction of Detective Stone.

"What are these?" he asked as he stood up to receive the documents.

"What you are looking at are the accounts for a shelf company I established many years ago. It's called Ailongam, my name spelled backwards. Not very clever but it was a joke at the time. Just leave it at that. I used this account to begin giving monthly payments to Darrian Conti. As I am sure my children have informed you," she lifted an eyebrow toward Oni, "he and I were entangled in an affair for over ten years. It ended when he was arrested."

Snapper began to say something, but Magnolia held a finger up to silence him.

"Let me get through this, Snapdragon, she requested. Her voice wasn't harsh, it had a tone of pleading.

"Please continue, Mrs. Blossom," Stone said as he shot a look at Snapper.

"That was all that Ailongam Limited was used for, until Darrian wanted to build a shelf company for his real estate holdings. I allowed him to attach it to my company. It was a good idea at the time. It made my company look more solid if I ever wanted to do something with it in the future. What I hadn't anticipated was what I would have to end up using it for six months before Helio was murdered." She sighed and placed her hand on her chest. A small tear escaped her left eye.

Snapper reached into his breast pocket and pulled out a handkerchief and took it to her. "Always prepared for a lady's needs," he said softly.

She nodded and accepted his offering. She dabbed her eye and continued, "Do you children remember when your father took you all to Paris in April of 2021?"

They all confirmed, "Yes, Mother."

"A woman showed up at the office looking for your father. She was refusing to leave until she spoke with him so I introduced myself and took her into my office. That woman was Rose," she paused as she remembered the meeting. "Her mother had just recently passed away and in cleaning her mother's home she found a letter addressed to her in the bottom of her mother's sock drawer. The basics of it, as I remember, were that she was the child of Heliotrope Blossom and that Rose should find him and make sure that he takes care of her."

Magnolia stood up and walked over to the window. Looking out she asked for a moment before she continued. The children could hear the pain in her voice and they all sat motionless as they had never seen their mother in that state. It was confusing and sad to them.

She didn't move from the window, but a few minutes later she began to tell the story again. "Rose was ranting and raving about how her mother had told her that her father had abandoned them and now she finds out that he is a rich and powerful man. She was appalled at the thought and would not listen when I told her that I'd never heard of her and that she was not about to come into my company with some fake letter and espouse that she was a Blossom. I asked her what it would take to get her to go away."

She slowly walked back to the desk and pulled out another piece of paper. It was a receipt for two million dollars. "That was her price. I told her I would set up an account that she could withdraw from and not have to pay taxes. I used my Ailongam Limited company to create an account – Rose. I even put a simple code on it that she had to have in order to access the money – RBJ. A bit reluctantly, she accepted the money, the account number, and that was it. She left and I never heard from her again."

Oni couldn't help herself but to ask, "Did you ever tell Father?"

Oni expected her mother to shoot daggers at her, but instead Magnolia calmly shook her head.

"He never knew. I was protecting the company. A scandal of this nature could have done untold damage to Helio's reputation. I wasn't willing to take that chance," she paused for a moment, looked up at her daughters and confessed, "honestly, I didn't want another Blossom woman in the family either."

Magnolia looked defeated, but she was glad that she had told the truth. "That's it. I washed my hands of her and never saw her again until your graduation party."

"I saw an exchange of looks between the two of you, but when I asked her about it all she said was 'ask your mother,'" Snapper stated.

"If she had someone kill your father, then I can only assume that she did it with the money I gave her. I was notified by the bank that the account had been depleted just days before your father's murder," she let out another heavy sigh. "I didn't think anything of it. I assumed she just withdrew the money and had her own reasons for doing so. I never thought…" she trailed off.

"What do we do now, Detective Stone," Magnolia asked.

"Nothing," Stone replied.

Everyone in the room snapped their heads toward him.

"I'm sorry, but we don't have anything that proves she used the two million dollars to have Mr. Blossom murdered."

"What about the hitman?" Snapper asked.

"The who?"

"So, there might be a few things you don't know," Snapper replied. "Mother, thank you for sharing all of this with us. I know it wasn't easy and that you wanted to keep all of this a secret. We all understand, but we have to find a way to prove that she hired the hit on Father." He stood up, went over, and kissed her on the cheek. "We need to take Detective Stone back to Freedom Flowers to show him some more evidence that will hopefully help. I hope you don't mind us leaving in a rush."

"No, in fact, I would appreciate some time alone. But please," she took his hand and looked up at him, "do everything you can to nail her ass to the wall."

With a slight chuckle, he assured her that they would.

Once they had left the library, Magnolia placed her head on the desk and began to weep.

Chapter 50

Snapper texted Sam and Rudy to meet them at the war room. Stone was none too happy that the siblings had been keeping things from him. Dio explained that it was best if Sam told what they knew, since he was the one who actually spoke to the alleged hitman. Oni and Nia sat in the back of Stone's SUV speaking softly about how they were afraid that Rose would not be brought to justice.

Mari overheard them, "She will. She has to pay for taking Father away from us. What I don't understand is why. Why would she not just want him dead, but to actually have him murdered?"

"Magnolia said that Rose's mother told her that her father abandoned them. To think that all of your life only to find out that he's one of the wealthiest people in Atlanta, in the fashion industry…I've said it before desperation makes people do desperate things," Stone answered.

"If Mother would have just told Father about Rose, none of this would have happened, "Oni said with anger.

"We don't know that. Probably, but there's no telling. I just can't believe I trusted her. I helped her," Snapper scolded himself. "She knew all along who we were. It was what…a game…to fuck with my head?"

"All of you need to stop the wondering and focus on what you know and how your information can translate into actual evidence because right now, we don't have shit on her," Stone fussed.

Sam and Rudy were waiting in the war room when the siblings and Stone arrived.

"What's the big emergency?" Sam asked.

Stone debriefed Sam and Rudy on what information they had obtained from Magnolia. It filled in most of the gaps in their own information and explained the connection between Rose and Magnolia.

"What I need from you, Sam, is to know exactly what transpired between you and this supposed hitman," Stone stated.

With precise details, Sam recounted how he received the burner phone and instructions from his contact and that he had followed directions that were texted. He couldn't identify the person's voice because they both used voice modulators.

"The why, he told me, was retribution. That makes much more sense now since she grew up poor and her mother had to struggle, meanwhile, her father was this rich guy who she thought had abandoned her," Sam deduced.

"I need to meet your contact," Stone told Sam.

"With all due respect, that's not happening," Sam replied with defiance.

"Sam, your contact is the only connection to the alleged hitman—"

Sam interrupted Stone, "Look I know where you're going with this, but all he had was the name Rose. They never made contact. If it was anything like our transaction, it was done with untraceable money to an untraceable account."

"The Rose account," Snapper hypothesized. "She gave him the account number and the code. He withdrew the money and did the hit.

The account was clean, untraceable, and if someone could trace it, they would find Mother."

"Rudy, is your team still working on that photo of the car?" Nia asked.

"What photo?" Stone inquired.

"There's a still frame from the video that my team has enhanced. We figured out that there is a second person in the car. There is a reflection that looks like a person sitting in the passenger seat," Rudy explained.

"What else aren't you guys telling me?" Stone asked with a tinge of anger.

They went back through everything they had with Stone. Most of it he knew but the possible second person in the car was new information.

"I can send this to the FBI, see if they can do something with it. I have a friend based out of the Atlanta office who would be more than willing to get in on this murder case. He worked at the police station with me before he became an agent. He knew your father too." Stone added.

Thirty minutes later, Agent Stackman entered the war room. Stone made the introductions and got him up to speed on the investigation thus far.

"You should have read me in sooner, Stone."

"I just found out most of this information tonight. There wasn't anything substantial to share until now," Stone replied.

"This photo is good. Can I see the actual video?" Stackman asked.

Rudy cued up the video and they all watched. Stackman asked if there were other angles and one by one they watched the CCTV footage. The siblings had never watched the video of when their father was gunned down. Oni screamed and Mari ran out of the room. Nia ran after her.

There was one piece of footage that Stackman had Rudy run back several times, then he asked him to play the view from the store across the street from the restaurant. He analyzed every frame and played several of them multiple times.

"There is definitely someone in the passenger seat. I just can't make out the face. Did your people try to enhance this frame?" Stackman went back to the frame from the signal light camera that displayed the windshield in full view. The glass had been tinted, but two people could be seen. It was also the best angle of the front of the vehicle.

"No, we got so focused on the passenger side mirror, that I don't think that we looked to see if there were any other possible hits," Rudy replied.

"Email me that footage. I'll send it to my guys and see what we can uncover. This goes without saying, but I have to say it so that everyone is clear, now that I am involved this is an FBI matter. You cannot pursue this any further. You've done good work and I'll need to get a statement from Mrs. Blossom, but no more amateur detective work. Understood?"

Everyone was clear on the instructions. The siblings were relieved to have Agent Stackman take over the case. They knew with his help Rose would finally be connected to their father's murder.

Chapter 51

Agent Stackman stood at the head of the briefing room, his gaze sweeping over the faces of the agents seated around the table. The air was charged with anticipation as he began to outline the plan to apprehend Jensen, the person at the center of a murder-for-hire plot against Heliotrope Blossom.

"Alright, team," Stackman began, his voice authoritative and commanding. "We've been tracking Jensen for months, and now we have enough evidence to move in. Our primary objective is to apprehend her safely. At the same time, another team of agents will go into her residence and execute a search warrant. The timing has to be precise to ensure that no one is at the residence. She is set to perform at the home of Mr. and Mrs. Penderbrook. I have spoken with them and they know we are coming. We will be there before the party during the sound check. The stage will be located here," he gestured to the large screen behind him, where a map of the target location was displayed. "We'll split into two teams: one to secure the perimeter and another to make the arrest."

As he spoke, Stackman outlined each team member's role and briefed them on the specific details of the operation. The tension in the room was palpable as they prepared to execute the plan even though they were prepared for any possible scenario.

"The perimeter team will take advantage of the two acres of woods that surround the back of the Penderbrook property. They will alert the arrest team when it is secure to advance on the target. Agent Pullman, of the perimeter team, will give the go command for the arrest.

"When the go command is given, the perimeter team will advance to block any possible escape routes. The Penderbrook family have been instructed to stay locked in the house. Agent Razter will be in the residence to secure their safety.

"This is the target, Rose Blossom Jensen," Stackman put her picture on the screen. "We do not know if she will put up a fight or run. Our perimeter teams are ready for the run. Arrest team, she will have numerous items that could be used as weapons, so stay sharp. If possible, and with a little luck, we can get her when she is not up on the stage.

"Once we are in position, it is radio silence until the go command. Is everyone clear on our objective and your part in it?"

"Yes sir," all of the agents said in unison.

"Let's move out."

With all agents in position, they held their breath until Agent Pullman gave the go command.

Jensen was on stage with her band as they checked the sound and strummed through a few songs.

"I think we're good guys. This is going to be a rockin' set and five Gs each isn't bad either."

All of the band members agreed with whoops and hollers.

Jensen took her guitar off and placed it on the stand. "I'll be right back. I'm going to grab a few bottles of water to place on the stage."

As she went down the steps, the go command was given.

All of the agents ran in and surrounded her. She tried to run back onto the stage and her band members jumped up to protect her. But it was too late. Stackman already had a hold on her arm and twisted her around to place the handcuffs on her.

She was kicking and screaming. "What in the fuck is going on! Who are you? What are you doing?"

"Rose Blossom Jensen, you are under arrest for the murder of Mr. Heliotrope Blossom," Stackman informed her.

Her bandmates backed down and held up their hands as they protested to know nothing about it.

The look on Jensen's face was one of complete shock. She stopped kicking and asked only one question, "How do you know it's me?"

Agent Stackman told her they would discuss everything at the precinct.

She professed her innocence and told her bandmates to play the gig without her. "Get that money guys," she yelled back to them as she was hauled away to the back seat of a patrol car.

At the police station she was taken into an interrogation room where Stackman and Stone questioned her.

They went through all of the information and evidence they had on her, but she refused to admit any guilt. She said that she didn't know anyone by the name Heliotrope Blossom, which was technically true. She said that she had talked to Magnolia Blossom, but she didn't know anything about two million dollars.

"Do you think I would live in my dump of a one bedroom apartment that doesn't have working air and where the management is shit if I had two million dollars? All of the money we make from gigs goes into a saving account so I can buy a house. You can check. There's about fifty grand in there, that's it. With my bad credit, I have to have twenty percent in cash just to qualify to look at a house. Do you know how much real estate is here in Atlanta? It's insane."

Jensen continued to babble on while Stone and Stackman just let her talk herself right into a hole. They were saving the best for last, the crystal clear, enhanced photo that clearly showed her sitting in the passenger seat of the Ford Expedition that was used in the commission of the murder.

"I don't know how y'all have me mixed up in this. I didn't murder anyone."

After three hours of questions without any response that was useful, Stackman opened a folder and slid the picture of her in the getaway car.

She looked down at the picture with intent. She was trying to figure out a way to explain why she was in the car with a man dressed in all black with a mask over his face as the driver. She had nothing.

"That's just a picture of someone in a car," she stated trying to buy time.

"That's you in the passenger seat," stated Stone as he pointed to her in the photo.

She brought the picture closer, like she was examining every detail. "You think that's me. Hell no. That doesn't even look like me."

"It looks exactly like you. In fact, if I'm not mistaken, you're wearing the same black, Jack Daniel's shirt now that you were wearing when this was taken,. All that's missing is the black beanie. I could get you one so we can do a true side-by-side comparison," Stackman pointed out.

"I'm done talking. I want a lawyer."

Chapter 52

At trial, the defense teams opening statement was strong. They pointed to no witnesses, no hitman, and their perception of an unreliable, enhanced photo that at best was pixelated and non-descript.

The prosecution saw things a little differently. They had the account where two million dollars just happened to disappear days before the shooting, yet Ms. Jensen had no explanation as to where the money went, the testimony from Mrs. Blossom about how angry Ms. Jensen was at Mr. Heliotrope Blossom, and in their opinion a very clear photo that showed Ms. Jensen in the getaway car from the shooting.

Both sides called witnesses, experts, photo analysts, crime scene examiners, police officers, and a veritable array of anyone and everyone who would corroborate their theory of the facts. The jury heard testimony for six days before both the prosecution and the defense rested.

The charges Rose Blossom Jensen was facing were severe and would place her behind bars for life. The jury had to consider the evidence for first degree murder and solicitation and conspiracy to commit murder. The prosecution decided not to allow lesser charges. They wanted her to face the maximum penalty for killing

Helio and despite her protests of innocence, they knew they had a strong case.

The jury was sequestered since the defense did not win their motion to move the trial to a different jurisdiction. They felt like with Mr. Blossom's much beloved status in Atlanta that Ms. Jensen would not get a fair trial. The judge, however, disagreed. She had been held in prison for the year it took to get the trial prepared and on the docket. She looked thin and exhausted when she showed up to court in a simple pair of black slacks and a blue button down top.

Both Magnolia and Snapper testified against her, but none of the girls felt like they had anything to add that would be useful or valuable to the case. They didn't want to parade all of the Blossoms up onto the stand as it might have come off to the jury as showing their power more than their solidarity.

After the jury left the courtroom to begin deliberation, Magnolia spoke to her children for the first time since the night they had confronted her with Stone at Flora Fields. The year had been hard on the siblings as they wrestled with the knowledge that Magnolia had held on to so many secrets and they couldn't help but to believe that if she would have just told Helio about Rose that maybe, possibly he'd still be alive.

"Hello children," she said in what sounded like a loving tone.

"Hello, Mother," they all replied.

"I know that we may never have a good relationship or any relationship, but I just wanted you all to know that if I could do it over, I would have told your father about Rose. I have always been so focused on saving the company and its reputation that I lost sight of saving my family. For that, I am sorry."

Her words sounded sincere and there was a part of them that wanted to believe her, especially Oni and Mari, but pretty words once in their lifetime could not erase all of the hurt she had inflicted on each of them.

Snapper spoke for the siblings, "Mother, we hear your words and we appreciate the strength it must have taken for you to say them. We will take them under advisement once the trial is over. If you will please be patient and let us focus on the situation at hand, we would be pleased to talk to you further at a later date."

He was so proper and polite, but blunt and dismissive at the same time. Magnolia knew that she had to wait and hope that her children would hear her sincerity. The previous year had taken a toll on her and the empty house and her thoughts had made her reflect on all she had done.

Six days later, the call came that the jury had reached a verdict. The prosecution was worried that it had taken the jury so long to deliberate. Most of the time it was a bad sign that they had not proven their case beyond a reasonable doubt.

The judge directed the foreperson to pass the verdict form. After reading it, the judge handed it to the clerk to read for the court.

"In the above and titled action, we the jury find the defendant not guilty of solicitation of murder."

There was an audible gasp in the courtroom.

"We the jury find the defendant not guilty of conspiracy to commit murder."

Snapper and his sisters all began to wipe tears from their eyes.

"We the jury find the defendant guilty of first-degree murder."

The judge banged the gavel as the courtroom erupted in cheers. Once everyone had settled the judge thanked and dismissed the jury.

"Sentencing will be held a week from today at ten. I will hear impact statements at that time before entering the sentence," the judge stated.

As they were dismissed from the courtroom and exited to the lobby, the family was bombarded by the press. They waded through the throngs who had been waiting to get that one soundbite or comment that would be exclusive for the evening news. All of the Blossoms gave the same two words, "no comment."

"Thank you your Honor," Magnolia said as she began her impact statement. "My husband, Heliotrope Blossom, was a kind and gentle man. He loved his family, he loved the community of Atlanta, and he loved his company." She looked at Rose, "He would have loved you, Ms. Jensen, had he known that you were his daughter. You lost the chance to know a wonderful man who would have embraced you into the Blossom family. You will miss the chance to know your five siblings and you will miss the chance to truly know what it is to be a Blossom. I know and understand my part in you missing those opportunities and for that I want you to know that I am truly sorry. However, you made the decision to have my husband and your father gunned down for no other reason than petty anger. Your heart has been filled with it for a long time and I hope that you find some way to extinguish it and find peace. I forgive you for your actions and I hold no malice toward you as a person."

Everyone in the courtroom was stunned by her words of forgiveness. The siblings had expected Magnolia to tell Rose to go to hell or to ask the judge to put her under the jail. They couldn't help but wonder if she really had been changed by all that had transpired.

The siblings and Helio's best friend, Harold Gill, also addressed the court with impact statements before the judge imposed the sentence. Rose informed the judge that she wanted to say she was sorry to the Blossom family and that she knew her words sounded hollow to them. With that, the judge addressed her for sentencing.

"Ms. Jensen, I am without sympathy for you in this matter. You made choices that have destroyed a family and saddened the entirety of Atlanta. I can only hope that you learn that your actions have consequences and that no bad deed goes unpunished. You manipulated the Blossom family and I can only imagine what your motives were for befriending Mr. Snapdragon Blossom. Ms. Jensen, please rise. As a jury of your peers has found you guilty of first-degree murder, I sentence you to a term of life in prison for a minimum of twenty-five years to be served before you may become eligible for parole."

Rose broke down in tears as the judge spoke. When the deputies came to take her back to jail she continued to say, "I'm sorry," until the door to the courtroom closed behind her.

Thank you for reading!
Please add a review on Amazon and share your thoughts!

Amazon reviews are extremely helpful to authors, and I thank you for taking the time to support my work. I would very much appreciate it if you would please share your review on social media and encourage others to read this story too! Thank you!

You can find more information about the author and her work on the following websites:

 Instagram: @karenraymondauthor

 TikTok: karen.raymond.author

 Author website: karenraymondauthor.com

 YouTube: Karen Raymond – Author

Please email to sign up for the author's newsletter.

Author email: karenraymond@karenraymondauthor.com

Acknowledgments

I am extremely lucky to have amazing friends who support my passion for writing and constantly encourage me to continue fulfilling my dream of writing books for the world to enjoy. The joy that I get from writing is unparalleled. It has allowed me to create characters who are robust and relatable. I have so many stories to tell that I find myself noting ideas and tidbits in my notebook for the future. I have enough to keep writing for many years to come.

Too many people deserve my thanks, my praise, and my devotion. They know who they are, and I tell them often how much their support and love mean to me. It is because of them that I spend my spare time creating the pages of my books. I will continue to work to make you all proud of the work I produce and the lessons I learn. Special thanks and love goes to Maggie Smith. She has been a cheerleader and great friend throughout my writing journey. With her massive talent for literature, she generously edited this book in exchange for a hug.

Equally as important are the readers who take their time to open the pages I have written and welcome the characters into their lives. I couldn't do this without my fantastic legion of ARC readers who ground me and lift me up all at the same time. It is truly thrilling to know that I am able to share my words because of you.

The value you bring to authors is immeasurable. Without your love for reading and your devotion to the written word, the authors of the world would be silenced. Thank you from the bottom of my heart for the opportunity to bring you my stories. I hope you enjoy this book. Happy reading!!

Karen Raymond is originally from South Carolina and currently resides in Savannah, Georgia. She has been writing poetry and short stories for most of her life but fell in love with creative writing in college.

She is the author of the three-part *Learning Series*.

House of Blossom is her first standalone novel.

She is an educator with a degree in English and a master's in education. She also has credentials in screenwriting. While she is trained in and teaches writing, she mostly enjoys developing strong characters and building real-life, relatable worlds around them. In her spare time, she loves to read, create graphic designs, and spend time with her Siamese cat, Mickie.

Made in the USA
Columbia, SC
08 December 2024

47636839R00200